Road to Kesar Khal

Devendra Dimri

First published in 2018 by

Becomeshakespeare.com
Wordit Content Design & Editing Services Pvt Ltd
Unit - 26, Building A-1, Nr Wadala RTO, Wadala (East),
Mumbai 400037, India
T:+91 8080226699

WORDIT ART FUND

This book has been funded by **WORDIT ART FUND**
WORDIT ART FUND helps deserving Authors publish their work.
To apply for funding, please visit us at
www.becomeshakespeare.com

©
ISBN: 978-93-87649-01-9

Disclaimer

This is a work of fiction. Names, characters, business, place, event and incidents are either the product of the author's imagination or used in a fictitious manner. Any resemblance to actual person, living or dead or actual event is purely coincidental.

Contents

Chapter 1

The roar of the bus could be heard from a distance as the village approached. The bus was still obscured by the long winding mountain road but the noise got louder. The road curving through rolling hills looked serene in the morning sun. A man and a woman standing close to each other, eagerly waiting for the bus to arrive stretched their necks in the direction of the vehicle. Their small village perched on a hill lay further below. The bus curved along a large mountain rock and made itself visible on a straight narrow road. A slight relief came over the couple as they signaled for the big vehicle to stop. The engine came to a grinding halt, just a few feet away from the couple. The man dressed in black pants and green woolen sweater, moved towards the vehicle. The female adorned in a colorful blue sari which covered her entire body followed her companion. It was still early on a Saturday morning and the bus gathered speed after picking up the couple who were the only ones waiting for it.

'Where to'? The conductor asked the recently seated couple in the middle seats. 'Kesar Khal' replied the female before the husband could mutter anything. 'It will be twenty rupees each' the conductor blurted, sleep still evident in his bleary eyes. The husband stretched his pockets and gave the conductor a hundred rupee bill as the wife looked. 'Do you have anything smaller'? The conductor asked. Husband shook his head and said 'No'. There was a brief pause as the three of them contemplated. 'Why don't you carry change with you'? The female admonished, taking out forty rupees from her purse and thrusting it forward. 'It is still early during the day and we don't have enough passengers yet' the conductor replied trying to conceal a smirk as he handed two tickets to the young couple. Apart from the couple, the bus had four other passengers. An old man sat at the front of the vehicle while a middle aged couple occupied the seat behind him. At the end of the bus, a man clad in saffron clothing was cheerfully playing with beads. The driver was focused on the road and the conductor on his watch. A crisp breeze crept into the vehicle.

Summer had just arrived in the high Hills and the surroundings were slowly coming to terms with it. A light fog partially covered the pine trees and the nearby mountains. Bright yellow flowers had bloomed on both side of the road and gave a strong scent in the early morning. Sound of the moving vehicle was scattering the birds on the road. Sunlight was piercing through the large glass pane on the front of the bus. The driver stylishly rolled down his colorful glasses and revved the engine. 'I had only brought forty rupees with me' Janki Devi complained to her husband about the bus fare. Manu Prasad just nodded in sympathy, his head drifting back and his eyes slightly closing. 'You don't like coming down this road, do you'? She asked her husband apprehensively. 'No' the husband replied pretending to sleep. The village of Gauri Ghat was fast disappearing behind as the large vehicle gathered speed. Kesar Khal was hour and half away from Gauri Ghat and at a much lower altitude. The bus eventually started making its downward descent. The road got narrower and curvier. There was little oncoming traffic for the bus to navigate and the driver was pleased about it. Still he would bring the vehicle to a stop around sharp mountain turns and peek out of his window to be safe. 'If he keeps driving like this, it will take us three hours to reach there!' Janki Devi complained. Manu Prasad managed to crack a smile. 'It will be late in the evening by the time we get back home, entire day just wasted' the wife lamented. Manu Prasad just listened as he mostly did when his wife spoke. 'Every month we have to do this', She muttered under her breath. Manu Prasad knew well that once a month this trip was necessary. After all, he was the one who planned the journey in advance.

Manu Prasad lived with his wife in the village of Gauri Ghat, located high in the Himalayan Hills of Northern India. The nearest town was about twenty kilometers from his village while the biggest city lay further two hundred kilometers away. Manu Prasad had often visited the town but the big city had remained a dream. His young life had mostly revolved around Gauri Ghat and the surrounding small villages. Along with his wife, the traditions and customs of the village were woven in Manu Prasad's fabric. He owned a small provision store in Gauri Ghat while his wife Janki Devi took care of the household. The store was about ten minutes walk from his house and Manu Prasad would get there around eight in the morning every day. He would work till six in the evening barring the lunch break for an hour when he would join his wife at home. The store was open on most days excluding special festivals or appointments suiting the couple. It was an ordinary village life which happily satisfied the couple. Their daily needs were sufficiently fulfilled from the income generated by the small business. Most villagers were actually envious of them. Still, the young couple knew something was missing in their life. Manu Prasad and Janki Devi were married for four years but had no children. Both were resigned to this fact and were trying their best to change the present. They had tried different things to no avail. A family friend had informed them about the fertility doctor few months back. Manu Prasad had convinced his wife to give it a try and she had apprehensively agreed. The monthly trip for a hopeful outcome was regarding this dilemma.

Manu Prasad had planned the trip in advance. He had kept the motive secret while informing most of the customers about his pending absence. The provision store was to remain close on Saturday so Manu and Janki could visit an ailing aunt in the town of Kesar Khal. This was the fabricated version to most and it suited the couple fine. The previous day, Manu Prasad had stocked up on his supplies at the store which meant paying extra for the Lorry that ferried goods to the village from the main town. He had even stayed open for an extra hour in the evening to cover for his anticipated trip. Once back home, he had helped his wife with household chores to ease her burden. Janki Devi herself had been busy before the morning journey. She had prepared lunch in advance for both and made sure her cattle herd had enough fodder and water for the entire day. This required making an extra trip to the animal shed which was a good fifteen minutes uphill walk. This was their second trip to the doctor so both were relatively calm. However as the moment for departure arrived, the couple got anxious. It subsided a little once they were seated on the bus.

The driver was maneuvering the bus through the narrow mountain road that snaked along the hills. He had an arduous task as the vehicle was going downhill and required constant speed adjustments. The road in itself was something to behold. On one side it was shielded by the hills while the other side was totally exposed to a deep valley. Vehicles going in both directions drove as close as possible to shielded side of the road, avoiding the end that was exposed to the valley. Drivers using the narrow road listened to sounds of oncoming traffic. Whenever two vehicles going in opposite direction came close to one another they would both stop and let the bigger vehicle drive ahead, smaller one moving subsequently. The terrain mostly enforced safety in the hills. Occasionally one had to be careful of large rocks coming down from the hillside on to the road. Navigating the mountain roads itself required special set of skills and a large vehicle just made it harder. The men who had been assigned this task had a thankless job. Poor pay and long hours were part of bus driver's life but it did have one advantage. It was a government job which meant stable income and hence attracted men from the lower rung of the economic ladder.

The steep decline was now clearly evident as the bus rolled down. The driver was listening to a song on his pocket radio and singing as he drove. Manu Prasad was sitting straight in his seat while Janki Devi rested her head on his shoulder. Thoughts went in and out of Manu Prasad's head. 'This visit should yield something; I followed his advice last time'. 'The doctor did say give it time, so we have to be patient'. Janki Devi too was drowning in thoughts. 'I wish the doctor still has that female assistant, I really don't like disclosing too much about myself to a male doctor'. 'Some of the questions are just too embarrassing'. The vehicle suddenly came to a screeching halt and this flung Manu and his wife forward. A tree had fallen on the road and the driver had seen it in time. The sudden stop had rattled the passengers. 'Are you okay' Manu looked at his wife. 'I'm fine, just a little nudge on the head' the wife replied. Manu Prasad rubbed her forehead while Janki Devi looked at him, her eyes closing. The driver along with the conductor got off the bus and walked towards the fallen tree. The road block was cleared and the large vehicle was on its way again. The bus had completed its downward descent and was now approaching the small town twenty kilometers away from Gauri Ghat. It was still another half an hour to Kesar Khal.

The town streets were crowded with people and the bus slowed down. It barely stopped as it picked up some passengers. The conductor quickly ticketed them and asked them to be seated. 'Looks like he was saving his change for them' Janki Devi complained. Manu Prasad knew it was an unscheduled stop but remained quiet. The bus was now approaching a bridge. Loud sounds of water getting splashed filled the air. Two Himalayan rivers coming from different directions were converging. The larger body of water was thumping the smaller one at the confluence. The result was a thick fountain of water that whipped across the rocks as the two rivers became one. On the banks people were bathing while some were performing Puja. Further down the confluence, a dead body was being given its final rite by a group of mourners. A temple stood close to the two emerging rivers and its long steps led to the merger of both. Water could be seen touching the final steps of the temple. A priest in white robes, holding a silver cup was looking in the direction of the sun with his eyes closed at the end of the steps. Further up, a small Ashram stood in front of a large tree. Holy men clad in saffron walked around the periphery. Confluence was a sacred place and its surrounding gave it a mystical look.

Janki Devi covered her ears with her hands as the bus made it past the long bridge. 'There is just so much noise out here' she said slumping in her seat. Manu Prasad nodded in agreement, his eyes looking straight. The holy confluence was now in the rear and most passengers in the bus hardly noticed. The bus had dropped down in altitude and the result was rise in temperature. Manu Prasad and his wife removed their thick sweaters and tied them across their waist. Janki Devi opened a bottle of water from her bag and took a sip. She offered the water to her husband who took a long drink. 'Do you want an orange'? Janki said. 'No' Manu Prasad quietly replied. Janki Devi picked an orange from her bag and started peeling it. 'We should be there soon' She whispered, slice of orange dangling from her mouth. Manu Prasad nodded in agreement, knowing that Kesar Khal was fast approaching. '2 Kilometers Kesar Khal' a sign on the road stated in broad letters. The bus driver looked at it and smiled. It was going to be his rest stop and he was looking forward to the break. He quickly glanced back at the conductor who was busy counting his money.

Kesar Khal was the District head quarters for a number of surrounding villages and small towns. The Court, District Magistrate and a Government hospital were all located in the big town of Kesar Khal. An aroma of scents and spices filled the air as the bus rolled into town. The streets on both sides were full of vendors, loudly boasting their identity. Various dishes were being prepared out in the open and this was attracting a decent crowd. Once the food stalls ended, small shops replaced them on the edge of the road. They sold items from shoes to clothing and everything in between. Most people who crowded them had come from far off small villages. Some were just struck by scope of things and their eyes wandered from one shop to the other. The vendors and shops eventually gave way to brick buildings and houses. The bus came to a small depot and stopped. Manu Prasad and Janki Devi gathered their belongings and prepared to disembark from the vehicle. The young couple felt the residue of the long trip as they walked out of the bus depot. 'In ten minutes we should be there' Manu consoled his wife. It was getting closer to noon. The bus trip had taken longer than anticipated.

The government hospital was located behind a small school. It was an old brick building which consisted of two floors. The paint on the structure had worn off and there was no effort to rectify. The small parking lot outside was also being used as a resting area. Two clear signs stating 'Parking for hospital doctors' were occupied by a couple of small cars. Manu Prasad and Janki Devi entered through the front door of the hospital. A hospital orderly lay slumping in his chair as they passed him. Sleep had overtaken him and his frail body seemed exhausted. Manu and his wife had been to the hospital in the past and knew the location of their doctor's office. The couple walked the stairs to the second floor, the scent of mopped floors still fresh in the air. Breathing heavily they reached their doctor's office only to find it empty. Frustration came upon them as they stepped outside and looked around. 'The doctor and his staff have gone for lunch and will be back in an hour' a passing hospital employee informed them. Manu and Janki located a bench and proceeded towards it. 'We should also have lunch' Janki Devi looked at her husband. Manu Prasad nodded in agreement and started helping his wife set up lunch on the wooden bench.

Janki Devi pulled out a plastic container from her bag and laid it out on the front. She opened it slightly and smelled the contents. 'Still looks good' she looked at her husband. The couple got comfortable on the wooden bench and slowly started eating. Janki Devi had prepared eight Rotis and a fried vegetable that consisted of cabbage and potatoes for both of them. She had also carefully placed a small serving of Mango pickle at the end of the plastic container. Soon the container was empty. Janki Devi licked her fingers after she was done while Manu Prasad picked out a napkin from his pocket and wiped his mouth. Janki Devi took a sip of water from her bottle and passed it to her husband who took a long drink. Manu looked at his watch; it was going to be another twenty minutes before the doctor returned. The second floor lobby of the hospital looked deserted; everyone it seemed took lunch at the same time. Once a while a visitor would come by and after peeping inside a window just lazily depart. 'Remember the first time we came here over a month ago'? Janki Devi asked her husband. 'It was lot quicker that time' Manu Prasad remembered.

During their first visit, the couple had come to the hospital at 10AM sharp in the morning. The doctor usually arrived at that time and they wanted to be the first to consult him. They were anxious about the visit and had arrived a day in advance. Janki's cousin lived close to Kesar Khal and the couple had made arrangements with him for their nightly stay. The motive of the visit was kept secret. As far as everyone knew the couple had fresh supplies of walnuts to pick from the big town for the provision store back in Gauri Ghat. Manu Prasad and Janki Devi had arrived at the hospital ahead of the doctor. Upon consulting the doctor they had been apprehensive. It was the first time both of them had been to the doctor in a long while. The size of the building had struck them along with the number of people in the facility. A one room medical clinic that functioned in Gauri Ghat was different from here. A single doctor attended all the patients in the village whose ailments ranged from common cold to back injuries. In Kesar Khal, the hospital had various wards tending to specific needs. It was still a far cry from a big city hospital boasting of state of the art facilities but for surrounding villages the government hospital was something to behold.

During their first visit, Manu Prasad and his wife most stayed quiet. The doctor's queries were answered by a simple 'yes' and 'no' by the young couple. The doctor had realized their anxiety and had asked his female assistant to join them. Janki Devi consulted with the assistant while the doctor interacted with the husband. The fertility doctor was also a gynecologist and his questions were more directed towards Janki Devi. The female assistant had been of help but still Janki felt uncomfortable. The first visit had been formal and the doctor had recommended the couple for a follow up. A preliminary test was performed on them as standard procedure. He had stressed the need for them to be more open on their second visit and assured them of confidentiality.

As Manu Prasad and Janki Devi relaxed on the bench, noises started echoing. The lunch hour was over and the hospital staff was getting back to work. The couple adjusted themselves upon seeing the doctor walking towards them. 'I will see you both in about two minutes'; the doctor assured them and entered his office. The couple packed their belongings and got ready for the meeting. 'Please be seated' the doctor informed the two upon entering. The two chairs facing the doctor were separated by a long glass table. A medical journal lay on it along with a sacred text. On the walls there hung academic certificates and mementos. Manu Prasad sat with his legs held closely together and his eyes staring at the glass table while Janki Devi clutched her bag and looked around the room, slightly tilting in her chair. 'My assistant is not going to be with us today, she had to leave early due to personal circumstances' the doctor informed the couple. Manu's expression remained unchanged, Janki Devi on the other hand felt unease upon hearing this.

'I'm going to ask you some personal details today' the doctor addressed them adjusting his glasses. Manu Prasad nodded his head in acknowledgment and his wife looked at the doctor, her mouth slightly open. The doctor continued 'You both have been married for over four years, correct.' The couple shook their heads in agreement. 'How long have you been trying to have a baby'? The doctor asked. 'Over two years' Janki replied. Manu just nodded as the doctor looked in his direction. 'Do you have problems during intimacy' the doctor looked at them. Janki Devi looked at her husband who slightly turned his head in her direction. 'We are okay' the words slowly came out of his mouth as he faced the doctor. 'Do you experience fluctuations in menstruation'? The doctor looked at Janki Devi. Janki paused and blurted 'Not really'. The doctor pulled out a piece of paper from his desk and carefully read it. 'Your initial tests seem to be fine' he assured the anxious couple. 'I will prescribe you some generic medicines, make sure you take it twice daily' he scribbled on a piece of paper. 'Few more visits will be helpful' He informed the couple, handing over his prescription. 'Our next meeting should take place in two months' the doctor decided. The couple breathed a sigh of relief. 'I think we can help you both' he assured the departing couple who were glad to exit the hospital.

After picking up their prescriptions from the hospital pharmacy, the young couple headed to the nearest Tea vendor. The sun was out in full force and the large canopy covering the Tea stall provided a welcome relief. Manu Prasad and Janki Devi sipped their hot beverage shielded from the sun. There was no place to sit and the couple huddled close together. 'Feel good after having hot Tea' Janki whispered to her husband in the crowded town square. Manu shook his head in agreement, taking his last sip. He paid for the Tea and started walking along with his wife. Janki Devi's eyes darted along the small shops and roadside vendors while Manu looked in the direction of the bus depot. 'Would you like to buy anything before we get on the buses? He asked his wife. 'I don't know' She replied apprehensively, her eyes fixed on a small dress shop.

Manu Prasad looked at his watch and said 'Let's walk to that shop'. Janki bristled a little and followed her husband. The dress shop was full of various garments and had attracted quite a crowd. The owner sat cross legged on the floor, supported by a fluffy cushion. He was meeting all the needs of impatient shoppers. A young boy pacing back and forth in the small shop was proving to be a worthy assistant. After bargaining with owner for the fourth time, Janki Devi picked up a Shawl for herself on her husband's insistence. 'A little expensive' she said to her husband as they walked away.

Upon reaching the bus depot, the departure schedule frustrated the couple. The next bus to Gauri Ghat was still two hours away. Manu looked at his watch and slightly shook his head. 'We better sit down somewhere' Janki quipped. They walked inside the depot and spotted empty chairs. It was going to be a long wait and there was little both of them could do about their predicament. Janki Devi carefully put her belongings close to her and seated herself. Manu Prasad slumped a bit in his chair, the long trip wearing on him. Soon, Janki was leaning on her husband, her eyes slowly closing. Her thoughts drifted towards her village. She would have to prepare dinner upon getting back home. She needed some fresh vegetables, having none left at the house. Her cows were most certainly out of fodder and water. They had been inside the shed all day and were probably cranky. She was unable to take them grazing due to her long trip. It was probably going to be dark by the time they both reached home. The trip was turning out to be lot longer than anticipated.

Manu Prasad rubbed his eyes, his mind drifting back. His provision store back in the village was closed for the entire day as a result no earnings were generated. The trip to Kesar Khal had been longer than originally planned. This was going to hamper his chances of ordering new supplies for the store. Most of the Lorries that ferried goods between Gauri Ghat and neighboring small towns stopped running after late evening. Manu Prasad also had a small patch of land in his village where he mostly grew vegetables for his daily needs along with some corn and wheat. Once a day his wife tended to the small field. Manu looked at his watch. He knew it would be close to dark by the time they both returned to Gauri Ghat. Manu Prasad just hoped they could avoid darkness before their trails on the long mountain road. With his hands folded and his wife leaning on him, he apprehensively seated inside the small waiting room.

Janki Devi felt someone tugging on her feet. She got up and looked down underneath the chair. A toddler barely six months old was clinging to her hind legs. For a minute she just looked at him. Janki Devi gently picked him up and put him in her arms. The child was smiling and pulling on her sleeves. Janki looked at his eyes as saliva started coming out from his little mouth. She pulled out a napkin and tenderly wiped the child's mouth. The child was seemingly enjoying the attention and looked for further more. The toddler grabbed Janki's fingers and started licking them. Janki Devi just smiled and obliged. She reached for the cheeks and gave the child a slight rub. The toddler grabbed her hair, making her scream. Janki Devi smiled and lightly moved the child's hand. Manu Prasad who at this point was oblivious to both of them just watched the spectacle.

'Oh my baby, there you are'! A young woman rushing towards Janki Devi screamed in satisfaction. A child probably three years old was following the woman. She got in front of Janki Devi and gathered herself. 'For the past fifteen minutes, I have been looking all over the bus depot for my child' she explained to Janki Devi. 'He has this habit of running away from me and wandering on his own' the mother further stated. Janki Devi handed the toddler to the young mother and straightened herself. 'Thanks for taking care of him' the mother said to Janki Devi and Manu Prasad as she walked away with her baby in tow. Janki Devi watched as the toddler merrily cuddled with his mother. The mother could be heard muttering stern warning to the child as they disappeared. Janki Devi started wiping her hands which were still wet. A little later she adjusted her sleeves and looked at her belongings. 'The bus should be arriving soon' Manu Prasad remarked, looking at his watch. Janki Devi silently nodded and looked outside.

The bus scheduled for departure to Gauri Ghat finally arrived. A long line of people was waiting anxiously for the vehicle. Manu Prasad had already purchased the tickets in advance and was guaranteed seats unlike some who had recently arrived and were having difficulty boarding. A little later, the bus was moving. Manu and Janki were seated in the front of the packed vehicle. Janki Devi wiped her brow and handed a napkin to her husband who was slightly sweating. Summer season had begun and large number of passengers inside the bus made for a sweaty commute. The town of Kesar Khal was now in the rear and the large bus was on the highway speeding ahead. Cool breeze coming through the open windows provided much relief to the passengers. 'Looks like we will get home before dark' Janki Devi quipped to her husband. 'I really hope so' Manu Prasad said, looking at his watch. Ten minutes later, the bus came to slow halt. Most passengers leaned forward and looked outside.

A caravan of different vehicles stretching for a mile had stopped on the highway. It seemed like an accident further down had stalled everyone. The two lane highway resembled a parking lot. The driver of the bus announced to everyone about a possible long delay. The conductor gave the passengers an option of exiting the vehicle till the logjam was cleared. Slowly most of the passengers cleared out and stretched in the open. 'Would you like to get some fresh air'? Janki Devi apprehensively asked her husband. 'Now we will definitely get back home after dark' Manu Prasad said dejectedly, firmly seated on the bus. 'Maybe, the highway will get cleared soon' Janki encouraged. Manu knew well a logjam like this would take few hours to clear. He had been involved in a few in the past. Luckily they all had been during the afternoon; he had made sure of it. His previous trips back to Gauri Ghat were well planned. The long mountain road back to his village Had to be avoided during dark! That possibility looked remote as Manu Prasad sat on the empty bus along with his wife, waiting for the highway to clear.

A large number of people had gathered outside on the highway from different stalled vehicles. Most of them were looking straight ahead on the road, hoping for the highway to clear. The older folks rested on the roadside curb while women huddled together with their small children. The brave ones darted ahead on the highway to get information on the deadlock. Soon, news started pouring into the rest. A deadly collision had blocked the highway according to few. Others blamed it on rockslide. No one knew when normalcy would resume again. Anxiety was slowly turning into anger but the predicament continued. Some passengers whose destination was close just picked up their belongings and started walking.

A river almost parallel to the highway was flowing through about half a mile down from the traffic logjam. Huge rocks stood in the middle of the gushing river, generating foam. The water was glistening in the setting sun and it was creating quite a spectacle. A Kingfisher was dipping in and out of water, hoping for a catch. Two Hawks circled high above the river, carefully studying the water shore. A cattle herd was grazing on the green grass close to the water. Two fishermen were folding their nets, having called it a day. Their catch lay next to them and they were examining it, accompanied by a song. They collected their belongings and rode away in their bicycles, hardly paying attention to the logjam further up. The dirt road running close to the river was wide open.

The highway slowly started clearing. The driver announced everyone to get inside the vehicle. Manu Prasad and Janki Devi had never left the bus. Slowly the bus moved ahead amid the setting sun. A little later, dead body of a huge farm animal could be seen on the side of the road. Dark stains on the middle of the highway clearly indicated it was removed with great difficulty. A scheduled stop approached and some passengers exited the bus. The bus unloaded more passengers on the way and kept moving forward. Eventually twilight gave way to darkness and the highway seemed quiet. Apart from the bus, few vehicles were still on the road. The driver was focused on the dark road while the conductor stretched in his seat. The vehicle was now three fourths empty.

Heavy sounds of water crashing in the dark reminded everyone that confluence of two rivers had arrived. The bus was soon treading on the large bridge. The long uphill mountain road to Gauri Ghat lay ahead. The bus still had six passengers left, most of who were sleeping. The responsibility to inform them of their respective stops lay with the conductor who himself seemed tired. Manu Prasad was awake while his wife soundly slept on his shoulder. He wished he could also sleep through the uphill journey. He even tried but he just couldn't. Memories hounded him! It was dark outside but Manu Prasad was well aware of his surroundings. Even the sound of the moving vehicle barely registered in his ears. The bus slowly navigated around a mountain curb and Manu Prasad gazed outside the window. His heart paced! The deep ravine on the other side of the narrow road was still visible to him. He stretched his neck and observed closely.

Six years ago, Manu Prasad's parents along with his younger brother had disappeared along this same spot. The driver of the small vehicle in which they were travelling during the night had lost control and plunged into the hollow ravine. No trace of the vehicle or the passengers was ever found. A large sack of rice and deep tire marks close to the accident site was the only evidence left of the disaster. The small vehicle in which the deceased were travelling was regularly used for transporting goods. Manu Prasad's family was not even supposed to be on this vehicle. 'Why did they have to miss the buses? Why was he not with them'? The thoughts remained with Manu Prasad for years. His life had changed after the tragic incident.

Manu Prasad's movements had woken up his wife. She looked at her husband who was almost leaning towards the window. 'Is this where it happened'? Janki Devi asked passively. 'Yes', Manu replied apologetically for making his wife uncomfortable and straightened back in his seat. It had been years since Manu Prasad had taken the mountain road back to his village after dark. He had traversed the road during the day but somehow night travel awoke past memories in him. 'We should be home soor.' Janki Devi said to her husband who was now looking straight at the night road. Manu Prasad just nodded and gave his wife a slight smile. 'Ten minutes to Gauri Ghat' the bus conductor loudly announced. Manu Prasad and Janki Devi started gathering their belongings. 'I still have to prepare dinner' Janki Devi remarked, getting off the bus. 'Don't worry; I picked something from the big town' Manu Prasad stated showing a neatly covered bag to his wife. 'When'? Janki Devi asked with a smile. 'While you were sleeping inside the bus depot' Manu Prasad replied looking at his wife. The two soon started carefully walking downhill towards their home.

Chapter 2

Gauri Ghat located at an elevation of about 1500 meters was nestled in the foothills of Southern Himalayas. The outer reaches of Himalayas provided the first layer of defense in the form of smaller mountain ranges. These hills closer to the village were rich in vegetation and home to various Flora and Fauna. The massive snow clad Himalayan peaks rose in the background and towered over the smaller hills. A pine forest about 200 meters from the village was easily visible on clear days. Deodar and Rhododendron trees were found closer to the village. Gauri Ghat was also close to various running streams and waterfalls. Cluster of houses and a wide open sky adorned the landscape.

Gauri Ghat had an approximate population of three hundred, depending on visitors and seasonal farm laborers. The village was birched on a small hill and most of the farmland was further down on even ground. Gauri Ghat like most villages in the hills was located close to water springs and small streams. The houses in the village were not built according to any town planning schemes but haphazardly put up on level ground in clusters. Houses in Gauri Ghat were built of stones and generally double- storeyed, few having more storeys. A mud or a stone stair case led to the upper level, the roof mostly being of wood. The top floor in most houses had a verandah which opened outside. A small prayer room adorned every house in the village. Some houses also kept a storage room. The cattle sheds were built at a distance from the house and required daily visits.

Most houses had a paved courtyard or a Chauk as it was commonly called out in the front. The Chauk was mostly used for spinning, weaving, thrashing and other household works. Women of the house mostly worked in the open Chauk. The Chauk was also used as a social set-up for family gatherings and other functions. During evenings, the men gathered around the Chauk and smoked tobacco. Daily lives and village gossip accompanied shared smoking. Keeping the Chauk nice and clean was considered noble. A person having a well paved and a large clean Chauk was held in high esteem by the villagers.

Manu Prasad's courtyard was of medium size but well maintained. Manu made sure of that every morning. It was around 7AM and he was busy cleaning his Chauk. Janki Devi walked outside from the kitchen and looked at the clean courtyard. 'You should have rested today, the trip was really tiresome yesterday' she advised her husband. 'Dust has settled on the ground' Manu Prasad replied continuing to sweep the courtyard with his hand broom. Janki Devi smiled, realizing it was futile to persuade her husband to change his mind. She picked up a bag along with some farming tools and prepared to leave the house. 'I have to go the field and then to the cow shed. It will take me few hours to come back home' she said and departed. Manu nodded and continued his cleaning.

An old lady was watching the proceedings in Manu Prasad's courtyard from her top floor verandah. She waited for Janki Devi to leave and then slowly made her way towards Manu Prasad. 'How was the trip' she asked getting closer to the courtyard. Manu Prasad turned around and noticed his neighbor dressed in familiar whites facing him. He paused from cleaning and replied 'it was good'. The old lady got a little closer and whispered 'What did the doctor say'? This puzzled Manu Prasad and he put down his broom. He looked at his neighbor who had a slight smile on her face. 'How did she know about the doctor'? Manu Prasad thought to himself. 'I will tell you later Mausi' Manu Prasad mumbled, words barely audible. 'Don't worry I will keep it a secret' Mausi replied and went inside her house. Manu Prasad sat in his courtyard and wondered. Except the family friend, no one had known about the trip to Kesar Khal. Aunt or Mausi as she was commonly known in the village had left Manu Prasad perplexed.

Mausi was Manu Prasad and Janki Devi's next door neighbor. She was a widow and her age could have been anywhere between sixty five or seventy, depending on who you asked in the village. Birth certificates were alien to people of her generation. She shared the house with her younger brother and his wife. The brother had retired from the Army and lived on a small pension. His wife, who was partly mute, took care of their small farm. Mausi helped in the household and kept things running smoothly. She cut a dominating figure, putting people around her mostly on the defensive.

Being a widow, Mausi was always clad in a plain white Sari as the village custom dictated. She wanted things done her way and was quick to point mistakes. Mausi also liked to gossip and occasionally pick on the unfortunates. Most people in the village avoided her and those who couldn't faced her antics. She had things to say to people which they didn't like, mostly annoying. Being her neighbor, Manu Prasad couldn't avoid Mausi even though he occasionally tried. Due to her age, Mausi hardly left the house. Besides Mausi's younger brother and his wife, Manu Prasad was the only one who put up with her. Janki Devi fitted differently in this equation. Apart from few formal greetings during the festival season, Mausi and Janki Devi hardly communicated. The dislike was mutual and Mausi usually avoided Janki Devi.

It was latter part of the morning and Manu Prasad was running late. He couldn't find the keys for his provision store. He had already checked his room closet twice, the usual place for the keys. He looked on the floors and the kitchen area but nothing. He had even looked in the courtyard unsuccessfully. Finally he decided to check his pants, the one he had used for his trip to the doctor. His wife had put those outside in the courtyard after wash for drying. They were hanging on a long string along with few other clothes. Manu Prasad rushed outside and checked his drying pants. He was relieved to find his keys in the pant pocket. He looked at his watch and trotted towards the provision store, a good ten minutes away.

Mausi stopped him halfway through. 'You seem in a hurry today Manu' she said walking towards him. 'Oh yes Mausi, I'm late already' Manu replied, pausing a little. 'You can spare few minutes for your old Mausi' she chuckled. 'Probably later, not now, customers are perhaps already gathering at the store' Manu stated, avoiding a direct gaze at the old lady. 'What did the doctor say'? You can tell me Manu, I will keep it under wraps' Mausi persisted. At this point Manu Prasad got defensive. He did not want anyone else to hear their conversation. 'I will tell you everything Mausi, it will take quite some time and right now I'm in a hurry' Manu Prasad requested. 'Okay, okay, you go to your provision store but I want to hear it all' Mausi replied walking back. Manu Prasad breathed a sigh of relief and quickly disappeared. 'Poor boy, he his having hard time making a baby' the old woman muttered to herself. 'Probably his wife's fault, she is too heavy for him' Mausi chuckled and went inside her house.

When Manu Prasad reached the provision store, ten customers were already waiting for him. He apologized to everyone and unlocked the store door. 'Just give me a few minutes and I will help each one of you' Manu asked the small crowd. The customers were impatient but realized the predicament. Manu Prasad was well liked by everyone due to his calm demeanor and

33

helpful nature. 'Okay, I'm ready for you all now' Manu Prasad proclaimed adjusting on the small chair inside his provision store. Soon, he was doing brisk business. Occasionally he would peep out of the store to look for someone and shake his head in disbelief. A young boy who usually helped him in the store was missing. This meant Manu Prasad had to do everything. First he would take orders from a customer, then find the particular item, properly bag it and eventually collect payment. 'Where is Bal today'? Manu exasperated wiping sweat from his forehead.

A little later, Bal arrived with his signature pocket transistor radio in hand. 'Where have you been' Manu looked in the direction of the young lad, his voice slightly rising. 'Sorry, I heard on the radio it was going to rain so I fell asleep' Bal replied and quickly started arranging things in the provision store. Manu just looked at the boy and shook his head. The provision store was now running smoothly due to extra help and this relieved Manu Prasad who was tending to more customers. Only problem was that chatter inside the store had picked up considerably. Bal hardly kept quiet when he worked. When he did, it was to listen to his pocket radio which was constantly running. Most customers avoided him and just talked to Manu who would then relay commands to the young boy. Speech impediment hampered the young boy's social skills. Apart from Manu Prasad and his own family members few comprehended Bal. The rest in Gauri Ghat considered him the village clown.

Manu Prasad had hired Bal out of goodwill. Actually, he was a good worker if one could put up with his chatter. Bal was about eighteen years old and lived with his mother and father. His pocket transistor never left his sight and he even slept with the device. All throughout the day and partly during the night, he would listen to the news. The problem was, he would hear one thing and comprehend something else. He would then describe the events to anyone who would listen. In this case it was mostly during his time at the provision store. It would give him great pride in describing things to Manu Prasad as customers would line up in front of the store. Manu would just nod his head in agreement to keep the young boy busy while most customers shook their heads in disbelief. Bal didn't mind as long as he had an audience and just kept busy. Manu Prasad had known Bal as a little boy and later as a good employee for almost four years. He actually enjoyed the young boy's company; it provided escape for him from his daily life which was lately becoming hectic.

For the next few days, Manu Prasad carefully avoided Mausi. She tried her best to approach Manu but it seemed Janki Devi was always in the vicinity. Manu Prasad had carefully arranged his schedule. This meant making two trips to the cow shed while his wife stretched in the courtyard. He even accompanied her to the small farm and helped plucking vegetables. Janki Devi was amused and pleased with this gesture and inquired about the sudden generosity. 'The doctor has advised easy workload for you' was the reason given by Manu Prasad to his wife. 'When did the doctor say that'? Janki asked. 'Oh, he informed me in private' Manu replied. 'Anything else the doctor said to you in private'? Janki smiled looking at her husband. Manu Prasad shook his head, his eyes scanning the neighbor's verandah. A figure in white Sari could be seen, disappearing inside the door.

Eventually Mausi got frustrated and stopped looking for her neighbor. Her brother and his partly mute wife now bore the brunt of her frustrations. It was mostly the mute woman who was about ten years younger than Mausi. The brother hardly stayed indoors, only coming to the house for eating and sleeping. His wife took care of the family farm during the day including the animal shed. She would milk the cows in the early morning and come back home to prepare tea for everyone. After this she would take them grazing in the pasture and return in the afternoon to help prepare lunch. After a short rest, she would leave again to toil in the family fields and call it a day in the evening. Mausi stayed in the house and helped with cooking. She also did some weaving, spinning and grinding in the courtyard. Mausi did all this and still followed most things around her.

It was still morning and Mausi had already finished her second cup of tea. Her brother had left the house after having breakfast while his wife was getting ready for a trip to the fields. 'Don't you get tired of working all the time'? She asked her sister in law. 'Not really' the sister in law mumbled, trying to avoid a direct gaze with her elder. 'You poor soul' Mausi exasperated looking at her sister in law. The younger woman just stood there, hoping for the encounter to end soon. 'Only if you had a son'! Mausi continued 'now you have to do everything yourself, work in the fields, milk the cows, collect fodder and take care of your husband'. The sister in law mumbled 'I don't mind'. Mausi gave her a disgusted look and said, 'Of course you don't mind, your three girls that are grown up and married won't come back to help you in old age'. The sister in law tried to speak but words deserted her. All she could do was mumble.

'You better get going now, the cows are probably starving and the field has to be tilled', Mausi lamented. 'I wish I could help but it is hard for me to walk, I can barely keep up with the household' She sighed. The sister in law gathered courage and coughed up, 'you do enough here'. Mausi shook her head as she watched her sister in slowly depart. 'God, we could use a man in this house' she blurted parting words at the sister in law. 'This woman has driven my brother to drinking, now the fool only comes home to eat and sleep' she said, slumping on the edge of the courtyard. 'My poor brother, god knows he tried his best for a son' she muttered to herself. A passer by looked at Mausi and quickly turned his gaze. 'What are you listening'? She said to the curious villager. 'Oh, nothing' the man replied picking up speed. 'Nothing is on the top of your bald head' she shouted at the man who quickly disappeared. Mausi looked across the neighbor's courtyard and found it empty. Manu Prasad was at the provision store and Janki Devi was grazing the cows. She wondered when Manu Prasad was going to be alone in the house.

Mausi remembered well the day a friend had visited Manu and his wife months ago. He had spent almost an hour with the couple in the courtyard. She had watched the proceedings from her verandah. All three of them were talking in hush tones and watching their surroundings. In the end, the friend had exchanged information with the couple. All this had peaked Mausi's curiosity. She knew Manu Prasad and Janki Devi wouldn't divulge anything about the meeting. Mausi would have to confront the friend for information and it wasn't going to be easy. When the friend eventually left, Mausi followed him on the dirt path for few minutes. After making sure no one was around, she approached him. 'You don't even say hello to me when you pass my house'! Mausi exclaimed to the surprised young man. 'Oh, Mausi I didn't see you' the man apologized. 'No one sees an old woman nowadays' Mausi sighed.

The young man was now feeling guilty and stopped walking. 'Let me walk you back home' he requested, realizing the old woman had veered off from her house. Mausi gladly accepted his help. 'It is the house next to Manu Prasad' she said. 'I know Mausi' the young man replied holding her hand as they both walked towards the house. 'Thank you' Mausi said upon reaching her house. It was farthest she had walked from the house in quite some time. 'I better get going now' the young man stated. 'At least let me offer you some tea while you are here' Mausi said looking at the young man. 'It will delay me' the man replied. 'This won't take long, what else you have to do in this small village' the old woman persisted. The young man smiled and agreed to have a cup of tea. Mausi pulled up a comfortable chair for him in the upstairs living room and disappeared in the downstairs kitchen. She appeared in ten minutes with her hands full. The young man was touched by the gesture. After two cups of tea and an array of delicious sweets, Manu Prasad's friend started opening up. Mausi eventually got the information she wanted in exchange for maintaining secrecy.

It was a late summer evening in Gauri Ghat. The sun was slowly setting in the west and this was creating quite a spectacle in the mountains to the east. The snow covered peaks in the back were glowing as the sunlight reflected on them. The color was almost golden brown. The mountains that were in the forefront and closer to the village adapted in their own way to the dwindling sunlight. Vegetation was clearly seen on the mountain side where light focused and the trees were slowly swinging in the wind. The side of the mountain obscured by the sunlight displayed a long shadow. It seemed quite but alive. Pine forest about two hundred meters from the village looked still amid the setting sun. The Rhododendron trees closer to the village were emanating scent from their flowers. Birds of various kinds were coming home to roost and their sounds filled the evening air. High in the sky a mountain eagle soared.

Gauri Ghat with a population of about three hundred was adjusting to the late evening. Farm animals were returning back from grazing and the small bells around their neck kept constantly ringing. Road above Gauri Ghat that connected to small towns seemed active. People were coming back home from their destinations. Women could be seen carrying utensils on their head filled with water from the spring. Few were still toiling in the fields but ready to call it a day. Men were gathering in the courtyard and getting ready to smoke. Hookah or a long smoke pipe was being passed around among constant chatter. The kids were running around, playing hide and seek. Temple bells in a distance could be heard ringing loudly followed by religious chants. Twilight hour was approaching and the villagers were now settling indoors. The women were busy preparing dinner and the men huddling in the courtyard. Time flew for some while waited for others.

Janki Devi was preparing dinner and talking to her husband at the same time who was sitting in the courtyard. 'How was your day at the provision store'? She asked. 'Just normal' Manu replied examining a small bag in his hand. 'Are those new medicines the doctor prescribed'? Janki continued. 'Yes, a friend dropped it in today from the town' Manu replied. 'Do you think all this will help'? She asked her voice rising.

'It will, just have patience, the doctor seems genuine' Manu assured. 'You know I have tried losing weight' Janki hushed. 'You are fine' Manu replied looking at his wife. 'I really want to have a baby' Janki said, her voice cracking a little. Manu Prasad listened in silence. 'God, I have tried so many things and revealed so much to doctors and others' Janki lamented. 'These villagers probably talk behind my back about my misfortune' she concluded. 'I know that old cow next door has nothing better to do than gossip. People tell me she comes over here and talks to you when I'm not around' Janki Devi stated looking at her husband who turned his head away from her.

Janki Devi was visibly disturbed and it reflected in her cooking. She was hastily preparing things. While looking for a frying pan, she inadvertently hit the small milk container and spilled everything on the floor. 'Oh no, I just spilled the last remaining milk on the floor' she sighed loudly. 'Don't worry; you can get some in the early morning' Manu Prasad assured. 'I need my tea in the morning, I don't like leaving the house without my daily cup' Janki replied. 'I will have to go milk the cow after dinner' she asserted. 'I can get some milk from the neighbor, it will save you a trip to the cow shed during the night' Manu intervened. 'Please don't get any favors from that old lady, it will prove costly' Janki Devi whispered to her husband. 'I don't mind the trip, the cows need extra water anyway during the summer' she assured her husband. Manu Prasad didn't mind his wife going to the cow shed but he was wary of being alone in the house. For days, he had carefully planned his schedule in the house. He knew accompanying his wife to the cow shed this late would just sound silly. He had already accompanied her early during the evening and placed enough fodder for the animals. Two people were not required to milk one cow. After dinner he was going to be alone in the house for some time. Manu Prasad turned his head. From his courtyard he could see Mausi sitting in her verandah smiling at him.

After dinner Mausi usually spent her time lounging in her top floor verandah. A large old wooden chair bent on the sides was her only companion. Her sister in law having worked all day would just fall asleep after dinner. The alcoholic brother would stumble in the house late at night and then leave in the morning. With so little activity inside her house, it was the outside that occupied the old lady. At night Mausi would gauge her surroundings from the verandah. Her eyes would look south and see the lights twinkling in a far off village. To her left was another house obscured by a large tree and a thick brush, making it difficult to see things clearly. The road that connected Gauri Ghat to other towns was behind her house. It was higher up and not visible from her verandah. There was one thing that was clearly visible from Mausi's verandah. It was Manu Prasad and Janki Devi's house which was to her right. She had always liked that house since childhood!

After dinner Janki Devi departed for the cow shed. She carried a small a vessel and a bucket of water with her. Manu Prasad was busy cleaning the kitchen for his wife. He realized the uphill trip back from the shed would be taxing on her. Manu was hurriedly arranging clean utensils wherever he could find empty space. Cleaning up the mess on the floor was taking longer but Manu was doing his best. He wanted to go upstairs to his room and relax. The kitchen was finally done Manu removed the apron from his front and hung it on the wall. A voice coming from the courtyard stopped him as he was walking towards the stairs.

'Manu, you still in the kitchen'? Mausi's unmistakable voice from outside stopped him in his tracks. For a minute Manu Prasad pondered about his next move. 'Should he quietly go to his room or meet Mausi in the courtyard'. Before he could decide, Mausi spoke again 'I heard the utensils clattering a few minutes ago, so you must be around in the kitchen somewhere'. Manu Prasad dejectedly walked out to the courtyard. 'There you are Manu'! The old lady said with a smile standing across from him. 'Hello Mausi' Manu mumbled looking at the old lady and then quickly turning away his gaze. 'You have been trying to avoid me for a long time son' Mausi stated, slowly sitting down on the edge of the courtyard. 'I have been busy Mausi' Manu replied, looking around him. 'Don't worry your wife is not coming back for another fifteen or twenty minutes. A big woman like her needs more time to do things' Mausi assured the impatient young man. Standing under a moonlit sky, Manu Prasad knew he would have to answer the old lady anxiously sitting across from him.

'So tell me, why did you have to go to the doctor in Kesar Khal'? Mausi said, hardly wasting any time. Manu Prasad took a deep breath and looked around his dark courtyard. 'We are having trouble conceiving, so a friend suggested going to the fertility doctor in the big town' he said to the old lady staring at him. 'Oh, you have been having trouble conceiving for years Manu' Mausi smiled at the young man. Manu was embarrassed but knew the truth. 'Both of us have tried various things in the past without success' Manu said, in a low tone. 'Did the doctor give you anything for this'? The old lady asked. 'He gave us both some medicines for a period of time' Manu replied. 'I'm sure you are taking those medicines every night' the old lady cracked, suppressing a smile. Manu Prasad just stood there looking at the ground. 'It is not your fault Manu, it is your wife. Not only is she older than you, she is also heavy' Mausi tried her best to assure. This irritated Manu Prasad but he maintained his composure against the elderly neighbor.

'The doctor checked her and said she was fine' Manu Prasad said calmly. 'Of course he is going to say that. He cannot change the obvious Manu, so the doctor is probably trying his best' the old lady defended. She continued 'you poor thing, you did not have a choice. You had to marry this woman out of need, now she can't give you a child'. Manu Prasad collected himself and said 'I think this doctor can really help us'. The old lady lifted herself and said, 'Well I have some ancient herbs that can help you in this matter. It will break the childless curse and probably deliver you a son'. Manu Prasad thanked the old lady for the offer and said 'I have to stick with the doctor for now'. Mausi was now standing up and replied 'Well if you ever need them, don't forget to ask me'. Manu Prasad just nodded. Sound of steps coming from a distance alerted the two neighbors in the courtyard. 'I better get going now before your wife arrives' Mausi said to her anxious neighbor. 'Okay' Manu replied, hoping the old lady would disappear soon. He did not want the two to meet, knowing well their mutual dislike. 'Don't worry I will keep this entire meeting secret' Mausi concluded and hurried indoors.

Manu Prasad rushed inside his house. He knew his wife would be surprised to see him in the courtyard this late. He quickly went upstairs to his room but realized he had forgotten the medicines in the kitchen. When he came downstairs to get them, Janki Devi was entering the house. 'What are you doing this late in the kitchen'? She asked her anxious husband. 'I had forgotten the medicines here' Manu replied, picking up the small bag. 'You are not the forgetting kind' Janki smiled. Manu Prasad shrugged on his way to the stairs. 'Looks like you have done the kitchen for me' Janki thanked. 'It only took a few minutes' Manu lied. They both made their way upstairs. 'I'm too tired today' Janki stated sitting on the bed. 'I will skip the medicines today and just go to sleep' she smiled. Manu Prasad placed the small bag in a corner. Few minutes later his wife was sound asleep while he lay on the bed looking at the ceiling.

Some things Mausi had stated in the courtyard stayed with him. He had definitely married Janki Devi because of his circumstances. There was little Manu Prasad could do! After the tragic demise of his family, he was caught in a downward spiral, economically and mentally. The provision store was in debt and took years to recover. The family of the girl he was supposed to marry suddenly disapproved of the union. Few in the village understood his predicament. Mausi was different! Apart from him she was the most distraught after his father's death in the village. She had consoled him on various occasions since the tragedy. He remembered she had arrived in Gauri Ghat a year before his father, mother and younger brother perished on the mountain road. Most in Gauri Ghat viewed her with contempt and fear. Mausi was definitely overbearing but she had a soft spot for Manu Prasad. He remembered his beloved late father was the only one in the village who had kind words for the old woman. After all Mausi was responsible for his marriage to Janki Devi!

After talking to Manu Prasad, Mausi slowly walked upstairs to her verandah and seated on the old chair. Every night, she usually looked at the village and the surroundings till her eyes stayed open and then retired in her room. Sometimes she would just fall asleep on her favorite chair. It was around 10pm and the night sky was full of stars and a partial full moon. Most of the villagers were asleep, early morning beckoned them to the fields. A handful was still in their respective courtyards winding down for the night. An abandoned shack at the end of the village was hosting few lost souls. A large bottle was passed around among them along with tales of misfortune. Mausi's bother was one of them. He would usually stumble home when both liquid and the talk dried up. There was little anyone could do to change his condition.

Mausi looked at the night sky and remembered a time when the villagers would line up in their courtyards and gaze at the moonlit sky. This was long before electricity was available in the village. In those days during the night, flashlight was required just to walk few feet. Mausi looked far south off Gauri Ghat and saw lights twinkling in a village. Long ago, the village was hardly visible in the dark. Lamps and lanterns ruled the roost. Mausi herself used to carry one of those during the night. Her older sister insisted on her company to tend call of nature during odd hours.

Mausi rubbed her eyes to scare away approaching sleep. She stretched back on her chair and relaxed. A sound of vehicle coming to a grinding halt awakened her senses. Mausi realized it was coming from the road higher up from the village. Even this late during the night, a vehicle would occasionally travel through the road that connected the village to bigger towns. Mausi reminisced the time when there was no road in Gauri Ghat. Large stretch of fields occupied the present road. When she was twelve year old, Mausi along with her friends used to graze their cattle on those fields. Few years later, plans were put forward for construction of a long road. It was a road that was going to connect Gauri Ghat and surrounding small villages to the big town of Kesar Khal along with other towns on the way. Lot of people was excited as the road would speed up travel. Few were against it as it meant losing of pasture land. As a young child, Mausi was one of those who were against the road as it meant end of long open fields. Later in life, she wished the road had never been built. It had taken a lot away from her.

It was getting late and Mausi slowly rose from her chair. The village was quiet and even an occasional breeze made noticeable sound. Mausi switched off the light in her verandah. Sounds of an animal coming from the forest high above the village stopped Mausi as she was walking to her room. The sound was heard again and then it stopped. Mausi looked in the direction of her cow shed and wondered. It was one of the most vivid memories she had of her childhood. The cries of 'Ruchi, Ruchi' still filled her ears. Mausi composed herself and made her way to the bed. She gently rolled on the small bed and pulled the pillow towards her. She wondered how time had passed since she was a little girl growing up in Gauri Ghat. Mausi wiped her tears as images flashed through her mind.

The transformation of Ruchi into Ruchitra Devi and eventually Mausi was slow and gradual.

Chapter 3

It was early in the morning and little Ruchi was still fast asleep. The school was closed today on account of a holiday and no one was going to bother her for some time. She and her older sister had stayed up late last night and played different games. First it was hide and seek. They both would take turns hiding from one another in different corners of the house until being caught. They would loudly scream upon getting found by the other forcing their mother to scold them on various occasions. After getting tired of playing, they started talking to each other in hush tones as most family members had fallen asleep. They were now trying to determine what the other was thinking by reading facial expressions. Ruchi was mostly wrong about her sister's thoughts but was proving to be an open book by her older sister. This continued for a while before sleep slowly started overtaking Ruchi. She tried to fight it off but soon fell asleep on her sister's lap. Her older sister picked her up and put little Ruchi on the bed. She kissed her on the forehead and departed.

'Ruchi, Ruchi' it was the older sister screaming at Ruchi in the morning who was still soundly sleeping. The screaming didn't help so the older sister slowly shook Ruchi. Ruchi arose from her bed, half dazed and half asleep. Her older sister was yelling at her but Ruchi didn't comprehend. She rubbed her eyes and looked at her sister who was crying. Ruchi was now awake and lunged at her sister who hugged her tightly. 'Our new born calf is gone' the older sister relayed to the younger one. Ruchi removed herself from the embrace and stared at her older sister. 'What are you saying'? She asked in anger. 'I'm saying the calf is dead. The leopard snatched him away' the older sister said dejectedly. 'When, how....'? Ruchi cried looking at her sister. The older sister put her arm around Ruchi and replied 'It happened during the night when everyone was asleep'. The sleep was now totally removed and anger had overtaken Ruchi. The newborn calf was her favorite; she used to visit him every day. It was born just ten days ago. The thought of him gone still wasn't sinking. Ruchi gathered herself and said, 'Let's go to the cow shed'. Her older sister replied 'Okay' and they both left, holding hands.

Every morning Ruchi washed her face before having hot tea. Today she had time for neither. When she arrived at the cow shed with her sister, a large group of people had gathered at the front door. The women were sobbing while the men were in disbelief. When Ruchi tried to enter the shed, a hand pulled her away. 'You should not go in there' her mother said emphatically; tear stains still visible on her cheeks. 'You shouldn't have brought her here' the mother scolded the older sister. 'She would have eventually found out and then gotten mad at me' the older sister pleaded sobbingly. The mother embraced the two daughters and held them tightly. 'You both should go back to the house now, we all are coming home soon' the mother comforted them both. 'I would like to go inside the shed' Ruchi pleaded, tears slowly drying up from her eyes. 'Ruchi there is nothing you can do now, you can come back to visit later' her mother replied as she fixed Ruchi's unkempt hair. After a little more cajoling, Ruchi and her older sister were on their way back home. 'She is only nine years old, how can I let her see the inside of the blood stained shed' the mother whispered to an old lady standing next to her. 'I can only imagine the suffering poor calf went through during the night' she murmured to herself.

Most animal sheds in the village were poorly built. They were partly made of wood and bricks. The front of the shed was usually strong but the roof made of patched wood was mostly venerable. In this case the leopard had come inside through the roof. The animal had sensed an opening in the wooden roof and torn through it. After getting inside the shed, the leopard had snatched the baby calf away. The calf itself had put up resistance and its mother tied close to him had made hysterical sounds but it was all in vain during middle of the night. The only proof left was blood stains and marks all over the rusty shed. In the end the wild beast had proven to be very powerful, disappearing in the forest with the young prey. Ruchi's mother had found out about the incident during early morning. She had almost fainted upon opening the cow shed. A passerby had noticed her and rushed for assistance. Eventually her husband and the older son helped her to regain composure. The rest of the family members had found out about the incident through neighbors.

After this incident, Ruchi remained quiet for days. Even in school, she hardly talked to anyone. All her mother's queries were answered by a simple 'yes' and 'no'. She would open up a little to her older sister but quickly return back to the shell. She would eat sparingly and this worried her mother who would bring sweets to her at odd hours. The mother had also encouraged her to visit the cow shed again but Ruchi had refused. She vowed never to visit the shed again. Her contempt for wild animals got stronger. It was the first time something dear was taken away from her.

It was after school and Ruchi was sitting on the edge of her courtyard. Her older sister who mostly accompanied her everywhere had been keeping her distance lately. She knew Ruchi was in no mood for company lately but kept an eye on her dear sister most of the time. Ruchi was slowly recovering from the painful incident of the past few days. 'How are you Ruchi'? A young boy's voice surprised her. Ruchi turned around and saw her neighbor. It was Dev Prasad, a boy her age who lived next door. For a few minutes, Ruchi remained perplexed. It was the first time; the young boy had said anything to her. They had exchanged casual greetings in the past as most neighbors usually do but it was devoid of conversation. 'Oh, I'm okay' Ruchi finally replied to her young neighbor who anxiously stood on his side of the courtyard. The meeting was brief and they both left after few more awkward minutes.

She returned back to her courtyard a little later and looked around but the young boy was gone. A smile descended on her little face. Ruchi turned to her old talkative self soon and her sister was the most pleased.

Ruchi was the second youngest of five siblings in her family which consisted of two older brothers, an older sister and a brother who was baby of the family. Her father a devoted man was a farmer and toiled in his fields. Ruchi's mother took care of the household and other domestic responsibilities. Her two older brothers usually picked on little Ruchi, so she mostly avoided them. The baby brother was still crawling and hence shielded by their mother. It was the older sister who Ruchi adored and the feeling was mutual. They were mostly together the whole day. The older sister dressed Ruchi in the morning and then fixed her breakfast. They would leave together for school and it was here that Ruchi was without her older sister for few hours. Different classrooms separated the two sisters in the small village school.

The school in Gauri Ghat attracted students from the surrounding smaller villages. Some kids would walk three to four kilometers just to attend the government run school as it was the only one available in the vicinity. Luckily for Ruchi and her sister, it was only a fifteen minute morning walk to the school. They both looked forward to this every morning. They discussed their plans for the day during the walk. Post school and evening plans were also chartered out by the two sisters on their way to the learning center. Sometimes the talk lasted longer than the walk for both of them. Once inside the small building, they would head to their respective classrooms.

Ruchi's class consisted of fifteen children. There were ten boys and five girls in her classroom. The boys kept to themselves and so did the girls. Ruchi's neighbor Dev Prasad was also in the same classroom but kept his distance. Their teacher, a young woman was a strict disciplinarian. She taught them an array of things suitable for their age and demanded respect. Ruchi was scared of her and hardly spoke in her presence. Everyday half an hour was devoted to sketching in the classroom. Kids would take turns and draw various things on the blackboard. This was Ruchi's favorite time in the class. She used to draw different things on the large board and forget about others. The teacher usually ended up reminding her about time constraints. Fellow students would nudge her about taking extra time. Ruchi would just smile and apologize. During recess she would meet her older sister again in the school yard and pick up where they had left. School would be over at noon and everyone would head home.

Hot lunch was always ready for the sisters when they arrived home. Most of their produce came from their fields, courtesy of their father's hard work. An assortment of vegetables and lentils filled Ruchi and her sister's plate. It was complemented by hot Rotis and saffron rice. The sisters would eat to their hearts content and wipe their plates clean. Their mother watched with smile from a distance, a toddler clinging on her. After lunch the older sister would help her mother clean up while Ruchi took care of the baby brother. The sisters would rest for few minutes and then look forward to their most favorite part of the day. It would keep them occupied till evening but they never complained.

It was time for Ruchi and her sister to graze their cattle. The older sister would unlock the cow shed and carefully take the herd outside where Ruchi anxiously awaited. They both would then march the herd towards long stretches of pasture above the village. Here they would meet up with other village kids who would also bring their cattle for grazing. The cattle would be untied and left to roam on the wide green pasture. Once free the herd would run towards the green grass. The kids would watch their respective cattle bask in freedom unshackled. They would then gather and start planning their activities. Here boys and girls played together unlike at school.

The kids would open up their small box and collect the marbles. A competition would be set up among them and the winner received the loser's marble. The marbles also had their own value depending on size and shine. The bigger and shinier marbles were envy of all and most kids tried their best to win them. Ruchi loved her precious marbles and hated to lose them. She was good at the game which was like playing billiards on the ground. The marbles were used as billiard balls and the most accurate person usually won. Ruchi was playing against a boy few years older than her. She was doing well in the beginning and smilingly adding more shine to her collection. The older boy was actually disguising his skills and letting little Ruchi win. This encouraged her to put the bigger and shinier marbles in play. The boy noticed this and changed his game.

To Ruchi's surprise, her precious marbles were now exchanging hands. She was not ready for this and refused to part with them. The older boy was having none of this and stated to everyone he had won fair and square. 'I'm not giving you my marbles' Ruchi protested. 'I have won them fairly' the boy replied. 'You cheated' she yelled. The older boy was adamant and refused to back down. A couple of kids tried to calm Ruchi but she started crying. She looked around and saw her sister playing further away, totally unaware of the situation. 'You can have my marbles, they are just as big' Dev Prasad said to the winner, opening a small box. The older boy didn't mind and took the offer. Ruchi got her precious stones back and was pleased. She thanked her kind neighbor who stood a few feet away from her and smiled. Soon everything was forgotten and the kids moved to their next venture. This required walking further up.

On the way, Ruchi along with her friends passed through small waterfalls and streams. Ruchi and her sister would wade through the stream and let crisp cool water splash on their legs. They would just stand in the middle of knee deep stream as other kids' sprinkled water on each other. The sisters tried their best not getting soaked but failing. Laughter and scream filled the air. They would emerge out of the mountain stream and dry themselves on the ground. 'Mother is going to be mad at us' the older sister usually stated. 'She would understand' was Ruchi's standard reply. The group would then wander around and pluck wild berries from their surroundings. Sometimes Ruchi and her sister would stumble upon apricot trees and devour the fruit. Her sister would hoist Ruchi on her shoulder. She would then pick ripe fruit from the wild tree. When the fruit hung too high, they would throw stones to get the desired result. The fruits of labor tasted so good!

As the evening approached the group would make their way downwards towards the pasture. Ruchi and her sister would check on their cattle and make sure they had not strayed into private farms. Occasionally a few cows would drift off into rich fields, requiring collective efforts from the kids to tame. Some bovines would veer further away and required more energy. The kids would then whistle to draw their attention. Once the herd was located, the kids secured their respective cattle. Ruchi would help her sister in this endeavor. The sisters would then bring the cattle down towards the shed. The downward slope was tricky and uneven. The older sister would hold Ruchi's hand while they descended with cattle in tow. They would slowly make their way to the cow shed. Here the cattle were safely led inside and secured. The shed door was properly checked and locked. Ruchi would then climb on her sister's shoulder and check the roof area. Her duty required inspecting the newly laid out hardwood. After all this, the two sisters would finally head home.

'Don't go inside without cleaning yourselves' the mother would yell at them upon their arrival. The sisters would take turn and thoroughly wash themselves, knowing well their mother's contempt for filth. After cleaning they would change their clothes and have freshly prepared hot tea, courtesy of their mother. Sometimes the mother would also include treats with tea, depending on her mood. The two sisters would rest for some time and then prepare for dinner. Ruchi would take care of her baby brother while her sister helped in the kitchen. The dinner would be eventually served and the entire family got together. They would all sit on the kitchen floor with their legs crossed and enjoy the evening meal. It was the only time during the day the whole family was in the same place. The older brothers would talk about their exploits in the field assisting their father. The old man himself would say little and just smile. The mother would describe her time at home with the toddler. The sisters in turn would narrate their day's events. Ruchi's description of her marble tales would draw laughter from the two brothers. The dinner would be soon over. Too soon for Ruchi, wishing it was longer. The sisters would help their mother clean up and then head to the courtyard.

A moonlit sky filled with night stars graced above. This was a boon to the village without electricity. It was quite a spectacle and most everyone in the village was out in their own courtyards. Like everyone else in the village, Ruchi and her sister spent the early part of night in their courtyard. Their father would gather around with few men and smoke tobacco in the middle of the courtyard. The two older brothers would disappear with friends their age and return home later. The mother would be busy putting the baby to sleep. The two sisters would find their own corner of the courtyard and huddle. They would look up and marvel at the sky. The configuration of nature would render them tongue tied but soon they would revert back.

'Is it a full moon today'? Ruchi asked gazing at the sky. 'Yes it is' the older sister replied with a smile. 'I'm trying to find the smallest star' Ruchi stated. 'Tonight it is going to be hard, the sky is full of stars Ruchi' the sister replied. 'How far do you think is the moon'? Ruchi asked. 'Too far' the sister stated. 'You think it is farther than the big town of Kesar Khal'? Ruchi inquired. 'Oh, a lot further away' the sister smiled. Ruchi suddenly looked at her sister and said, 'I never want to leave our home'. The older sister put her arm around Ruchi and said 'Eventually you will have to leave home'. Ruchi failed to comprehend and asked her sister to elaborate. Her sister tried to shrug it off but Ruchi persisted. 'All little girls eventually get married and leave their home' the sister spoke with a hint of regret. A night worm raced across shining brightly but Ruchi hardly noticed. Her sister's words had left her thinking.

'Where do the girls go after getting married'? Ruchi asked showing concern. 'To their husband's home' the sister replied. 'Do they have to'? Ruchi inquired. 'Yes dear, it is the tradition' the older sister said with a shrug. Ruchi scratched her head and pondered for a minute. 'The husband can still be in Gauri Ghat, right' Ruchi asked apprehensively. 'No' the sister replied with a hint of regret. 'What do you mean'? Ruchi asked, her voice rising. 'The girl's husband has to be from another village, it is the age old custom' the older sister stated. Little Ruchi looked at her sister. She hoped it was just a joke her older sister was playing to tease her. She was waiting for the moment her older sister would laugh like she had many times in the past. The moment never came and her older sister's expression remained the same. 'Ruchi, you know our parents are already looking for my suitor' the older sister confided. 'But you are only twelve years old' Ruchi protested. She realized she had spoken loudly and quickly covered her mouth. 'Well they plan to get me married in a few years' the sister replied. 'Where will you go then'? Ruchi asked anxiously. 'I don't know it may be a village three kilometers from here or a village close to Kesar Khal' the sister answered. 'It better not be that far' Ruchi demanded. 'It is not up to us Ruchi' the sister stated. 'How will I see you if you are far'? Ruchi asked, tears rolling down her eyes. The older sister put her arms around Ruchi and said, 'After marriage we won't be able to see much of each other'. Little Ruchi prayed this would never happen.

Few years passed and Ruchi had now grown up. Marriage plans for her older sister had been finalized by the family. The long and drawn out process of finding the best possible suitor had been finally achieved. This required meeting and talking to various families but was necessary. It was customary and Ruchi's parents just followed the old tradition. It was the first marriage in the family and they wanted the best for their oldest daughter. The first prospective suitor lived five kilometers away from Gauri Ghat. He was a young man about four years older than their daughter and a farmer in his village. Apart from having a slight limp due to childhood injury, he seemed like a good match. Their daughter wasn't sure, so they looked further. They found a possible match in a village far from Gauri Ghat. It was arranged by a family relative. The boy too was a farmer but the family hardly owned enough land. This search also failed to get the desired result. The parents continued to look without success. They wanted a boy financially stable for their child. Someone who could take care of their daughter the way they did. To the parent's great relief, the search finally ended.

A distant relative from a nearby town had arranged the match involving a family with ties close to the village. The boy's parents wanted a girl with a familiar background for their son. He lived in the big city which was state capital and about three hundred kilometers from Gauri Ghat. The young man was also six years older than his future bride but he possessed something no other suitors did. He had a well paid government job in the city. This sold Ruchi's parents. They realized their older daughter would never have to toil in the fields later. The distance was far but their oldest daughter would have comfortable life. The initial formalities were finalized after meeting the young man's parents who themselves had migrated to the big city from a village close to Gauri Ghat. As the custom dictated in those times, the bride and the groom met during the wedding. The auspicious day had arrived and everyone was looking forward to it except Ruchi.

Ruchi's house in the village was colorfully decorated for the wedding. Leaflets hanging from strings circled around the house and people were streaming in and out. After a ceremonial bath for the bride in morning, a Henna ceremony had been arranged. Women had anxiously gathered around Ruchi and her older sister. They were all waiting for the Henna artist from the village, an older lady running a little late. The idea of sharing her sister with everyone wasn't sitting well with Ruchi. It was Ruchi's last day with her dear sister and this thought kept bothering her. She looked at her sister adorned in a beautiful red Sari and smiling. 'Stop smiling, you will be gone for a long time soon' Ruchi thought to herself. The older sister looked at Ruchi and smiled some more. Ruchi was having none of this and turned around, trying to hide her emotions. The older sister just shook her head and fixed her Sari. Ruchi had been the same way during the night.

The night before the wedding Ruchi and her sister had stayed up late and talked. 'You are going to be three hundred kilometers away from Gauri Ghat'! Ruchi exclaimed. 'Don't worry I will come see you occasionally Ruchi' the older sister assured. 'It has to be farther than the moon' Ruchi stated. 'No it is not, you are old enough to know that' her sister interjected. 'I thought Kesar Khal was far but this is ten times further' Ruchi said dejectedly. 'Well my husband has a government car so I don't have to walk there' the older sister smiled. 'Have you seen your husband'? Ruchi asked looking at her sister. 'Not yet, but we will see each other during the evening' the older sister replied. 'He is ten years older than you'! Ruchi said rolling her eyes. 'He is only six years older, silly' the sister shot back. 'He better treat you properly' Ruchi demanded. 'Oh he will, otherwise I will come get you' the older sister smiled. Ruchi cracked a sarcastic smile still finding hard to comprehend. The older sister put her arms around Ruchi and they held each other. Soon they fell asleep in the same bed.

The Henna ceremony was finally over and the all the women had dispersed. Ruchi's hands were covered in delightful red with distinctly carved designs. Her older sister displayed similar patterns. A Puja was organized in the middle of the courtyard and the priest was getting ready for the ritual. Ruchi along with her parents, two older brothers, the youngest one and her older sister were all sitting in a makeshift stage. The priest was going around sprinkling holy water on the immediate family. Scent of sandalwood and incense filled the air. People were taking turns wishing the family and this was taking time. The noon hour was approaching and lunch was being prepared in one corner of the courtyard. Huge utensils had been set and cooks were busy preparing a large feast. Scent of spices and smoke heightened the senses. Soon lunch was served for the eager guests. Long rows of sheet were laid on the courtyard and people were sitting side by side. Ruchi along with her brothers was serving hot meals to the hungry guests. Everyone from the village was at the Ruchi family courtyard. Some waited for others to finish and then joined the afternoon feast. This lasted for almost two hours and Ruchi was tired of playing host. Finally it was her turn to eat but she was too tired and nervous as the day progressed. She still managed to get a mouthful, knowing well energy was required for the evening festivities.

After lunch, Ruchi and her family got some rest to get ready for the hectic evening. The evening arrived and Ruchi was fast asleep. Her younger brother had to intervene and push her. Ruchi thanked him and rushed outside. 'You better get ready soon' her mother yelled at Ruchi. She asked about her sister and was told the bride was getting ready in her room. Ruchi rushed upstairs and saw three women dressing her older sister. She was clad in a light red Sari with a matching blouse. The women were putting ornaments around her sister's arms and neck. 'Hey you' the older sister smiled upon seeing Ruchi. 'You better get ready, the groom and his party will be here in few hours' the sister continued. She turned around and picked up a bag close to her. 'This is for you little sister' the older one said, handing the bag to Ruchi. The three women smiled and continued with their work. Ruchi picked up the bag and looked inside. A light red Sari along with the blouse adorned the small bag. Ruchi carefully took the content out and thanked her older sister. 'You should get ready in this room, one of these women will help you' the sister stated. Ruchi was led to the corner of the room by a middle age woman. 'This will take time Ruchi as you have to look just like me' the older sister yelled to her. Ruchi didn't mind, she was just thrilled having the same matching dress as the bride.

It was late in the evening. Sounds of drums coming from a distance signaled the arrival of the groom and his wedding party. The drums got louder as the destination approached and most of Gauri Ghat was anxious to catch the first glimpse of the arriving guests. The villagers queued up in front of their homes and jostled for a better view. Ruchi was with her sister in the upstairs room and heard the drums. Her heart skipped a few beat as she made her way to the courtyard. 'Where are you going'? Her sister asked. 'Oh, just to get a view' Ruchi replied. 'You can't go there yourself, you have to be seen with me' the older sister demanded. 'Don't worry, I will stay invisible' Ruchi assured and disappeared. She was now in her courtyard which was full of people. Her parents along with her brothers were all ready to welcome the groom. Ruchi's father was dressed in matching black pants and blazer while her mother adorned a bright yellow Sari. She had never seen her parents look so sharp and happy. Ruchi made sure she wasn't visible and consciously hid behind people. She noticed her two older brothers dressed in white slacks and shirts. A bright red turban was neatly wrapped around their head. The youngest brother was also dressed in whites and hid behind his mother. His red turban was partly visible to Ruchi. The groom and his party were about to enter the family courtyard and the band got louder.

The groom entered the courtyard along with his family to a grand welcome. Ruchi's parents embraced their son in law and led him to the make shift stage towards the end of the courtyard. Two big empty chairs adorned with flowers were set on the stage. The groom was on his way to occupying one of them as the onlookers gazed. Ruchi was trying to get a good look at her future brother in law but a crowd gathered in front was obscuring her view. She discreetly moved her position but was still unable see clearly upfront. All she could see was the back of her brother in law. He was clad in matching light pink attire and a yellow turban which was partly visible. He seemed to be a man of medium built but walked with confidence. Ruchi was hoping for the groom to sit in order to get a proper view. She positioned herself behind two older women and was now able to see clearly. Her delight was disrupted by soft sounds of 'Ruchi, Ruchi'. It was her youngest brother tugging on her dress. Ruchi motioned him to be quiet and pulled the sibling towards her. 'You are needed upstairs, the sister has sent me to get you' her brother whispered. Ruchi was required to accompany her older sister to the stage according to tradition. After all she was the bridesmaid! Ruchi looked up and noticed two women in the verandah motioning her to hurry upstairs. She fixed her dress and quietly started walking.

Ruchi was leading her older sister to the stage amid anxiety and anticipation. The large crowd in the courtyard was admiring the new bride as she made her way towards the unoccupied chair. Ruchi's parents were standing in the middle of the courtyard and observing their two daughters. The mother wiped her eyes as the bride passed by her. Her oldest daughter looked beautiful in the wedding dress, her forehead partly covered by the Light red Sari. Ruchi seated her sister next to the groom and slowly departed. Keeping with tradition, she avoided a direct look at her brother in law. Ruchi elbowed her way to the opposite end of the courtyard. Here she was clearly able to see her older sister and her husband without being noticed. She leaned forward and started observing.

First thing that struck her was the glasses. Her brother in law had horn rimmed glasses that gave him an older look. He also had a moustache but no other facial hair. He seemed to be a young man of decent looks but Ruchi wasn't impressed. Her older sister was a princess and deserved better. The groom sat expressionless while the bride displayed a smile. Guests were taking turns greeting the newlyweds and the makeshift stage was the center of attraction. Standing in the corner, Ruchi realized her older sister was so close yet so far. Now she just couldn't walk over and talk to her. Someone else had more access to her. More rituals and ceremonies followed as Ruchi watched from a distance. Now it was all about her older sister and her husband. Ruchi walked around the courtyard trying to get closer to her sister. Her attempts were thwarted by one ceremony or the other. She finally took refuge on the edge of the courtyard. 'They make a lovely pair' a voice whispered next to her. It was Dev Prasad her neighbor standing few feet away. 'Yes, I guess' Ruchi replied. 'You don't seem too happy' the young boy stated. 'I'm happy but sad to see her leave' Ruchi remarked. 'Well your sister is going to a nice place, I hear the husband has a good government job' Dev Prasad said looking at the couple still going through few rituals. 'He also has glasses' Ruchi lamented. 'Intelligent people have glasses; it means they are good at studies' Dev Prasad added. 'You are too mature for your age' Ruchi smiled looking at her neighbor. Dev Prasad just shrugged. The night feast was getting ready to be served and Ruchi's assistance was required.

Entire Gauri Ghat had descended on Ruchi's courtyard for the wedding feast and it was proving to be hectic. Ruchi along with her family members and few relatives were doing their best to cater the hungry guests. The groom's family and his group were being served first and the rest followed afterwards. People were devouring the hot delicious dishes. Bride and the groom who were patiently waiting finally got their chance to feast. The groom whispered something in his bride's ears who nodded in agreement. Ruchi looked at her sister who was talking to relatives while eating. The groom quickly finished the meal and looked at his watch. He waited for his bride and they both arose from their seats. They slowly walked around and started bidding their farewell. The final departure for the bride was arriving! Ruchi went upstairs and watched the proceedings in the courtyard from her verandah. Her older sister was now hugging close relatives and friends. The immediate family would follow next. Ruchi wanted time to stop and go back. She just wished the previous night with her older sister could be revisited. They were so many more things she wanted to share with her. The entire day had awakened new emotions in Ruchi and she wanted to confide in her older sister. Now that was not going to happen, a man would always be her side. Her older sister was now hugging the little brother in the courtyard and tears rolled out from her eyes. 'Where is Ruchi'? She asked her mother. Ruchi was hiding in the corner of the verandah but couldn't escape her mother's sharp eyes. Her mother walked a little closer and angrily remarked' come down'.

The older sister had tightly grasped Ruchi with both hands and was gently talking to her. The husband was standing close by and observing the exchange. Ruchi hardly looked at him, her head firmly resting on her sister's chest. 'I will come see you soon' the sister remarked tears flowing from her eyes. 'Say something Ruchi' the sister requested. Nothing! Ruchi stood there speechless firmly holding her sister. Her eyes were droopy but tears stayed inside. 'Okay that is enough' the mother intervened and tried to separate the two sisters. It took a while and Ruchi finally relented. Finally the mother and her departing daughter embraced. They both were crying hysterically and had to be separated by relatives. The farewell was officially over and now preparations were made for the departure.

A small wooden gondola was brought in the courtyard by hired help. A little later two men placed a large chair decorated like a throne in the courtyard. Ruchi father was discussing travel arrangements with some people as the bride and the groom anxiously awaited. A group of people emerged with lanterns and flashlights to the delight of everyone. The bride was to be seated in the gondola and carried by four men, holding it from the front and back. The groom was going to be hoisted in the throne and moved by another four men. The bride and groom made their way forward. Ruchi was being held back by her mother as she watched her sister get inside the small gondola. She tried to move but her mother held her tightly. 'You know they have a long journey' her mother stated. Ruchi knew well about the journey, her sister had explained to her during the afternoon Henna ceremony. The bride and the groom along with the rest of the wedding party were going to spend the night in a hotel. The hotel was located in the town by the confluence of two rivers, about twenty kilometers from Gauri Ghat. It was probably going to take the wedding party about hour and half to reach their destination in the night. Lack of proper road meant a long walk in the dark aided by lanterns and flashlight. In the morning the bride and the groom were going to travel in car towards the big city.

The wooden gondola was moving and people gathered around showered it with flowers. The wedding party along with lanterns and flashlights was departing. A somber mood prevailed in the courtyard. Ruchi managed to free herself from her mother's clutches. She lunged forward and ran towards the gondola which had moved far from the courtyard. 'Someone get Ruchi' her mother screamed. Ruchi picked by speed and was now by the side of the gondola. 'Sister, Sister' she cried getting close to the wooden structure. Her older sister peeked out of the small window of the gondola and held Ruchi's hand. 'Don't leave, don't leave' Ruchi screamed, tightly holding her sister's hand. Tears were now freely from her eyes swollen eyes. The four men carrying the gondola had stopped as the two sisters held each other. 'Ruchi you have to leave' a voice screamed from behind. It was the older brother holding Ruchi. She was in mood to leave her older sister and clutched her tightly. It was with great difficulty the brother separated the two sisters. As she was being dragged away, Ruchi saw her sister disappearing inside the small wooden window.

When she reached home, Ruchi was exhausted. Her mother embraced her and was crying. Ruchi herself had run out of tears. She looked in the direction of the wedding party which had completely disappeared from sight. Her courtyard which was bustling with activities just a few hours ago was now silent. The makeshift stage had been removed but the decorations still adorned her house. Her parents along with her brothers were sitting in the corner of courtyard while she stood in the middle gazing at the night sky. A little later she went upstairs to her room. She was looking for her night dress, something she never did in the past. Ruchi looked around and the silence made her realize about sleeping alone.

It took two weeks for Ruchi to get over her older sister's departure. She was never going to be fully recovered but at least the initial symptoms had disappeared. Her appetite had returned and she was definitely more talkative. With her sister gone, the task of helping her mother in the household fell on Ruchi. Now she assisted her mother in cooking and washing. She also had to take care of her younger brother. This required bathing, feeding and occasionally clothing him. Ruchi still had to go to school and graze her cattle. The walk to school seemed longer to her. She would mostly walk alone to the school, her neighbor Dev Prasad accompanying her on few occasions. They both would talk about various things but quickly separate as the school approached. This was done to avoid passing remarks from other boys at the school. Ruchi liked her village school but knew in a few years this would change. The small school only had a limited curriculum for students and the course for further studies required moving to the nearby town. Those who could afford the bigger school moved, the unfortunate ones stayed in the village. Ruchi definitely wanted to learn more. She hoped in a few years she still would be studying and not getting married like her older sister. Her older sister was smart but had little choice. She was required to help in the household and take care of her younger siblings. Now it was Ruchi's turn!

High above the village, Ruchi was grazing her flock in the vast green pasture. Her friends from the village were also present and talking among each other. 'You know they are planning to build a road in the village' a girl few years older than Ruchi remarked. This took most by surprise and their curiosity was aroused. 'How do you know' Ruchi asked the older girl. 'Well my older brother works in Kesar Khal at the government building and got the information' the girl replied with a sense of pride. Everyone started surrounding the news breaker who was now the center of attention. 'How long will this take'? Ruchi asked standing away from the crowd. 'Soon' the girl replied with a smile. 'Can you imagine buses and cars coming up here'! The older girl exclaimed. 'It won't take hours anymore to reach the town by the confluence of rivers' a boy in the group remarked enthusiastically. 'Where will they build the road' Ruchi asked after a pause. Everyone looked around but no one had an answer including the news breaker. The group talked about various possibilities as they herded their cattle from the long stretch of green pasture.

Ruchi's sister had well settled in the faraway big city and was enjoying her married life. Her letters addressed to Ruchi and the family arrived every two months. The older sister detailed the contrasting lifestyle in big city and the village. Amenities and opportunities, the villagers could only dream was easily available to the older sister. Time was of essence and people hardly had any surplus in the big city. The older sister and her husband were also planning to have a family. Her plans of visiting Gauri Ghat in the near future were going to be altered. Ruchi read all the letters meticulously and hoped to meet her sister soon who was caught up in married life. Eventually the letters started arriving randomly. Some would take four months while others took five months to arrive at the family home in Gauri Ghat. Ruchi was getting disappointed but her mother consoled her. 'Her home is in the city now' the mother tried to pacify. Ruchi wondered if her older sister still felt the same way.

Ruchi's oldest brother was getting married soon and the second oldest had joined the Army. The older sister was unable to attend the wedding. She was expecting a child and her husband was against the idea of coming to the village. He wanted his wife in the city where hospitals could cater to her needs. There was not much they could do so Ruchi and her family accepted the predicament. 'Well she really can't come here under the circumstances' the mother rationalized. Ruchi just shook her head. 'They don't have any doctors here in case of emergency' the mother lamented. 'She is still a few months away from delivery' Ruchi intervened. 'Her husband probably doesn't want to take a chance in case of complications' the mother pleaded. Ruchi realized arguing with her mother was futile. She wondered about writing a letter to her sister but soon abandoned the idea. Ruchi had to accept things as they presented themselves. She was an adult and mature now. The brother's wedding commenced without the sister. His younger brother was also unable to attend the wedding. He could not get his leave sanctioned by the Army in time.

Ruchi was watching her little brother in the courtyard who was now grown up. He was refusing to be bathed by his sister insisting on taking care of him. 'I don't need your help anymore' the brother giggled. 'You are not that old yet' Ruchi shot back. Sound of boots entering the courtyard broke the brother and sister argument. Ruchi and her younger brother turned around. Two men dressed in clean and crisp army uniform were walking towards them. 'Where are your parents'? One of them asked Ruchi who seemed to be an officer. 'They are inside the house' she replied. 'Can you ask them to come outside' the officer requested in a somber tone. Few minutes later the parents emerged. They both were surprised to see the two army men in their courtyard. The officer got closer to them and said, 'It is with great sorrow I inform you of your son's demise. He has sacrificed his life for the nation'. The mother and father started trembling and asked the officer to repeat. The army officer put his arm around the father and elaborated as the mother stood close. Ruchi's second youngest brother had been stationed in the Himalayan border with his unit. A fast moving avalanche had buried him along with his unit. A search part was unable to recover the bodies due to extreme weather.

Ruchi's mother had lost her senses after getting the tragic news and had to be helped by relatives from totally breaking down. Her father also was deeply affected but seemed to keep everything inside. Ruchi herself was devastated. She realized how little she knew of her army brother. Most of her time growing up was spent with older sister and her friends. Ruchi remembered her brother occasionally teasing her. She wished he had teased her more. This wasn't going to happen anymore and she fought back tears. The family was distraught. Ruchi's mother suffered a partial loss of memory and required help. Ruchi and her older sister in law assisted in the household. Ruchi eventually had to skip school to help the family. Her older brother quit his job in the neighboring town and helped his father in the fields. It was more for moral than physical support. A month later the father passed away. Loss of a young son and toiling in the fields his entire life had taken a fatal toll on the old man.

The older sister arrived for her father's funeral. She was accompanied by her husband and their toddler son. It was with great difficulty they made the trip as she was expecting another child. The old man's final rites were performed at the confluence of the two mighty rivers while the women mostly stayed indoors. Ruchi was filled with mixed emotions. She was sad about the family tragedy but glad to see her older sister. The sisters hugged and cried reminiscing about their childhood but something was different. A space had been created between Ruchi and her older sister. The toddler son and the one inside her sister's belly occupied that space. The husband got some and Ruchi got the rest. The husband was wary about spending time in the village and had brought his own sheets and pillows for the brood. His servant walked every morning to the nearby town and brought drinking water for them. The older sister was also careful and scolded her son when he played in the courtyard. 'You will get germs in your body playing out there' the mother yelled at the toddler who enjoyed the open space. She herself was careful and washed her hands upon touching things in the house. Occasionally Ruchi was the recipient of her sermon regarding cleanliness. For a person who had passed most of her life in the village, the older sister seemed to have adapted to the big city quickly. The mourning period was over and the older sister was ready for departure. She volunteered to take her mother along but the older brother denied the request. 'Our mother has lived in the village her whole life and will live here the rest' he proudly stated. 'We can take better care of her in the city with all the hospitals' the sister protested. The older brother didn't budge.

'Have you washed your hands properly'? The older sister asked her son as they prepared to leave. The toddler just smiled and nodded his head holding Ruchi's hand. 'Be careful with the luggage' the husband scolded his servant. Ruchi and her older sister embraced in the courtyard. The sister waved her hand walking away as Ruchi smiled. Without realizing Ruchi also raised her hand and waved back. The older sister and her family carefully treaded through the village path. Ruchi watched them from her courtyard with a strange feeling. She was glad they had left!

Ruchi's family now consisted of her mother, older brother along with his wife and the younger brother. Her mother's condition deteriorated further and she required assistance for most of her normal activities. Majority of the work load fell on the brother's wife as Ruchi also attended school. The sister in law cooked for everyone and then took care of the household. Ruchi did her best to help but the sister in law felt like a beast of burden. The mother in law required constant assistance along with morale uplifting. This fell on the brother's wife when her husband was working in the fields and Ruchi was attending school. The younger brother also had his own needs. The rest of the household activities occupied Ruchi's sister in law throughout the day. Soon she started having long conversations with her husband during the night. 'I need help taking care of the family' the wife complained to the husband. 'Ruchi helps you as much as she can' the brother replied. 'She needs to be here all the time, it is just too much for me' the wife demanded. 'Well she also goes to school so that is going to be hard' the brother stated. 'Why does she need school? Most of the girls her age are either helping in the household or getting married' the wife asked, her voice slightly rising. The husband remained quiet and contemplated. They both talked some more about the current family situation and possible solutions.

It was late in the evening and Ruchi had just returned from grazing the cattle. It had taken her longer than usual to come home. Two district officials from Kesar Khal had been inspecting the wide green pasture above the village. Ruchi and her friends had been following them around and asking random questions. The answers were not satisfactory but the kids followed the two gentlemen closely. This resulted in Ruchi being late to her sister in law's dismay. Ruchi quickly cleaned up and tended to her mother. 'I would like to speak with you Ruchi' her older brother asked, standing few feet away. This surprised Ruchi and she turned back. Her older brother hardly spoke to her unless something was needed. 'Sure' Ruchi replied with little anxiety. 'Let's go upstairs in the family room. Don't worry my wife will take of our mother' the older brother assured. They both walked upstairs to the family room and settled. For a minute there was silence in the room. The deadlock was broken by the brother. 'Ruchi you know it has been a difficult time for our family lately. The untimely death of our dear brother and subsequently our beloved father has taxed us all'. Ruchi nodded somberly. 'God knows how long mother will survive'? The brother wondered looking at his sister. 'Some villagers think evil spirits have entered our house' he said shaking his head. 'Really'? Ruchi asked in disgust. 'Oh yes, people say things behind our backs' the brother replied. 'You have been of great help Ruchi but I think time has come for your marriage' the brother stated looking away from his younger sister.

The revelation took Ruchi by surprise. For a minute she just looked at her brother and stayed quiet. 'I would like to continue with my studies' she finally replied. 'I understand but with passing of our father it will unwise for us to wait longer. Some people will be hesitant to entertain marriage proposal from our family' the brother said with regret. 'Why'? Ruchi asked confusingly. 'A daughter getting married without the father is considered bad omen' the brother stated according to village traditions. Too much information and thoughts were going through Ruchi's head and she was puzzled. She wanted to speak but just looked at her older brother. 'You know, it is better if we hurry while mother is still with us. Only god knows what will happen if you are still unmarried and she is gone' the brother sighed. The thought frightened Ruchi and tears dropped down from her eyes. 'I thought marriage was still far away for me' she said wiping her face, slowly coming to harsh realization. The older brother put his arm around her and they embraced. 'You are a grown woman now, Ruchitra Devi' the brother confided. Ruchi had now become Ruchitra Devi and was coming to grips with it.

Ruchitra Devi and Dev Prasad were walking to school in the morning. 'I won't be coming to school soon' Ruchitra Devi said with a shrug. 'Why'? Dev Prasad asked with a surprise. 'My brother is looking for possible suitors and planning to get me married soon' she replied devoid of emotion. Dev Prasad looked at her and kept walking. 'I guess your brother is looking in the surrounding villages according to tradition' he finally said. Ruchitra Devi nodded her head in agreement and kept walking. 'You know my father is planning to open a provision store in the village. The proposal to build a road has opened up various possibilities' Dev Prasad stated with enthusiasm. Ruchitra Devi looked at him and smiled. 'I too will probably miss school to help my father' he said with pride. 'You never liked school anyway' Ruchitra Devi teased. The school arrived and they both walked inside together oblivious of others around them.

Surrounding villages in the mountains had their own codes and customs. The villagers abided by them religiously. Centuries of traditions were passed down and people adhered to them. Occasionally some questioned the norms but their voices got drowned by the overwhelming majority. Few bold ones that strayed were made social outcast and the stigma remained forever. The villagers were mostly content following their ancestors as it gave them a special sense of belonging. Marriage among men and women of the same village were forbidden. Girls were married off at a younger age than the boys and were mostly discouraged from pursuing higher studies. After marriage they were basically property of the husband and his family. This meant having children and taking care of the entire household. Most married women in the villages worked all the time except for eating and sleeping. They hardly complained and considered it part of life. The boys helped in the farms after formal schooling unless a government job blessed them which raised the young adult's social status. The opportunities were limited for young men, hence they toiled in the fields the entire life. Upon death of an elder, the final rites were performed by the eldest sibling, preferably a male. The boys were considered an asset compared to the girls who were looked as a liability. The villages followed these norms along with few more and Gauri Ghat was no different.

Ruchitra Devi's family was in a dilemma. The death of her father and deteriorating condition of her mother had pushed the older brother in the forefront. He was now the decision maker in the family, something he was unaccustomed. The task of finding a suitable husband for his younger sister fell on him. This required travelling to different villages. His fields remained unattended most of the time while his search continued. Occasionally his wife tended the fields when she could find time from her hectic daily schedule. They both wanted to make sure Ruchitra Devi got married while the mother was still alive. Ruchitra Devi herself had little say in the matter and did not want to disappoint the family especially her sister in law who considered her a burden. The prospect of sudden marriage still frightened Ruchitra Devi but she accepted her fate. She just hoped she would be wanted wherever destiny took her.

Finding suitors was turning out to be harder than the brother had anticipated. People in neighboring villages knew about Ruchitra Devi's family. The demise of her brother and father was considered bad omen which turned away lot of suitable families. Some still showed interest but paused after inquiring about the mother. The older brother could not hide the obvious from the neighborhood villagers who were bound to find out the facts eventually. The parents of the prospective bride and groom were required to meet before the final commitment according to tradition. The older brother tried his best to highlight his sister's qualities. 'She is pretty and good with household activities' he would stress to the families. 'She is also a little educated and can take care of kids' the brother emphasized. Eventually two families agreed and the older brother was keen to meet the possible suitors. The first suitor was ten years older than Ruchitra Devi and had lost his wife few years back. This fact was hid from the older brother initially by suitor's family. The second suitor was four years older but he also came with a surprise. He was blind in one eye and glasses accompanied him everywhere. The older brother was desperate to marry his sister but he wasn't cruel. He loved her and wasn't going to dispose her to anyone.

Discouraged by his recent experiences, the older brother changed his course. He was now travelling to far away villages to find a suitable match. He figured the recent family tragedies wouldn't dominate the social dialogue. His persistence and hard work eventually paid dividends. It was a village about twenty five kilometers north east of Gauri Ghat. A chance encounter at the village tea stall had led him to the prospective family. Far from Gauri Ghat, the brother was taking a break from his search and having tea at a vendor. A young man from the village spotted him and inquired about his whereabouts. 'Where are you from'? The villager asked sipping his tea. 'About twenty five kilometers from here' the brother replied with a smile. The conversation continued and the brother gave his reasons for the long journey. The young villager informed him about his younger brother who was unmarried and looking for a match. The older brother was pleased and requested to meet the family. Soon he was led to a house in the village.

The older brother first met the parents. He explained to them about his dutiful sister and her need for a good husband. The parents wanted to know about his father and mother. The brother stated that his father had died of a recent heart attack and avoided the deceased younger brother in the conversation. 'My mother is still in shock from this and unable to leave the house as a result' the older brother emphasized. The parents empathized and did not mind meeting the mother later. 'We are not well off and survive on a small piece of land in the village' the father stated. The mother interrupted 'But we are from good lineage and also have two cows and a healthy buffalo'. The older brother looked around and could see the humble dwellings. After a long search, he realized his options were currently limited. The family wasn't rich but they were self sufficient and his beloved sister would be content here. Soon the younger son arrived and the older brother observed him closely.

He slowly walked in the room and seated himself. His mother proudly stated 'This is my son, Mohit Lal'. The young Lal had a thin moustache and neatly groomed hair. He seemed few years older than Ruchitra Devi. Upon insistence of his mother he greeted the guest. 'He helps in the field' the mother said looking at her guest. 'He has finished his high school and was going for higher studies but…' the father stopped and looked at his wife. 'Well his older brother needed help in the farm as my husband is getting old' the mother interjected. Ruchitra Devi's brother watched his future brother in law and noticed a young man of few words. Apart from formal greetings, the son hardly spoke. His mother did most of the talking for him and he just looked in her direction. 'You have to excuse my son, he is a little shy' the mother apologized to her anxious guest. 'He might be quiet but he seems fine' the older brother thought to himself. 'Well if you are interested we can move forward' the mother opinioned. The older brother adjusted himself and said, 'Yes, let's do that'. The mother smiled and put her arm around the son. The young man displayed a slight smile and looked in the direction of his guest. 'You know it is hard to find a good boy nowadays for a girl' the mother said as her husband watched closely. The older brother caught her drift and replied 'Your family will be adequately taken care of during marriage. The mother smiled looking at her son. The older brother visited the family few more times and eventually it was official. Mohit Lal and Ruchitra Devi were getting married soon.

The wedding day had commenced and Ruchitra Devi was getting her ceremonial bath. The older sister had failed to arrive for the wedding. Her husband had moved further away and couldn't get leave from his recently promoted job. His wife now had three kids and was unwilling to travel to the village alone. Her own wedding four years ago seemed eternity. Ruchitra Devi's sister in law along with two women was assisting her in the ritual. The house had been decorated as per tradition and a small makeshift stage adorned the courtyard. Ruchitra Devi's marriage ceremony compared to her older sister was understandably a low key event. The family had passed through a difficult phase in the past few months due to the tragic demise of the brother and father. This had resulted in the mother being partially incapacitated. Still the rest of the family had pulled together and lifted their spirits for the wedding. The older brother was mostly responsible for this outcome. He also had lot of responsibility on his shoulders. Unlike the wedding of his other sister where his younger brother and father along with his mother assisted the entire family, he was the only adult in the family for this ceremony. His wife also helped but she mostly took care of Ruchitra Devi. The entire burden of conducting the marriage fell on the older brother's shoulder. Few of the villagers offered assistance, the exception being Dev Prasad.

The Henna ceremony was being performed and Ruchitra Devi was surprised to see so few women. It seemed lot of her friends had stayed away from the event. Few years back the same event had attracted most of the women from the village at the family home. The Henna artists had failed to appear and hence the sister in law was doing her best for Ruchitra Devi. 'You know some people in the village consider it bad omen to attend the wedding' the sister in law narrated as she applied the red paste on Ruchitra Devi. The bride just nodded her head. 'We are just glad the marriage is finally commencing' the sister in law said with a hint of relief. Ruchitra Devi knew the spate of events in the past few months had cast a doubt on the family. Some villagers had come up with strange excuses not attend her wedding. Annual pilgrimage to the holy shrines and sacred dip at the confluence of the rivers coincided with wedding! 'What a contrast it was from her older sister's wedding'? Ruchitra Devi wondered when the entire Gauri Ghat seemed to have come together. The long ceremony four years ago seemed to have ended too quickly for some while the current one kept dragging. The bridal departure was in the evening but for Ruchitra Devi's family it couldn't come faster and this included her anxious older brother. Ruchitra Devi sensed this and wished she could leave soon. Gauri Ghat didn't have the same appeal for her anymore.

The sister in law was yelling at Ruchitra Devi's younger brother about the priest's whereabouts. 'Go find him quickly' she yelled at the young boy. He obediently went looking around the house. The older brother was assisting in the preparation of afternoon feast. Dev Prasad was by his side and churning a giant pot. Two other men were busy cooking rice in a large utensil. The resources were limited and the older brother was trying his best to help. The priest finally arrived and the family got together for Puja ceremony. A fire was set up in the middle of the courtyard and a sheet was spread around it. Ruchitra Devi, the older brother, his wife and the baby brother seated on the covered floor as the priest chanted sacred hymns. Dev Prasad watched from a distance with smoke and fire around him. 'You look beautiful today' he wanted to tell Ruchitra

Devi. The heat around the makeshift open kitchen was causing to him perspire and he wiped his brow with a towel. 'You look like an elegant bride in the yellow sari' Dev Prasad wanted to convey. He knew today his communication with Ruchitra Devi was going to be limited. She was going to be around her family most of the time during the day and with the groom during the evening. 'You better stir the pot or the lentils will get overcooked' a cook yelled him. Dev Prasad apologized and got back to his duty.

The groom's village from Gauri Ghat was almost a two hour walk. Keeping this in mind, the evening ceremony had been scheduled a little early and this suited everyone. The groom's family wanted to be home before nightfall. They couldn't afford an army of people with lanterns and torches to help them on their return journey. This task was delegated to Ruchitra Devi's older brother. He had hired some seasonal farm workers for this job along with lanterns and flashlights. The groom's family had also demanded a silver coin for each member of their wedding party. This wish was also fulfilled by the older brother without the knowledge of his wife. The older brother knew this was part and parcel of the wedding agreement. It was bridal family tradition for centuries in the villages to satisfy the demands of the groom and his family. Ruchitra Devi was just another statistic.

It was still early in the evening and the sounds of the drums could be heard above Gauri Ghat. The groom and his party were on their way to Ruchitra Devi's courtyard. Like any other wedding procession, the villagers had lined up outside their homes to watch the proceedings. Some whispered among each other as the groom passed. As per tradition the groom's mother had stayed home and he was led by his father and older brother. The groom was walking slowly and was partly shielded by his brother. When the party reached the courtyard, Ruchitra Devi's older brother greeted them with a warm embrace. The groom was led to the makeshift stage and seated. His bride was to follow suit soon. Ruchitra Devi was getting her final makeover and things were hectic. Even her mother had joined in decorating her. The sister in law had pleaded but Ruchitra Devi's mother was unmoved. 'We will take care of Ruchitra Devi, you don't have to worry' the sister in law had argued to no avail. 'I want to be with my little girl' the mother said with great difficulty. Here she was trying her best to help but ending up being an obstacle due to limited mobility. 'It is okay, I want her here' Ruchitra Devi finally calmed everyone around her.

By the time Ruchitra Devi was led to the wedding stage, some people had already started feasting. Mohit Lal and Ruchitra Devi were closely seated but hardly looked at each other. Ruchitra Devi was clad in a bright red sari and the top of her head was partially covered with the garment. Mohit Lal was dressed in a black suit and a pink tie. He seemed devoid of emotions and was looking in the direction of his brother who was seated few feet away from him. The priest arrived for the customary rituals as the bride and groom arose from their seats. The close family members from both sides joined the sacred ceremony and the rest of the guests followed later. 'This is going according to schedule' the older brother whispered to his wife in the courtyard. 'Wouldn't mind if it went a little faster, it is a long walk to the groom's village' his wife opinioned. The sun was slowly drifting behind the mountains and the late evening rays were splashing on the courtyard. The evening feast was now being served and to the assembled guests. Ruchitra Devi and Mohit Lal also joined the wedding feast. Ruchitra Devi wasn't too hungry but she forced herself to eat. Her husband had a moderate appetite and was joined by his older brother. The brother whispered something in groom's ears and departed. Mohit Lal quickly finished his meal and looked in the direction of his wife. It was the first time Ruchitra Devi caught a glimpse of her husband. She quickly turned her gaze and finished her early dinner.

It was time for bridal departure and Ruchitra Devi's older brother was busy making preparations. The wooden gondola for the bride and medium sized throne for the groom were now available in the courtyard. Ruchitra Devi was now bidding goodbye to close relatives. She would be leaving her village soon but strangely she felt no emotion. Her sister in law was embracing her for the final time. Tears were raining from her eyes but Ruchitra Devi's somber eyes remained dry. The baby brother was the next to embrace and Ruchitra Devi held him tightly. The older brother embraced her as she bent and touched his feet.

'Hope you find joy in your new home' the brother said wiping his tears. 'Thanks for everything' Ruchitra Devi replied, her eyes filled with emotion. Now she had to say final goodbye to her mother who was inside the house because of her condition. Ruchitra Devi walked inside the house and went upstairs. Her mother was seated on the floor and looking in her direction. Ruchitra Devi lunged forward and embraced her. 'I have to leave soon' she yelled to her mother. 'Ruchi, Ruchi 'was all her mother could muster. They both started crying and had to be separated by the older brother. 'The groom and his party are waiting for you' he pleaded with his sister.

As she was being led away in the wooden gondola, Ruchitra Devi's mind raced back to her older sister's departure four years ago. She remembered well that darkness had fallen by the time her older sister bid goodbye. The village path was covered with guests as her older sister's gondola was carried away. The scene of her running towards the older sister played in Ruchitra Devi's eyes. Except for a late arriving apology letter, she had not heard from her older sister. 'Was it the same sister that carefully fixed my hair as a little girl'? Ruchitra Devi wondered. It was twilight hour and Ruchitra Devi had moved away from the courtyard. A handful of guests stood along the village path as the gondola made its way forward. Ruchitra Devi's family remained in the courtyard after bidding her final goodbye. Upstairs in a closed room, her mother wept alone. The four men carrying the wooden gondola had picked up pace. Ruchitra Devi opened the small window and peeked outside the wooden structure for one final look at her departing village. A familiar figure struck her sight! She leaned forward and saw Dev Prasad slowly following the wooden gondola with folded hands. Ruchitra Devi screamed but quickly covered her face realizing people around her. She kept looking out of her small window. Soon Dev Prasad and Gauri Ghat had disappeared from view.

Chapter 4

The land surveyors and government officials descended on Gauri Ghat and surrounding villages. The proposal to build a road that connected the villages to the big town of Kesar Khal was initially cleared by the district officials. Now they had to convince the villagers about it to get the final approval. After all the road was to be built on vast stretches of pasture land that trespassed through private fields. The land surveyors mapped and checked the soil density of the area. It also included elevation and surrounding connectivity. The government officials focused on costs and the villagers. The villagers had to be convinced about relinquishing their private lands and this wasn't going to be easy. Meetings were conducted and grand plans were laid out. The government was building the long road for the benefit of the villagers. The road would make it possible for vehicles to enter the villages, something that was currently unavailable. A trip to the district headquarters could be completed in a matter of few hours from Gauri Ghat. Currently this trip required an entire day of travelling, mostly by foot and the remaining by the bus. The government officials stressed this to the villagers. The ones giving up their land for the road would be compensated by the government.

The government had the right to grab land deemed fit for constructing the road as stated by the law. It was better for the villagers to bargain with the officials. They knew eventually the government will have its way with them. The other benefits of building the long road were laid out by the officials. The construction would require a large amount of manpower. Employment would be provided to young men from surrounding villages for an extended period of time. This prospect excited the villagers. A government income and not working in the fields was enticing for them. Those still hesitant to give their land to the government now softened their stand. A few still resisted about forfeiting their land cheaply but they were silenced by the overwhelming majority. The road would bring connectivity along with prosperity to the villagers. This was stressed by the officials and the villagers agreed. The goods and other services could be eventually ferried back and forth from the villages to the surrounding towns. The government wasn't asking much. Most of the road was to be built on vast abandoned pasture land. Few private fields had to be sacrificed for the greater benefit of all. It took some time but soon everyone was on board. The foundation for the long road to Kesar Khal was eventually laid. The work began soon after and young men started assisting in the laborious task. Dev Prasad and his father were excited about their provision store in Gauri Ghat. The road construction was a blessing for them and their business was thriving. Once in awhile Dev Prasad wondered about Ruchitra Devi between his busy schedules. Gauri Ghat was changing and she was far away.

The wedding night of Ruchitra Devi was a revelation! After a long trip from Gauri Ghat to her new home Ruchitra Devi was tired. Still there were some formalities that had to be finished. First it was her mother in law. Ruchitra Devi had a quick introduction with her and wasn't able to deduce much about her mother in law. It was probably because by the time the wedding party made it back everyone was exhausted. There was also a sister in law in the house and Ruchitra Devi only exchanged formal greetings with her. Her husband Mohit Lal had quickly disappeared inside the house upon his arrival back home. Ruchitra Devi's mother in law guided her to the bedroom. 'Make yourself comfortable, your husband will join you soon' the mother in law smiled. Ruchitra Devi removed the partial covering from her forehead and looked around the room. It felt good to remove the covering as she had it on throughout the wedding. The room was about the same size as the one in her house in Gauri Ghat. A small bed lay in the middle of the room. It seemed poorly and hastily decorated. Two candles burned at the edge of the room thus illuminating it in the dark. Ruchitra Devi sat apprehensively on the edge of the bed and waited for husband. She had been with him throughout the wedding but barely had a chance to know him. He hardly spoke to her and was mostly surrounded by his brother during the wedding. Now she was going to finally meet him all alone! Noises outside the room captured Ruchitra Devi's attention.

'You go inside now' a female voice said forcefully in a hushed tone. 'I don't know' a male voice pleaded. 'You

will be fine, just go' the female voice got more forceful.
'I like sleeping alone' the male pleaded further. 'You
are a married man now, you have to be with your wife'
the female said in a gentle tone. Ruchitra Devi could
make out it was her mother in law and guessed she
was talking to her newly married son. A little later the
door cracked open and Mohit Lal entered the room.
Ruchitra Devi pulled her sari and partially covered her
forehead. She looked in the direction of her husband
who was walking towards her. Mohit Lal came towards
the bed and sat on the opposite edge away from his
wife. He just sat there without looking at Ruchitra Devi
who also avoided a direct gaze. This continued for few
minutes. Ruchitra Devi partially lifted her forehead
covering and looked in the direction of her husband.
This seemed to have irritated Mohit Lal as he got up
and moved towards the other end of the bed. Now he
was further away from his wife. Ruchitra Devi quickly
covered her forehead again and looked away from
her husband. One of the candles finally extinguished
and the room was dim. Mohit Lal got up and walked
towards an old closet. His back was in full view of
Ruchitra Devi. She noticed he was walking slowly
and his two feet were almost touching. 'Probably just
being careful in the dark' she wondered. Mohit Lal
opened the closet and looked for a candle inside. He
was having a difficult time finding one and was getting
frustrated. He looked a little lower and found a bunch.
As he picked them up and closed the closet, Mohit Lal
slipped and fell on the floor. 'I have spilled the candles'
he moaned to no one particular.

Ruchitra Devi rushed towards her husband. 'Get the candles' Mohit Lal said to his wife. 'We will get them later' Ruchitra Devi replied as she helped her husband back on his feet. Mohit Lal was in obvious pain as he stood up. Ruchitra Devi held his hand and they both walked towards the bed. Mohit Lal removed his slippers and stretched in the middle of the bed. His wife adjusted the pillow on his head and Mohit Lal turned sideways, partially covering his head with his right arm. 'Can I get you water'? Ruchitra Devi asked anxiously. 'I'm fine' Mohit Lal replied slowly. Ruchitra Devi stood close to the bed and watched her husband. 'Candles have to be picked up from floor or mother will get angry' Mohit Lal stated softly to his wife. 'Okay' Ruchitra Devi replied and walked towards the scattered candles. She picked two of them up and lit them in front of the only burning candle in the room. The rest she carefully put in the closet. Ruchitra Devi stood in the middle of the room perplexed. She herself was tired and wanted to sleep without disturbing her husband. His earlier indications suggested he didn't want her close to him. She slowly walked back and forth in the small room and observed her husband. 'All this jewelry is weighing me down' Ruchitra Devi whispered to herself. She carefully started removing ornaments from her body. First it was the heavy necklace, flowed by bangles. She then carefully removed her large nose ring. It wasn't easy removing things in the dark but Ruchitra Devi succeeded. She felt like a load had been removed from her body. There were still more ornaments left but Ruchitra Devi felt comfortable with them. Ruchitra Devi gathered her ornaments and placed them deep inside the closet aided by a candle. She looked in the direction of her husband who seemed to be sleeping soundly. He was sleeping sideways and his face was turned away from Ruchitra Devi, covered by his right arm. Ruchitra Devi tenderly walked towards the bed and sat on the edge. A strange sound coming from her husband intrigued her.

Ruchitra Devi didn't know what to make of it and moved her ears closer to the sound. After listening to it for few minutes, Ruchitra Devi realized her husband was moaning. His face was turned away from her so Ruchitra Devi walked towards the other end of the bed. When she got close, Ruchitra Devi couldn't believe her eyes. Mohit Lal was sobbing and tears were running down his cheeks. Ruchitra Devi grabbed his hand and asked 'What is wrong, are you okay'? Mohit Lal just shook his head and continued sobbing slowly. 'Are you hurt because of the fall'? Ruchitra Devi asked nervously. 'No' Mohit Lal replied, his tears drying up slowly. 'Is it something I did'? Ruchitra Devi asked again, hoping to get a proper answer. Mohit Lal just shook his head and straightened himself on the bed. Ruchitra Devi looked at Mohit Lal who was somberly gazing straight up. She herself was overcome with emotions but was holding them back. At this moment she was more concerned about her husband who had completely thrown her off guard. She had even forgotten to cover her forehead as she sat close to Mohit Lal. 'I can never be a proper husband to you'

Mohit Lal uttered looking away From Ruchitra Devi. The statement confused Ruchitra Devi and she shook her head. 'What is he saying'? She thought to herself for few minutes. 'We have been only married for a day' Ruchitra Devi relayed to her husband. Mohit Lal turned his face towards his wife and it was the first time they were facing each other. Ruchitra Devi tried to hurriedly cover forehead but Mohit Lal stopped her midway. A slight smile descended on her face due to his gesture. 'Everything will be fine by tomorrow' she comforted her husband. 'You don't understand' Mohit Lal replied looking at her. Ruchitra Devi put her hand on his forehead rubbing it slightly. 'My condition will never change' he stated to his shocked wife.

As Ruchitra Devi sat close to her husband on the bed, she found it difficult to comprehend him. She realized he wanted her to know something but was hesitant. Ruchitra Devi wanted her husband to elaborate without being embarrassed. She held his hand which was slightly trembling and looked at him. This calmed Mohit Lal and his eyes were fixed on his wife. There was enough candle light in the room and Ruchitra Devi observed her husband closely. He had an innocent face which betrayed his age. A thin moustache gave him a slightly older look. He had dark pretty eyes which were a little swollen because of his sobbing. His hair was oiled and nicely cropped in the back. Ruchitra Devi observed that Mohit Lal was a decent looking young man. He looked apprehensive in his current state but seem to be slowly gathering his composure. 'You are Beautiful' Mohit Lal whispered to his wife who was holding his hand. This pleasantly surprised Ruchitra Devi and she turned her face away. She turned back and looked at him concealing a smile. Mohit Lal just looked at his wife with droopy eyes. He held her hand tightly and cracked a light smile. 'Do you want to tell me something'? Ruchitra Devi asked her husband getting a little closer. Mohit Lal shook his head in affirmative and mumbled few words. 'I will get you some water' Ruchitra Devi announced and got up. She walked to the edge of the room and picked a small container filled with water. Her mother in law had placed it there for both of them. She raised the container and took a sip without letting it touch her lips. She then brought the container to her husband. Mohit Lal picked it up and emptied half of the water quickly. He gave the container back to his wife and took a deep breath. 'I feel better now' Mohit Lal said to his wife and started narrating. Ruchitra Devi sat next to him and listened closely to his words. 'My condition will never change', still played in her mind. 'It all happened about six years ago' Mohit Lal began.

Mohit Lal was sixteen years old and was out with his friends in the village. They all had left their cattle to graze and had strayed from their usual path. 'Let's go further up today' one of the boys had challenged the group. All six of them had agreed to venture further. The group had passed through streams and waterfalls on their way upwards. They swam and played around the waterfall with abandon and continued further. The activities had left them hungry and they were looking for something to eat. Big Apple trees surrounded their higher terrain. The fruit looked delicious to the hungry boys but it was hanging away from their reach. They picked up stones and started pelting the fruit. This brought limited success and frustrated the boys. They were all hungry and had expended most of their energy on the trip. 'Let's climb on the trees' a boy yelled. This proposition was turned down by most as they were too tired. 'I guess I will climb alone' the boy stated. 'I will climb with you' Mohit Lal volunteered. 'Be careful Mohit, you are the smartest among us' one of the boy's yelled. 'You mean I'm dumb' the original climber shot back. 'Yes' the rest of the boys replied in chorus. Laughter erupted among the hungry group. Mohit Lal and his friend began the climb.

Soon, the two started plucking Apples and throwing them down. The rest of the boys on the ground eagerly started collecting the rich fruit. A plucking contest ensued between Mohit Lal and his climber friend to determine the winner. Who was going to get the most Apples? They started climber higher as all the fruit on the lower end got plucked. The two were pretty much even but Mohit Lal was now pulling away from his friend. He had climbed further up and was raining Apples down to his excited friends. They were all cheering him and Mohit Lal kept leaping from one branch to the other. Even the other climber had conceded defeat and was now in awe of Mohit Lal. The Apples were piling up on the ground and the group was screaming in delight. Mohit Lal felt invincible and continued with his endeavor. Now his pant pockets were filled with the fruit but he wanted more. A large bunch of Apples hung from a branch away from Mohit Lal. He made a giant leap but lost his balance and slipped. It was the last thing Mohit Lal remembered as he came crashing down to the ground.

The rest of the boys were in shock as Mohit Lal lay unconscious on the ground. A few started crying upon seeing their friend in an unresponsive state. 'We have to get him home' one of the boys screamed. They all agreed and slowly started lifting their friend. It wasn't easy but the group managed to get Mohit Lal back to his house. Mohit Lal was slowly regaining conscious but was in excruciating pain. His mother saw his friends carrying him and rushed towards them. 'What happened' she shrieked looking at her semi conscious son. 'We need to rest him on the bed,' one of the boys suggested. 'Someone get his father and brother, they are at the farm' the mother said almost fainting. One of the boys departed and the rest helped Mohit Lal on the bed. The mother was crying hysterically holding Mohit Lal's head as the rest of the boys stood around. The father and brother arrived in a hurry and rushed to Mohit Lal's side. 'We have to get him to a doctor immediately' the father stated looking at his younger son. 'This will require travelling to the big town' his older son interjected. A proposition that currently wasn't feasible due to lack of a proper road. They would probably have to walk for hours and then catch a bus to reach the big town of Kesar Khal where a government hospital was located. Mohit Lal was withering in acute pain and was in no condition to move. 'The longer we wait the worse it will get' the father said somberly to everyone around him. His current options were limited and this frustrated him. Mohit Lal's mother appeared with a freshly prepared bowl of herbal paste. 'Where does it hurt my child'? She tenderly asked Mohit Lal. He slowly lifted his hand and pointed to his lower back. The mother lifted his shirt and gingerly started applying paste on his back. The pain was unbearable and tears were running down Mohit Lal's cheeks. His father and brother watched in agony and so did his friends around him. 'God, why did you have to do this to my boy'? The mother cried as she applied the herbal paste on Mohit Lal. 'He was the smartest in the village, I told him not to hang out with these fools' she said, her voice rising in anger.

'You know I was preparing for engineering studies' Mohit Lal said softly as he took a break from his long narration. Ruchitra Devi looked at her husband and wiped her eyes. 'I will get you some more water' she said and brought the container to her husband. Mohit Lal took a nice sip and handed the container back to his wife who put it away. 'When did they finally take you to the hospital'? Ruchitra Devi asked anxiously. 'The next day and with great difficulty' Mohit Lal replied. He explained the rest of the events to Ruchitra Devi. The doctor in Kesar Khal did not possess the expertise required to deal with serious back injury but he did his best. He urged the family to move Mohit Lal to a big city for better medical care. The family already had spent a fortune and was in poor financial condition.

They decide to stay with the doctor in Kesar Khal who prescribed lot of painkillers and extended physical therapy. 'He has sustained a serious back injury and will take long time to heal' the doctor emphasized. 'I wish you could have brought him the same day' the doctor concluded. It was a miracle that the family had brought Mohit Lal to hospital the very next day. The boy was paralyzed from waist down and had to be carried on a makeshift wooden shaft. The family had hired four people for this endeavor. Lack of proper road meant walking for two hours. A small vehicle was later rented and Mohit Lal was carefully transferred inside for the trip to the hospital. It was more emotionally draining for the family than financially but they did their best.

'I was bed ridden for almost a year' Mohit Lal continued as Ruchitra Devi listened closely. 'My plans for further studies were shattered' he said with regret. Ruchitra Devi felt a connection with her husband upon hearing this. 'I too wanted to study further' she said softly. 'Really'! Mohit Lal exclaimed. Ruchitra Devi nodded her head. 'What stopped you'? Her husband asked. 'Marriage' Ruchitra Devi replied with a smile. A broad smile descended on Mohit Lal's face. 'I was going to be first in my family to pursue higher studies' Mohit Lal continued. Ruchitra Devi listened enthusiastically. 'My older brother never liked school and dropped out early to help in the fields' Mohit Lal stated. His father had also been a farmer his whole life but wanted something else for his two sons. The mother and father realized early that their younger son was special. He was a prize student from the beginning and was also very athletic. His father wanted him to join the army and become an officer. His mother was against it and wanted something safer. 'He should be an engineer and build things' she proclaimed to everyone in the family. Her wishes mostly prevailed in the family and eventually Mohit Lal was encouraged to be an engineer. Mohit Lal himself liked the idea as it required moving to the big city eventually. The engineering college was located there about three hundred kilometers from his small village. First he would have to graduate from high school with honors which was no problem for a brilliant mind like him. Mohit Lal was gearing up for this till that fateful evening on the Apple tree.

'How long did it take you to walk again'? Ruchitra Devi asked her husband. 'A year after my injury, although it took me two years to walk comfortably' Mohit Lal responded. 'All this time you were mostly in bed'? Ruchitra Devi asked innocently. 'Yes, I'm heavily indebted to my mother, she took care of all my needs during this time' Mohit Lal replied, his eyes drifting back in time. 'I don't think I would have recovered without her' he relayed to his wife. 'You are very obedient of your mother' Ruchitra Devi noted to her husband. 'Yes I'm, although sometimes she can be overbearing' Mohit Lal said with faint a smile. 'How is your mother'? He suddenly asked Ruchitra Devi. The question took her by surprise and Ruchitra Devi paused for few seconds. 'Oh, she is very caring but I will tell you more about her later' Ruchitra Devi replied. Mohit Lal looked at his wife and held her hand. 'I would also like to know about you' he said to his wife. 'Okay, but right now we should get some sleep, the night is almost over' Ruchitra Devi said to her husband. 'I didn't realize this' Mohit Lal responded. 'We have been up all night but I don't feel tired' Ruchitra Devi stated. 'I'm not tired either but we have to get some sleep, the morning is approaching' Mohit Lal suggested. 'You are right' Ruchitra Devi concurred. They both straightened themselves and lay side by side on the small bed. 'I feel like talking some more' Mohit Lal whispered to his wife. 'We have our entire lives' Ruchitra Devi smiled. Mohit Lal imagined the possibilities. It had been years since he was this optimistic. The long night was ending but the young couple was soon sound asleep.

No one exactly knew when Mohit Lal and Ruchitra Devi woke up but it was well past morning. Mohit Lal's father had got worried and asked his wife about the couple. 'They should be awake now, it is past 10am' he wondered. 'They are newlyweds'! His wife smiled. 'You know our son's condition' the father shook his head. 'He is getting better' the wife replied firmly. 'You better go to the fields, it is already late' the wife added. 'I was hoping to see my daughter in law before leaving' the father replied apprehensively. 'She will be here when you get back' the wife stated. The father finished his cup of tea and started walking towards his fields where his older son was already toiling. A little later the mother gently knocked on the door. There was no response from inside so she knocked harder. 'Looks like they are tired' the mother whispered to herself. She waited a little and then knocked harder, followed by a scream. 'Sorry we overslept' Ruchitra Devi apologized to her mother in law upon opening the door. 'There is tea for both of you in the kitchen so hurry before it gets cold' the mother in law stated to Ruchitra Devi. 'We will be there soon' Ruchitra Devi replied. 'Also make sure to cover your forehead in the house' the mother in law demanded. Ruchitra Devi quickly covered her forehead with her sari and disappeared inside. 'Was mother upset'? Mohit Lal asked his wife. ''No, she just wanted us in the kitchen for tea' his wife replied. 'God, it is really late in the morning' Mohit Lal said looking at his newly gifted wedding watch. 'It is the most I've ever slept' Ruchitra Devi regretted. They both slipped into something more comfortable and headed to the kitchen.

As she was sipping tea in the kitchen with her husband, the sun was brightly coming inside through a small window. 'How is the tea'? Mohit Lal asked his wife. 'I've had better' Ruchitra Devi joked. Her husband smiled and continued sipping. His mother slowly entered the kitchen and Mohit Lal suddenly became quiet. 'From tomorrow you will have to prepare tea early in the morning' the mother in law said looking in the direction of Ruchitra Devi who nodded her head. 'There is lot of work to be done in the house' she stated further. 'You should get ready soon, I will have lunch for you' the mother said to Mohit Lal. The son just acknowledged his mother. 'You have to relieve your brother in the fields, he has been there since early morning' the mother added further. She turned to Ruchitra Devi 'We need some work done; you can have something to eat later'. Ruchitra Devi lowered her head and softly replied 'Okay'. The mother in law motioned to a pile of dirty utensils outside, 'Can you take care of them soon'? Ruchitra Devi was put to work while her husband got ready for the fields. She was out in the courtyard and it was her first time observing the new surroundings. She picked up a utensil and slowly started scrubbing. Many more needed cleaning and Ruchitra Devi dug herself closely. High noon was approaching and sun was shining brightly. Ruchitra Devi wiped her brow and continued cleaning.

As she was cleaning, Ruchitra Devi got a full view of her new home. It was definitely smaller than her house in Gauri Ghat. The courtyard too was small but well maintained. A small patch of land bordered one side of the courtyard where shrubs flourished. On the other side of the courtyard, a large grapevine circled. The verandah was partially visible from Ruchitra Devi's work station and she stretched her neck to get a better view. Sound of footsteps broke Ruchitra Devi's concentration and she turned around. It was her sister in law walking towards the house. There was a large basket on her head filled with fodder. A toddler hung on her arms. Ruchitra Devi remembered briefly meeting her the previous evening but had no recollection of the child. 'I guess the older brother is also a father' she thought to herself. The sister in law smiled looking at Ruchitra Devi and went inside the house with her child. A little later Ruchitra Devi was finished with the utensils. She carefully picked them up and walked inside the kitchen. She now started arranging the utensils as requested by her mother in law. 'You are finally done' the mother said upon entering the kitchen. 'Do you want to eat something before leaving the house'? The mother in law asked Ruchitra Devi. 'I'm hungry, so I better eat something' Ruchitra Devi noted as she looked at her husband finishing his lunch. She wondered if she was also accompanying her husband to the fields, a desiring prospect for Ruchitra Devi. 'Guess you better eat first, you need to collect a lot of firewood today' the mother in law said, shattering her prospects of joining Mohit Lal in the fields. 'Also from tomorrow you will have to prepare lunch' the mother in law stated to Ruchitra Devi who listened with her head partially covered. 'I need some help, I'm getting old' the mother in law lamented.

After Ruchitra Devi finished her lunch, her mother in law placed a strong Sickle in her hands, 'Your sister in law will show you the place where you can get firewood'. Ruchitra Devi was also required to carry a large basket made of bamboo sticks. 'Have you collected firewood in the past'? The sister in law asked Ruchitra Devi as they both departed the house. 'Yes' Ruchitra Devi smiled adjusting the large basket on her head. A narrow dusty path led both of them on their way. The sister in law motioned towards a spot high above the village. Ruchitra Devi looked up and noticed miniscule looking women gathering things far above. 'You will collect the firewood out there' the sister in law stated. Ruchitra Devi acknowledged and got ready for a long uphill walk. 'I have to assist in the fields' the sister in law said and departed. After her sister in law left, Ruchitra Devi stopped for a while and observed her surroundings. The village was smaller than Gauri Ghat but also perched on a hill. The houses were similar in shape but further apart from each other. From her position, Ruchitra Devi could see her father in law and brother in law working in the fields further below. Few other scattered villages could also be seen in the vicinity. The snow clad mountains reminded her of Gauri Ghat but they seemed further away. A dense forest lay further up from the village. Ruchitra Devi closely observed all this and her eyes looked for more. After all, this was going to be her new home! As her eyes wandered around, she caught a glimpse of her sister in law looking at her from further below. Ruchitra Devi picked up her basket and started walking uphill.

When Ruchitra Devi finally reached her destination, she was exhausted. Thirst had overcome her but she had no water. She wished she had brought some along. Two women not far from her were busy picking up some dry branches. A water container stood on the ground close to one of them. Ruchitra Devi hardly knew the women but her mouth was parched. She walked towards them and asked for water. One of the women looked at her and offered the water container. Ruchitra Devi quickly quenched her thirst and thanked the woman. 'Where are you from'? The woman asked. 'From the village downhill' Ruchitra Devi replied. 'Really, we are from the village on the other side but have never seen you before' the second woman interjected. 'It is my first day here, I'm married to Mohit Lal' Ruchitra Devi replied with a slight smile.

'Oh, they finally found a wife for him' both of them almost said condescendingly. Ruchitra Devi just stood there and looked away from both women. 'Where is your village'? One of the women asked. 'About two hour walk from here' Ruchitra Devi replied. 'Mohit Lal's mother is clever' the woman smiled. Her friend chuckled, 'It was going to be difficult for them to find someone closer'. Ruchitra Devi picked up her basket and walked away from the two women. 'Poor soul' the two women whispered to each other. Ruchitra Devi was angry and wished she had brought some water along. Soon she started picking up dry firewood from the ground. Some she chopped from the trees using her Sickle. Thus began her married life in a new village.

Ruchitra Devi's daily routine hardly changed. After waking up at five in the morning, she washed and cleaned up as her husband still slept. She then prepared tea for rest of the family. Apart from her father in law, no one greeted her in the morning. The old man was always courteous and flashed a smile. Ruchitra Devi hardly talked to him and answered her father in law with head gestures. She also made sure her forehead was partially covered in the house. Her mother in law kept her in check. Most of the family worked in the fields; hence lunch had to be prepared early. Her sister in law was responsible for cooking in the past but this task now fell on Ruchitra Devi. The mother in law also assisted in cooking but slowly her duties started shrinking. 'I'm getting too old' was her constant complain. Ruchitra Devi was basically cooking for the entire household. After lunch, cleaning and other household duties also rested on her shoulders. A little rest and the daily search for firewood took Ruchitra Devi on the uphill journey again. Here the women from the village and around never failed to cheer her up. 'Is he capable of starting a family'? The women would whisper to each other in Ruchitra Devi's presence. 'He can barely walk properly' others would interject. 'The family just needed a caretaker' some in the group whispered. Ruchitra Devi did her best to block the gossip but it would still bother her. She wondered if her older brother was apprised of Mohit Lal's condition before her marriage. Strangely she didn't feel sorry for herself but the whispers about her husband hurt Ruchitra Devi. Sometimes Ruchitra Devi wished a fitting reply to those gossiping women but she held her tongue. She would move away from the group and gather her firewood. After collecting the necessary amount, she would load the firewood on her basket and head home. A long and careful downhill walk culminated her evening. She would then prepare tea for herself and rest in the kitchen. 'It is getting late' the mother in law usually yelled from the courtyard. It was signal for Ruchitra Devi to start preparing dinner. Her mother in law offered assistance later. Soon the rest of the family would arrive from the fields. After cleaning up and changing they would get ready for dinner. The males ate first and the women served. After that the mother in law and sister in law had dinner usually followed by a long conversation. Ruchitra Devi was last to have dinner in the house and she didn't mind. She could quietly have her meal without being interrupted. A pile of dirty utensils awaited Ruchitra

Devi after dinner and she eagerly looked forward to cleaning them. She knew the most entertaining part of the day was now approaching!

'You are already done'? The mother in law asked. 'Yes' Ruchitra Devi smiled. 'I've noticed, you seem to enjoying cleaning those dishes every night' the mother in law stated curiously. Ruchitra Devi turned her head away. 'Can't wait to join your husband upstairs' the mother in law smiled. Ruchitra Devi blushed. 'Come with me, I've something for you' the mother in law whispered. Ruchitra Devi followed her mother in law to the small storage room next to the kitchen. A candle burning in her right hand lit up the dark room as the two women entered inside. The mother in law opened a rusty closet and took out a bottle. She smiled and handed the bottle to Ruchitra Devi. 'There are ancient magical herbs in this bottle, you should mix some in the milk and serve your husband' the mother in law opinioned. Ruchitra Devi was a little perplexed. 'You two have been married for months now, this should help you start a family' the mother in law smiled. 'Mohit Lal was going to need lot more than herbs in this endeavor' Ruchitra Devi thought to herself. Nevertheless, she mixed some herbs in a glass of milk to satisfy her mother in law and headed to her husband. Now they both could be with each other uninterrupted for hours. Ruchitra Devi looked forward to this throughout the day. Mohit Lal and Ruchitra Devi would talk till midnight about their day and everything else. The husband who barely acknowledged her in front of his mother and others would open his soul when they were alone in the night.

Ruchitra Devi too emptied herself out in his presence. In the past few months, she had already informed her husband about her life in Gauri Ghat. Mohit Lal had listened carefully and admired her courage. She still thought it was him who was courageous. After all he had gone through tremendous hardships after his tragic fall. Every passing night they got closer without the need to be physical.

'What is in the glass'? Mohit Lal asked his wife as she entered the room. 'I mean that reddish powder mixed in the milk' Mohit Lal smiled. 'Oh, your mother insisted on the herbs' Ruchitra Devi said, concealing a smile. Mohit Lal was confused. Ruchitra Devi slowly explained the reasons behind the mix. 'I wish it was that simple' Mohit Lal lamented. 'It might help you' Ruchitra Devi said handing the glass to her husband. 'You don't want to disappoint your mother' she added further. 'Actually I don't want to disappoint you'! Mohit Lal remarked taking the milk glass from his wife. They both smiled and Mohit Lal soon finished his milk. 'It was sweeter than usual' he said wiping his chin. 'Probably the herbs' Ruchitra Devi replied. Mohit Lal stretched on the bed and Ruchitra Devi lay next to him. 'How was your day'? He asked his wife. 'Pretty much the same as every day' Ruchitra Devi replied taking a deep breath. 'Is mother still hard on you'? Mohit Lal asked looking at her. 'She is the same, just getting older' Ruchitra Devi said with a hint of frustration. 'Mother will eventually get better, give her some time' Mohit Lal stated. 'She will, if you are not so scared in front of her' Ruchitra Devi said with a smile.

'I've to be that way in her presence otherwise she will start suspecting something' Mohit Lal said to his wife. 'She has always been the head of the household and I don't want to undermine her authority' Mohit Lal added. Ruchitra Devi slowly started comprehending the dynamics of social life in a large family. 'Was your mother the same way'? Mohit Lal asked his wife. 'No' Ruchitra Devi replied as tears came down from her eyes. 'Sorry' Mohit Lal apologized. 'It is fine; you are only one who cares' Ruchitra Devi said wiping her face. 'Your father does seem caring but it is awkward for me to talk to him' Ruchitra Devi stated. Mohit Lal nodded his head in agreement.

'Do those women collecting firewood still bother you'? Mohit Lal asked. 'Yes they do but it is fine, they have nothing better in their life' Ruchitra Devi replied. 'Enough about me how was your day'? Ruchitra Devi asked her husband. 'Well, as usual I was busy in the fields' Mohit Lal replied. 'Do you have difficulty performing tasks'? Ruchitra Devi asked apprehensively. 'Not really, I can do lot of work without assistance' Mohit Lal assured. He paused a little and continued,' my brother does help in plough and tilling the fields'. Ruchitra Devi looked at her husband and smiled. 'What about your father, he seems weak'? Ruchitra Devi asked. 'He tries his best but I don't want him working in the fields' Mohit Lal said to his wife. 'He used to be strong but his health has deteriorated after my injury' Mohit Lal said with regret. 'He had such high hopes for me' Mohit Lal sighed. 'The whole family did' he added, his voice slightly fainting. 'You are getting better, you are still young' Ruchitra Devi encouraged her husband. 'Give it some time, you will be your old self again' his wife added. This cheered Mohit Lal and he looked in her eyes. 'You know eyes tell a lot about a person' Mohitl Lal said to his wife. 'What does mine say'? Ruchitra Devi asked mysteriously. Mohitl Lal again looked in her eyes and smiled. 'You were mischievous as a child' Mohit Lal deduced. Ruchitra Devi burst out laughing and then quickly controlled herself. 'Were you always like this'? Ruchitra Devi teased her husband. 'They said I was different' Mohit Lal replied. 'Everyone says you were the most popular boy in the village growing up' Ruchitra Devi stated. 'I was definitely good in studies' Mohit Lal responded. 'You really wanted to be an engineer'! Ruchitra Devi exclaimed. Mohit Lal slowly nodded his head. 'You know the government is building a road that is going to connect a lot of villages to the district headquarters' Mohit Lal said to his wife. 'I know my village of Gauri Ghat is the focal point of construction' Ruchitra Devi informed. 'I would have graduated from engineering college by now' Mohit Lal lamented. Ruchitra Devi held his hands. 'They would have definitely needed my help in road construction' Mohit Lal wondered. It was getting late and they both wanted to talk further but their bodies didn't cooperate. Mohit Lal and Ruchitra Devi lay next to each other, hand in hand. They were overcome by exhaustion and soon fell fast asleep.

Ruchitra Devi had adapted to her new home as time progressed. Her memories of Gauri Ghat and her family started thinning out. She did worry about her mother and the thought got her emotional. Ruchitra Devi knew it was going to be a while before she returned to Gauri Ghat. Most newlywed women in the villages returned to their maternal home during childbirth or a sudden death in the family. The first scenario in Ruchitra Devi's case was unlikely for a long time and she hoped the second one remained a distant future. Occasional her older brother would send a message through someone coming her way. Everyone was doing fine but her mother's condition was still the same. Her older sister had lost touch with the family and Ruchitra Devi didn't care. She wondered about Dev Prasad but never asked her brother's messenger about him. She realized Gauri Ghat wasn't her home anymore. Ruchitra Devi belonged to Mohit Lal and his family. Life in her new home was difficult but she was content.

It was around dinner time and Ruchitra Devi was busy in the kitchen. Her mother in law and father in law were whispering in the courtyard but Ruchitra Devi could hear them inside through the open door. 'It is getting hard to sustain our extended family just through farming' the mother in law stated to her husband. 'I know, we don't have enough land and out our yield is not enough' her husband replied. 'We need another source of income' his wife added. 'I don't know how'? Her husband responded. 'You know the government is building a long road through surrounding villages and needs help in construction' the wife said to her husband. The old man took a deep breath and pondered. 'Young men from our village are earning daily wages building the roads' the wife stated. 'We need our older son in the fields, you know Mohit Lal can't do the required heavy farm work' the husband said to his eager wife. 'I know it is better if Mohit Lal does the road work' the mother whispered to her husband. This surprised Ruchitra Devi and she moved closer to the kitchen door. She leaned forward and intently listened to the conversation in the courtyard. 'I don't think Mohit Lal is capable of doing construction' the father in law opinioned. 'He doesn't have to do any heavy work, just pass gravel in a container to the person in front of him' the wife assured her husband. 'I've been asking young men in the village about the road work. They said all they do is pick gravel and pass it along a human chain the entire day' the wife stated. 'At the end of the day they all get paid in cash' the wife said and her eyes sparkled. 'I still don't know, we will have to ask Mohit Lal about this' the father replied thoughtfully. 'Of course we will need to apprise him' the mother responded sincerely. 'Believe me I wouldn't send him out to work if it wasn't safe. After all he is my baby' the mother added. 'The daily income would be nice but....' The father pondered. 'Don't worry everything will be fine' the mother assured.

'We will also need to ask his wife' the father interjected. 'Why'? The mother asked angrily. Ruchitra Devi wanted to listen but something burning in the kitchen made her run towards the fireplace. 'She is his wife' the father stated. Ruchitra Devi quickly returned back to the kitchen door and leaned forward. 'She is his wife but does not provide for the family' the mother said, her voice rising. The husband just listened and mumbled few words. 'We have an extra mouth to feed since she arrived here' the wife added firmly. 'You are getting old and cannot work longer. Soon the family will need another source of income' the wife stated to her husband. Ruchitra Devi kept an eye on cooking but closely listened to her mother in law and father in law. She did not like the idea of her husband working outside the family fields. The thought of Mohit Lal doing daily labor upset her. His condition was getting better but was far from satisfactory. She knew the family wasn't going to ask her opinion in this matter. The mother in law had made this clear and no one in the household was going to challenge her. Ruchitra Devi hoped Mohit Lal would object doing construction. This did not happen. During dinner, the mother in law sat next to Mohit Lal and her husband in the courtyard. The rest of the family members were required to eat later. Ruchitra Devi watched the developments from the kitchen. Mohit Lal's mother explained the family situation to him as his father quietly listened. The family need for extra source of income was stressed. Relatively safe work environment was illustrated by the mother to Mohit Lal who listened carefully. 'Young men from the village are working there every day and earning daily cash' the mother added. 'I would never put my boy in harm's way' the mother concluded. Mohit Lal listened to everything and then looked at his father sitting next to him. The old man looked at his son and quietly nodded. 'Okay, I will help building the roads' Mohit Lal stated to his father and mother.

The mother was ecstatic but her husband remained expressionless.

'Why did you agree to work on the roads'? Ruchitra Devi angrily asked her husband when they were alone. Mohit Lal was taken aback by her demeanor and slightly smiled. He knew she cared for him. 'What is so funny'? Ruchitra Devi demanded. 'I've never seen you angry before' Mohit Lal said to his wife. 'I have good reasons' Ruchitra Devi replied, her anger slowly subsiding. Mohit Lal moved closer to his wife and held her hand. A smile replaced on Ruchitra Devi's face and she tried her best to conceal it. 'Let me explain you the reasons' Mohit Lal said to his wife who listened intently. 'The family needs more resources as we are expanding' Mohit Lal slowly started. 'Do you think I'm a burden'? Ruchitra Devi asked anxiously. 'No you are not; you actually help the family in many ways' Mohit Lal replied. 'My sister in law is expecting another child in future and won't be able to help in the farms. My father is in deteriorating health and has to stop working soon' Mohit Lal continued. 'My brother alone cannot support the entire family on a small piece of land. We need new source of income' Mohit Lal added. 'I'm just concerned about you' Ruchitra Devi stated to her husband. 'I don't know if you ready for this kind of work' Ruchitra Devi added. 'I've been working in the fields for quite some time now' Mohit Lal said to his wife. 'Apart from some heavy work, I perform various tasks on the fields' Mohit Lal added. 'Yes but you are with your family in the fields' Ruchitra Devi interjected. 'Believe me the road work is safe' Mohit Lal assured.

'I've actually been talking to some of my friends from the village building the roads' Mohit Lal revealed to his wife. 'They have detailed the workload to me' Mohit Lal continued. Ruchitra Devi listened to her husband and felt a little relieved. 'Actually I've wanted to work on the roads for some time' Mohit Lal said to his wife. Ruchitra Devi looked at him with a frown. 'I'm just glad my parents brought it up first' Mohit Lal added. He paused and took a sip of water. His thoughts wandered off and he looked at his wife. 'The day of my injury I couldn't be transported to the hospital in the big town due to lack of a connecting road' Mohit Lal stated to his wife. 'Had I been in the hospital the same day, my condition would be different today' Mohit Lal regretted. Ruchitra Devi knew the surrounding villages nestled in the hills had poor connectivity. 'My small role in building the road would help someone in the future' Mohit Lal concluded.

It was Mohit Lal's first day at his new job. He was excited and also nervous. What if they didn't need his help? What if they thought he was too slow? These thoughts occupied him. He mentioned some of this to his friends as they made their way to work. 'Don't worry about all this, those people just need more bodies over there to help' his friends assured. Mohit Lal had bid goodbye to his family and his wife had prepared early lunch for him. They had all wished him well on his new endeavor. Ruchitra Devi had apprehensively watched him depart with his friends. Mohit Lal and his village friends walked for two kilometers. Here they were supposed to wait for an old army vehicle. It was the pickup point for daily labor from the surrounding villages. They were then transported to the work site which stretched for more than fifty kilometers covering hundreds of villages. It wasn't easy building roads through mountains and deep valleys but the government was determined. Heavy machinery and equipment had to be moved around and the army was required for assistance. The government still needed massive manpower to accomplish the task. This was gladly filled by hundreds of villagers looking for steady employment. Some abandoned farming and lined up for government work. The lure of daily cash was hard too hard to resist. It was a favorable situation both for the government and the villagers. A long and laborious task was undertaken whose end seemed distant. Mohit Lal was now part of this, a prospect that delighted him.

Mohit Lal and his friends from the village were dropped off close to a large hilltop. On the other side of the hill lay a deep ravine. It seemed part of the hill had been dynamited leaving rocks of various shapes and sizes scattered on the ground. Mohit Lal and the rest of the laborers were required to form a long human chain. A second group was given a round metal container and asked to fill it with rocks and gravel from the ground. The filled container was then passed on to the human chain which stretched to the end of the hill. Here the container was emptied into a giant pit. An industrial grinder picked up the gravel from the pit and emptied it inside a huge crusher. This process was repeated for hours by both men and the machine. It wasn't back breaking work but passing the container filled with gravel for hours was definitely laborious. The men were allowed breaks when the machine got overloaded at regular intervals. Lunch was the only extended break the laborers enjoyed. Otherwise they were required to stand for hours passing rocks. The rocks that were too big were crushed by a giant crane. It was difficult for men to hear each other during work due to constant clattering of heavy machinery. Some just covered their ears to block the noise. After all, the job description required movement of hands and not mouth. A site supervisor monitored the proceedings closely. His main concern was getting the maximum work done for the day. The superiors had made this abundantly clear to all site supervisors. The workers safety was definitely a concern but accomplishing the task was paramount. The supervisor at Mohit Lal's work site was probably few years older than him. The supervisor was quite conscious of his status and occasionally admonished the workers for being slow. Mohit Lal did his best and generally escaped the supervisor's sermon.

Mohit Lal continued going to the construction site every day. The days turned into weeks and weeks into months. The young man was now a regular at the construction site. Some of his friends from the village had discontinued going to work. The workload and constant noise at the construction site was too much for them. Mohit Lal actually looked forward to work every morning. His dedication and work ethic were appreciated by his superiors at work and his he was made the leader of his crew. This resulted in slightly higher pay along with added responsibilities. His family was pleased as their financial condition improved. The mother boasted about her son to the villagers. 'I told you he would be fine' she said to her husband who was now declining in health. The old man's fear were now gone and he was pleased by his wife's earlier decision to let their son work. There was one person in the family who was still apprehensive. Ruchitra Devi was pleased that her husband was able to work under normal conditions but she still had lingering doubts but his continued involvement. She didn't care about the financial implications; it was Mohit Lal's safety that was paramount to her.

Mohit Lal had finished his glass of milk mixed with herbs. Ruchitra Devi had changed into something more comfortable for the night. She lit up two candles to brighten the dark room. 'You know when the road is eventually completed; electricity will come to the villages' Mohit Lal said to his wife as she walked towards him. Ruchitra Devi took a deep breath and lay next to her husband on the small bed. 'It will take years for that to happen' she said to her husband. 'I know, it will take years to build the road first but it will happen in the future' Mohit Lal stated. 'How long do you plan to work there' Ruchitra Devi quickly got to the point. 'I'm progressing at the construction site' Mohit Lal assured his wife. 'Yes they have moved you up but they will not make you an engineer without proper expertise' Ruchitra Devi said to her husband. Mohit Lal realized his wife was right and nodded his head in agreement. Every night he would apprise her of his daily work. 'Only the engineers and your superiors are relatively safe at the construction site. The rest of the workers are exposed to dangers of machine and nature' Ruchitra Devi opinioned. Mohit Lal faced this predicament every day and was aware of his work environment. 'Some of those Engineers are so naïve' Mohit Lal said and his eyes drifted way. 'What do you mean'? Ruchitra Devi asked. 'I've only been there few months but I know more about the road work than them' Mohit Lal sighed. 'Yes but they have a college degree' Ruchitra Devi said slowly. Mohit Lal's eyes drifted away and Ruchitra Devi held his hand. 'Your hands are getting so rough' Ruchitra Devi remarked to her husband. 'Yes, those rocks do take a heavy toll on the hands' Mohit Lal said softly. Ruchitra Devi held his two hands and rubbed them. 'I cannot quit going to the construction site soon' Mohit Lal said to his wife who listened closely. 'The family is heavily dependent on me' he added. 'The work is not safe and it is taking a physical toll on you' Ruchitra Devi remarked. 'Maybe a little later I can stop going there' Mohit Lal pondered. This brought a smile on his wife's face and Mohit Lal was pleased. 'We can then buy some more farming land' Ruchitra Devi said to her husband who nodded in agreement. 'I actually like working in the fields' Mohit Lal mentioned. 'It will be our farm and I will help you do the work' Ruchitra Devi said to her husband. This prospect pleased the husband and wife. They imagined the possibilities of working on their own piece of land as they lay next to each other.

It was getting late as Mohit Lal drew close to his wife and mumbled something. Ruchitra Devi couldn't comprehend him. 'Do you want to say something'? She asked her husband. Mohit Lal hesitated and replied' Yes'. He wanted to say something but wasn't sure. Ruchitra Devi was puzzled and looked at him. 'Those herbs you have been mixing with my milk are proving to be beneficial' Mohit Lal finally stated to his wife. 'What do you mean'? Ruchitra Devi asked with a pleasant surprise. 'I'm having sensations in my lower body that were absent in the past' Mohit Lal revealed to his wife who was overcome with emotion. Sleep soon overtook both of them, followed by dreams. This was the last nightly conversation Mohit Lal had with his wife Ruchitra Devi.

The details from Mohit Lal's construction site were sketchy. Few actually saw the accident. Most workers were busy transporting rocks and gravel upwards the human chain. The supervisor was close to the giant concrete mixer on top of the hill. The driver handling the moving crane was the only credible eye witness. He described the events to the site supervisor. Mohit Lal was inspecting huge rocks being crushed by the giant crane on the edge of a dug out mountain pass. His job consisted of emptying the crushed rocks in a makeshift trolley and moving it towards the human chain. The process was going smoothly until a glitch developed. The crane unexpectedly stopped moving as it was going forward. The driver tried his best to start the machinery but failed. Mohit Lal observed the stalled crane for a while and then got back to his duty. After the Driver's various attempts the crane finally started moving and he was pleased at the outcome. In his enthusiasm, the driver picked up more speed than was necessary on the narrow path. Mohit Lal was in the direct path of the moving crane and panicked. The driver screamed to announce the imminent danger to everyone before he could apply his breaks. Instincts made Mohit Lal run backwards to avoid the rushing crane. It was the right thing to do but unfortunately a deep ravine lay on the edge of the narrow path. Mohit Lal disappeared in the ravine and his body was never found.

When the news finally reached his family the shock was soon overtaken by hysterical cries of women. The villagers started gathering at the small family home offering condolences. Mohit La's mother and his sister in law were crying in the courtyard along with women from the village. Ruchitra Devi had locked herself in the upstairs room was crying in anger. Various attempts made by others to console her proved to be unsuccessful. 'Go away' Ruchitra Devi yelled few times to chase women away from her door. Mohit Lal's brother was distraught in the courtyard surrounded by men from the village. Mohit Lal's father was too shocked after hearing the grave news and was speechless. Older men from the village tried talking to him but he remained emotionless. The family grieved throughout the night into the morning. Everyone had been awake except the father. When his older son tried to wake him the father didn't move. They soon found out he had been dead for hours. Mohit Lal's demise was too much for him and the father had suffered a heart attack. The family had another tragedy to face. In her locked room, Ruchitra Devi couldn't face the prospect of losing her husband. She remembered talking to him the previous night. How could it all end so fast? She just failed to comprehend. In less than a year after her marriage, Ruchitra Devi was a widow!

Chapter 5

For two weeks after her husband's demise, Ruchitra Devi dreaded the nights. In the morning the household duties occupied her. She had to prepare tea about three times during early morning hour. The first serving was right after waking up in the morning. The brother in law and his wife departed for the fields soon after having their tea. This left Ruchitra Devi and her mother in law in the house along with the sister in law's young toddler. The mother in law would go back to sleep with the toddler after her first cup of tea and wake up later. When she would wake up, a second cup of tea was needed to recharge her. A third cup was required to calm her nerves a little later. Ruchitra Devi provided this in the middle of her cooking duties. After the demise of her son and husband, the mother in law had withdrawn from most household activities. Her day was mostly spent brooding over the family tragedy. Cooking for the entire family was now done by Ruchitra Devi in addition to cleaning. The mother in law had assigned her new tasks and Ruchitra Devi readily accepted. Ruchitra Devi just wanted her mind to remain occupied. She diligently worked in the kitchen preparing meals and then washing utensils in the courtyard. Noon would arrive and Ruchitra Devi would barely notice. Her brother in law and his wife would arrive from the fields and get ready for lunch.

Ruchitra Devi would feed the entire family and then later eat herself. As rest of the family rested in their rooms, Ruchitra Devi just relaxed in the corner of the courtyard. Her body was tired but her mind wandered. Ruchitra Devi would get up and prepare for her next endeavor. It was the only way her mind remained detached from thoughts. Thus, she constantly worked the entire day.

Collecting firewood high above the village took hours and Ruchitra Devi stretched it even more. The tragic death of her husband had garnered Ruchitra Devi some sympathy among the women of the surrounding villages but there were always a few standout. As she collected firewood, whispers of compassion and evil luck echoed in the background. 'She is too young to be a widow. What is she going to do? The family is cursed. The mother in law is probably going to blame this poor thing' the village women chattered away from Ruchitra Devi but she could still hear them. Nonetheless, Ruchitra Devi kept herself busy collecting firewood. She would move away from the women but a new group would soon emerge. 'Why did they have to make the poor soul work in the roads'? Some women would whisper to each other. This would make Ruchitra Devi angry but she still maintained composure. She couldn't argue with all those women on her own. They were in a bunch and she was alone. So Ruchitra Devi listened to all the whispering and continued picking firewood. When she couldn't find anything on the ground, Ruchitra Devi chopped low lying dry tree branches. The rest of the women would eventually leave after collecting a set amount of firewood but Ruchitra Devi continued. She would assemble the collected firewood on the ground and chop it evenly. The heavier wood was arranged on the bottom of the basket and the lighter one on the top. Some of the departing women would look at her and wonder, 'Why is she doing so much extra work'? Ruchitra Devi wanted to stay up and work even more but approaching evening would deter her plans. Dinner had to be cooked for the family along with cleaning and washing. Ruchitra Devi didn't mind as long as she was busy doing something. She would pick up the large basket of firewood and make her long slow descent downwards. The setting sun would lighten up the snow clad mountains surrounding the small village but Ruchitra Devi barely noticed.

After getting back home, Ruchitra Devi would make herself some tea. 'Make some for me too' the mother in law would yell and extra water filled the black kettle. Ruchitra Devi would hurriedly finish her tea and start preparing dinner. She would slowly chop onions and then prepare to cut tomatoes. Strong onions would moisten her eyes but she continued. Sometimes she would run out of firewood and get more from the dark storage room adjacent to the kitchen. She would hear her mother in law and brother in law talking in the courtyard along with her sister in law. Conversation mostly focused on financial constraints and the recent family deaths. The mother in law would occasionally yell to Ruchitra Devi from the courtyard 'Are you okay in there'? Ruchitra Devi would calmly reply,' Yes' and continue working. When the conversation shifted to Ruchitra Devi in the courtyard, the three would talk in hush tones. Ruchitra Devi didn't care anymore. She knew the family talked about her behind her back. She wanted her mind to be busy with work and not thoughts. Dinner was ready and Ruchitra Devi informed everyone. 'It is taking you longer every night to prepare dinner' the mother in law opinioned as Ruchitra Devi set the dinner plate in front of her. Ruchitra Devi would just nod her head and accept the mistake. She would wait for everyone to finish dinner and then prepare to eat. Out in the courtyard she would have dinner all alone. She would eat slowly and look at the approaching dark night. Ruchitra Devi knew soon there would be no work left. It would take her quite some time to finish dinner and small portions still remained on her plate. She would get up and empty the remaining food in bushes across the courtyard, hoping a hungry bird or a cat would be the beneficiary.

Ruchitra Devi would then walk towards the pile of dirty utensils on the corner of the courtyard. She would adjust herself on the ground and start cleaning. A large bucket of water on the side would help her rinse the utensils. She made sure each utensil was spotless and shining after being finished. Ruchitra Devi would then arrange the utensils in the kitchen. Finally she would clean the kitchen and douse some water on the fireplace. Soon she would realize there was no more work left! Ruchitra Devi would head to the courtyard and sit on the edge facing the kitchen. The mother in law had long retired in her room. The same held for the brother in law and his wife, both tired from the day's work in the fields. Ruchitra Devi too was tired but she wanted to continue. As everyone slept, she gazed at the night sky lit with stars. For a moment it transformed her back to her childhood with her older sister. She wondered how the rest of her family was doing. She had almost forgotten about them. The thought of her ailing mother touched her. She had not been back to Gauri Ghat since her marriage. She wanted to visit but that prospect looked bleak at the moment. Her thoughts were disrupted by sounds coming from the house. Ruchitra Devi moved a little closer to the noise and realized it was her brother in law and his wife arguing about finances. The argument ended soon and Ruchitra Devi was again alone in the courtyard. She wanted to stay there but the progressing night got colder. Ruchitra Devi realized she was going to freeze if she stayed outdoors too long. She would have to go back to her room eventually and this prospect scared her. Every night since the passing of her husband, Ruchitra Devi had been going through this feeling. There was no remedy in sight. The night had just begun and the morning was far away. Ruchitra Devi got up from the edge of the courtyard and slowly made her way to the upstairs room.

Ruchitra Devi entered the room and closed it from inside. She walked towards the small table near the old closet and lit two candles. The memory of Mohit Lal slipping and spilling the candles during her wedding night flashed through her mind. She turned around looked at the small empty bed. An empty milk glass stood on the side of the bed. It had been there for almost two weeks and Ruchitra Devi never picked it up. She walked up to the bed and sat on the edge of it. After sitting for a while she got up and changed into her night dress. Her mind began drifting so she started fixing the bed. First, she removed the sheet and put it aside along with the thin blanket. She then dusted the old mattress lightly and turned it on the other side. Mohit Lal always wanted the bed to be dusted during the night. 'It is the only way bugs can be removed' he had mentioned to her in the beginning of their marriage. Ruchitra Devi wanted the thoughts to go away but they kept drifting in and out of her mind. Once the bed was properly arranged, she stretched in the middle of it. Mohit Lal always liked sleeping in the middle and she slept on his left. His arm would occasionally touch her face and Ruchitra Devi liked the soft feel. Once fast asleep, Mohit Lal had a slight snoring habit. The thought made Ruchitra Devi smile and she turned away her position. She was now looking at the empty milk glass at the edge of the bed. The lip stains from than two weeks were still visible on the glass. Occasionally she felt like cleaning the stained glass but just couldn't follow through with the task. Mohit Lal's words would ring in her head, 'I think I'm feeling sensations in my lower body'. As she lay on the bed hoping to stay wake, her body would not co-operate. Ruchitra Devi would fall asleep but her mind would start drifting.

Mohit Lal is next to her sleeping soundly. The snoring has picked up but it is barely audible to his exhausted wife from the day's work. A hand slowly rests on her face. Ruchitra Devi touches it and pulls it a little closer. It is a strange feeling as it seems to cause a little pain. She pulls the hand more and the pain increases. Ruchitra Devi wakes up from her deep sleep and notices she has been pulling her own hand. 'Where is Mohit Lal'? She wonders rubbing her eyes. As far as she knows he was just sleeping beside her. There is no one next to her and this crushes her sleep. She gathers herself and sits upright on the bed. She glances again to her side and nothing! Ruchitra Devi starts sobbing. It was just a dream like so many in the past weeks. Dreams Ruchitra Devi had been trying very hard to unsuccessfully avoid. Mohit Lal is not coming back. He is only retuning in her dreams. Ruchitra Devi is tired sitting upright on the small bed. She wants to go back to sleep but is hesitant. Ruchitra Devi knows the dreams will return and give her momentary pleasure. The rest of the day she will have to face the harsh reality. Ruchitra Devi gets up from the bed and walks towards the closet. She pulls out Mohit Lal's watch and lights a candle. Dawn is still few hours away and Ruchitra Devi reluctantly walks back to the bed. She stretches herself and closer her eyes, making sure her mind stay awake. She fights off sleep by occasionally getting up. Sleep eventually gets the better of her exhausted body. When she hurriedly awakes, dawn has arrived. She doesn't need a watch to verify this, light comes inside her dark room through small wooden cracks. The night is finally over and Ruchitra Devi is pleased. She starts getting ready for the long day. A plain white sari inside the closet waits for her. It has been her attire for the past few weeks as the local custom dictates for a widow. She carefully wraps it around her and looks in the small mirror. Her forehead is devoid of a bindi or a small red dot. Mohit Lal used to admire her bindi. Now he is gone and so is the ceremonial red dot. All the jewelry and ornaments that adorned her married body have been placed away in the closet. Ruchitra Devi is coming to grips with the sudden changes in her life. She is a young widow and unfortunately nothing is going to alter it. As time passed the memories started to fade but her fate remained the same.

It was still morning and Ruchitra Devi was cleaning utensils in the courtyard. Her brother in law and his wife were working in the fields. The mother in law was taking care of the newest arrival in the family, a baby girl. Her son and his wife were thrilled at having another child. The mother in law wasn't too pleased, 'Now we have two daughters in the family'. She was hoping for a male but her older daughter in law had delivered another baby girl to her dismay. The older child was demanding things and the mother in law was telling her to be quiet as the little baby was still soundly sleeping. 'Keep an eye on her, I've to check on the little girl' the mother in law said to Ruchitra Devi who gladly agreed. The utensils were finally cleaned and Ruchitra Devi was arranging them in the kitchen along with watching her little niece. The little girl seemed to have liked her Aunt and was quietly observing the work. After she was finished with the utensils, Ruchitra Devi took her little niece in the courtyard. Here she carefully arranged her ruffled hair, delighting the little girl. The sun was now out in full bright so Ruchitra Devi along with her niece moved to the shaded part of the courtyard. A young man walking towards the courtyard disrupted Ruchitra Devi's attention from her niece. 'I'm coming from Gauri Ghat' the young man announced to Ruchitra Devi. 'Please sit down' Ruchitra Devi excitedly said to the visitor pointing towards the shaded area of the courtyard. 'Can you get some water from the kitchen'? Ruchitra Devi asked her little niece. The girl quickly disappeared in the kitchen. The young man took few sips of water and wiped his sweaty brow. 'How is everything back in the village'? Ruchitra Devi asked the visitor. The young man paused for a moment and said, 'Your mother passed away last night'. For a minute Ruchitra Devi remained quiet and then she started crying. The little niece got startled and ran inside the house to her grandmother.

The grandmother hurriedly came outside in the courtyard. 'What happened'? The old lady asked her daughter in law. Ruchitra Devi was still distraught and was unable to answer. The young man finally introduced himself and gave the news to the old lady. 'Oh no, not another death in the family' the mother in law started weeping. The commotion had attracted some women from the surrounding houses and they were assembling in the courtyard. Grief was being expressed to Ruchitra Devi and her mother in law as both of them had continued weeping. The young messenger stood in the corner of the courtyard feeling guilty of bringing the tragic news. Ruchitra Devi's older brother had asked him to deliver the news to his sister. He had walked almost two hours to reach his destination and now he was surrounded by grief stricken women. Soon the crowd in the courtyard started swelling and Ruchitra Devi's brother in law along with his wife had also joined the mourners. Bad news travelled quickly to them in the fields and they rushed back. Mother in law's weeping slowly turned into anger as the village gathered in her courtyard. She had vivid memory of the similar event months ago. Her dear son and his father had passed away almost simultaneously, generating large gathering of the villagers for days in her courtyard. The mother in law had been holding back lot of her anger for months. She had been simmering but had managed to keep a lid on things. The grieving faces in the courtyard revived her tragedy. 'The evil spirits have entered our house' the mother in law screamed in the middle of the mourning.

'First they took my young son and then his father' the old woman cried. The crowd gathered in the courtyard had now stopped mourning and was glued to the mother in law. 'Now her mother passes away' the mother in law continued. 'Only god knows when this will stop' the mother in law screamed as the crowd listened closely. 'Her young brother and father had also passed away before her marriage' the mother in law accused looking in the direction of Ruchitra Devi who was aghast. 'They hid all this from us during marriage' the old mother in law barked loudly. Apparently she had been gathering information from different messengers coming from Gauri Ghat to see her younger daughter in law. 'My poor boy, he didn't deserve this fate' the old lady cried in the courtyard. People slowly started spilling out of the family courtyard. They whispered and hushed to each other as they left. The brother in law and his wife went back to the fields, taking their oldest daughter with them. Now the young visitor from Gauri Ghat along with the mother in law and Ruchitra Devi remained in the small courtyard. 'Are you coming to Gauri Ghat with me'? The young man asked Ruchitra Devi.

Before Ruchitra Devi could answer her mother in law angrily remarked, 'Who is going to help us if she leaves'? The young man was perplexed and sheepishly looked in the direction of the old lady. 'Her older brother has asked me to bring Ruchitra Devi along' the young man said to the impatient old lady. 'Her presence is required in the village before the final rites of her mother' the young man concluded. The old woman was quite familiar with rituals and customs and reluctantly understood the situation. The villagers would cast her in bad light if she refused her daughter in law. 'How long will she be gone'? The old lady asked anxiously. 'I will be back the following evening' Ruchitra Devi hastily interjected. The young visitor watched the two women from a close distance. 'Okay but you better be back by tomorrow evening, I'm too old to work around the house and your sister in law is busy with the farm and two kids' the mother in law stated. Ruchitra Devi bowed her head and nodded. 'I will gather my things from the room and meet you here in a few minutes' Ruchitra Devi said to the young visitor from Gauri Ghat. She arrived trembling a little later in the courtyard with a small bag. After touching her mother in law's feet as a mark of respect, Ruchitra

Devi departed with the young visitor. It was going to be a long walk and the two slowly started walking through the village trail.

It was the first time Ruchitra Devi was going back to Gauri Ghat since her wedding and she was understandably sad and anxious. The tragic news of her mother had her distraught but her mother in law's outburst in the family courtyard among the villagers had left her shaken. She had composed herself but pain lingered inside as she prepared for the trip. The sun was now out in full force and Ruchitra Devi covered her head with a long scarf. Her young companion on the journey wrapped a napkin around his head to shield it from the heat. 'How long will it take to get there'? Ruchitra Devi asked her young guide. 'About two hours, if we keep a steady pace' the guide replied. 'Have you travelled back to Gauri Ghat since your marriage'? The young man asked. 'No but I do remember walking from Gauri Ghat to this village after my wedding' Ruchitra Devi informed the young man. 'You really didn't walk, you were probably carried away in a gondola that evening' the young guide smiled. Ruchitra Devi blushed as she walked through the hilly terrain. They both were walking on a foot trail used by villagers to traverse far away villages. The trail passed through peaks and valleys depending on a traveler's destination village. 'I don't remember seeing you at my wedding' Ruchitra Devi said to the young man who was probably few years older than her. 'I attend college in the big city and have just returned to Gauri Ghat for my holidays' the young visitor answered. Ruchitra Devi liked the pleasant demeanor of her young guide and they talked more as they hiked through the rough trail.

Ruchitra Devi and her young guide were now approaching a valley dotted with small villages. High above the valley, men had lined up on a narrow path. They were all busy building the long road. Giant machinery could be seen moving slowly down the narrow path. Ruchitra Devi paused and looked high in the direction of the mountain road. She wondered how all those men got transported to such heights. 'They are almost half done, the entire road should be finished in a few more years' the young guide opinioned standing next to Ruchitra Devi. 'In Gauri Ghat, the road construction is almost finished' the young guide stated further. Ruchitra Devi heard everything but her gaze was fixed high above on the road. 'Once the road is complete, there will be no need to walk' the young man said and his eyes widened. Ruchitra Devi agreed nodding her head. She took out a bottle of water from her bag and took a sip, then offering it to her young companion. Soon they were back on the trail again. Occasionally they met weary travelers on the way going to various destinations. Apricot and Apple trees lined up on some of the higher terrain, transforming Ruchitra Devi back to her childhood. Her young guide offered to climb the trees and pluck the fruit but Ruchitra Devi vehemently refused. He ended up throwing small rocks at the fruit and picking them up from the ground. They both ate the delicious fruit and continued their journey forward. Gauri Ghat was now approaching but Ruchitra Devi couldn't recognize her surroundings. A new road passed above the village but the vast green pastures had disappeared. 'Well this is home' the young man said pointing to Gauri Ghat which lay further down the walk trail. Ruchitra Devi had a strange feeling upon entering her old village. She thanked her young companion who promised to escort her back the following day.

A large group of people had gathered at the family courtyard as Ruchitra Devi walked towards her childhood home. Her older brother raced forward and embraced his younger sister. They both began sobbing and were joined by other relatives. The grieving continued for a while and then Ruchitra Devi was escorted upstairs in a room where her mother's body lay wrapped in long white sheet. Ruchitra Devi screamed and grabbed the motionless body. 'They were waiting for you; the body has to be taken for the final rites at the holy confluence of the rivers' a young voice spoke to her. Ruchitra Devi turned around and saw a young boy standing behind her. It was her younger brother who had physically quite matured. She hugged him and gently fixed his long hair. 'I've missed you sister' the boy stated and Ruchitra Devi held him tightly. 'You have grown so much' Ruchitra Devi said to her young brother. 'So have you' the brother replied apprehensively who was seeing his sister for the first time since her wedding. The plain white sari and lack of jewelry had given Ruchitra Devi a much older look. Her ceremonial bindi on the forehead or the red dot was also missing. The brother and sister reminisced about the past as their mother's body lay on the floor. A little later the older brother arrived with three other men and hoisted the lifeless body on a wooden shaft. Ruchitra Devi sobbingly bid her mother a final goodbye. A long and arduous journey for the men began to the holy confluence of two rivers. Ruchitra Devi and the women stayed in the village.

Ruchitra Devi was tired from her long trip and decided to rest. When she finally awoke it was late in the evening. The men had still not returned from the ritual and a handful of women still grieved around Ruchitra Devi's house. Her sister in law offered hot tea and some snacks which Ruchitra Devi ate slowly. She walked outside in the family courtyard and looked around. A group of older women were talking to each other in hush tones. Ruchitra Devi recognized two and walked towards them. The group stopped chatting upon seeing her approaching and made space for her on the edge of the courtyard. Ruchitra Devi sat beside them and the group offered their condolences. The group was apprehensive in the beginning but eventually started opening up. Soon everything about Gauri Ghat came to the forefront and Ruchitra Devi quietly listened. The new road had opened up various possibilities. Young men from the village had abandoned farming and were now making good money building the government road. This prospect had condemned the old to farming and it was taking a heavy toll on them. The village had become prosperous and the young men were the most sought out bachelors in the surrounding areas. Some had saved money and moved to the big city for higher studies. Gauri Ghat was losing its younger population and the old felt venerable at this development. The road had brought changes to the village. It had absorbed most of the pasture land and the cattle had to be herded far for normal grazing. The gossip among the group then turned to individual families and Ruchitra Devi listened closely. Someone's daughter couldn't find a proper groom while some had too many suitors. Some men had to travel distant villages for brides of the same caste. 'By the way Dev Prasad found a match in the neighboring village' one of the women from the group declared. This got Ruchitra Devi's attention. 'They are planning to get married soon' the women concluded. The group of women continued talking but carefully avoided Ruchitra Devi and her family from the conversations. Ruchitra Devi eventually departed from the group as twilight approached. As she was walking away she heard the whispers, 'Poor soul, she has lost so much'. Some whispered,' God she looks really old'.

The next day Ruchitra Devi was ready to go back to her paternal home. She had bid goodbye to her family and was waiting for her young guide to arrive in the courtyard. The young man was running a little late and Ruchitra Devi and her older brother were waiting for him in the family courtyard. 'How are you Ruchitra'? Dev Prasad said softly from across the courtyard. Ruchitra Devi turned around and looked at her neighbor. He had a slight smile on his face and seemed a little taller since the last time she had seen him during her wedding. A thin moustache adorned his young face and his hair was nicely trimmed. 'Hello' Ruchitra Devi said walking towards him. 'I couldn't see you yesterday as I had accompanied the men to the ritual by the rivers' Dev Prasad stated. 'By the time we got back it was dark and you had already fallen asleep' Dev Prasad informed Ruchitra Devi. 'I understand' Ruchitra Devi assured her neighbor. The two exchanged smiles for a minute and observed each other. Both wondering how the other had changed! 'I heard you are getting married soon' Ruchitra Devi said to her neighbor. 'Yes in a few months to a girl from the other side of Gauri Ghat' Dev Prasad replied sheepishly. 'Lucky woman' Ruchitra Devi said with a smile. Dev Prasad looked away from her and gently stroked his moustache. 'How do you like your new home'? He asked looking at her. 'It is fine' Ruchitra Devi replied concealing her emotions. 'I......I was sorry to hear about your husband' Dev Prasad finally said to her. Ruchitra Devi acknowledged him in an awkward moment of silence. 'Here he comes' the older brother screamed upon seeing Ruchitra Devi's young guide. He handed the young man some tokens and said, 'Make sure she reaches the village safely'. The young man smiled, 'Don't worry'.

'I have to leave now' Ruchitra Devi said to Dev Prasad standing across from her. Dev Prasad smiled and silently acknowledged. Ruchitra Devi hugged her older brother and departed with her young guide. She looked back and Dev Prasad was still standing in his courtyard watching them. 'You still look nice' the words were barely audible from his mouth. Dev Prasad looked at her as she disappeared along the village trail with her companion. High above the village army vehicles were humming down the new road. Men were being transported to various construction sites. Dev Prasad had almost forgotten about his provision store. His father probably needed him and Dev Prasad quickly made his way towards the store. When he reached the provision store it was bustling with business. The road workers were busy stocking up supply for the entire day. His father had his hands full and was doing his best to satisfy the eager customers. Dev Prasad discreetly entered the provision store and started assisting. His father just smiled looking at him and carried on his business.

The return trip for Ruchitra Devi and her young companion seemed relatively easy. It probably had to do with her being familiar with the trail. When they finally approached the village, clouds had started gathering in the sky. 'I need to get back to Gauri Ghat before the skies open up' the young guide said to Ruchitra Devi. 'Yes, you better hurry back now, I can walk from here to the house' Ruchitra Devi said to the young man. 'Are you sure'? The guide asked. 'My house is only ten minutes away' Ruchitra Devi assured the anxious young guide. She thanked him for his company and they went separate ways. When Ruchitra Devi entered the courtyard a large pile of dirty utensils greeted her just outside the kitchen door. 'Didn't your brother send someone along'? The mother in law asked her as she entered the kitchen. 'Oh, the young man just left as the weather was turning bad' Ruchitra Devi answered. 'He could have at least waited for a cup of water or tea' the mother in law opinioned. 'People nowadays'! She lamented. 'Glad you are back my body is too tired from all the work' the mother in law said to Ruchitra Devi. 'Make yourself some tea, I can use a little myself' she moaned stretching her back. Ruchitra Devi hardly had time for stretching, after tea, dinner had to be prepared. The brother in law disappeared in his room after dinner. The mother in law and sister in law talked for some time and then walked inside their respective rooms. A large pile of dirty utensils still waited for Ruchitra Devi. She positioned herself and started cleaning them slowly. The night sky was covered with dark clouds signaling the arrival of monsoon. The summer months were coming to an end. The monsoon would give way to autumn eventually and autumn to winter. The harsh winter would yield to spring and spring would then to summer again. Ruchitra Devi experienced all this and more that came her way!

The mother in law started deteriorating physically but still complained about the family condition. Years had passed since the demise of her young son and her husband but she still couldn't come to terms with the tragedy. Her eldest daughter in law now had three daughters and this worried the mother in law. She longed for a male heir but kept getting disappointed. 'How will the family blood line continue'? She lamented to anyone who would listen. 'My boy Mohit Lal would have definitely fulfilled my dreams' the mother in law cried occasionally in the courtyard. She blamed the evil spirits for the family misfortune to the village women who would visit her. When Ruchitra Devi wasn't around the house she bore the brunt of her mother in law's vitriol. 'It has been downhill for the family since that woman arrived' the mother in law would inform the village women gathered in her courtyard. 'I hear her own family in Gauri Ghat is cursed' the mother in law opined to the gathering. 'Wish we had known all this before the wedding' she would sigh in the courtyard. The news would eventually reach Ruchitra Devi in the small village where gossip mongers abound. Ruchitra Devi herself started slowly indulging in gossip. In a small village there was little else for a widow besides work.

The sister in law mostly assisted in the fields. She also took care of the cattle shed twice a day and milked the cows. The birth of her third child left her little time for anything else. Ruchitra Devi was now responsible for cattle shed and milking the cows. It was something Ruchitra Devi disliked but she had no option. 'She has no children to look after, little more work won't hurt' the sister in law had opined to the family. The mother in law had agreed and Ruchitra Devi was quickly taught the art of milking the cows by her eager sister in law. Now she just took care of her newborn in the house while the mother in law tended to her other two daughters. Eventually they both would huddle in the courtyard with the kids and empty their hearts out. The mother in law still had a soft spot for her hoping the desire for a grandson would eventually be fulfilled. The family was surviving on meager means courtesy of a small patch of ancestral land. It was difficult to make ends meet with each new arriving member but this did not deter the mother in law and sister in law from yearning for a male heir. 'Someone should assist in the fields, it is hard for my husband all alone since arrival of my new child' the sister in law stated to her mother in law who shook her head in agreement. 'My poor son, he has been toiling in the fields forever' the mother in law concluded.

Ruchitra Devi and her brother in law hardly ever talked. It had mostly to with circumstances and customs. He was mostly working in the fields while Ruchitra Devi was busy with household activities. The local custom also discouraged unnecessary communication between a brother in law and the sister in law. There was some communication between them when Mohit Lal was alive but since his demise Ruchitra Devi and her brother in law hardly engaged in any conversation. Ruchitra Devi would serve him early lunch regularly before his departure for the fields. She would neatly fill his clean plate with an assortment of lentils and vegetables along with daily staple and then bring it to the courtyard where the brother in law quietly finished his meal. He barely looked in her direction or acknowledged her hospitality. Ruchitra Devi didn't mind and continued with her work. During the evening, dinner would be served and he would sit in the courtyard along with his mother and wife. Ruchitra Devi would serve all three of them and fulfill their needs. During dinner the three would talk about various things and offer divergent views. They mostly agreed on the matters pertaining to the family. Ruchitra Devi would quietly listen to all of them from inside the kitchen. When the mother in law and sister in law talked about Ruchitra Devi in hushed tones, the brother in law strangely stayed out of the conversation. A gentle nod of the head was all the brother in law indicated when the two looked in his direction. He would quickly offer his opinion when the topic shifted back to other matters. This puzzled Ruchitra Devi. The brother in law was mostly indifferent to her in the household. Ruchitra Devi secretly wished her mother in law and sister in law also showed the same emotions.

Autumn had arrived in the surrounding hills and Ruchitra Devi's village reflected the changing season. The trees had started shedding their leaves and they lay scattered on the ground. The summer fruits had disappeared and the winter ones started appearing on the trees. The flowers too had changed appearance and scent. High above the small village, the pine forest seemed dense. The snow clad mountains looked majestic in a distance. The sun shined brightly but the rays were gentle. The late morning air was cool and the villagers had appropriately attired themselves. Ruchitra Devi was in the courtyard spreading grain on the courtyard. A light red sweater adorned her body on top of the pale white sari, giving her a distinct look. She was busy separating the grain on a large cloth which covered the ground. The brother in law was working in the fields and his wife still slept. Her young child had kept her up all night and now both of them soundly rested. The mother in law was in her room taking care of her two other granddaughters. Her physical condition had deteriorated further and required assistance. 'How long do I have'? She moaned to family members frequently. Ruchitra Devi was about to check up on her mother in law when a neatly dressed man entered the courtyard.

'Did Mohit Lal live here'? The man asked Ruchitra Devi as she was leaving the courtyard. 'Yes he did, I'm his wife' Ruchitra Devi replied anxiously facing the visitor. 'Well I'm a government official and I've come to your house to verify things' the visitor stated. He narrated the events that led to his sudden arrival at the family home and Ruchitra Devi listened intently. After Mohit Lal's tragic death the government had been sending monthly checks to the deceased family. It was monetary compensation for the next of kin which was legally Ruchitra Devi, the deceased's wife. The checks were delivered at the local post office few kilometers from the small village. Each check had been picked up and cashed at the post office for the past few years. Once a year it was mandatory for the person cashing the check to be interviewed by the government official at the post office. The person cashing Mohit Lal's check had been missing the yearly mandatory meeting. The government had issued notices regarding this matter to no avail. An official had finally been sent to meet the check recipient. 'Have you been cashing your late husband's check'? The official asked Ruchitra Devi who stood shocked in the courtyard. She wanted to say something but words fumbled out of her mouth. The government official observed the young widow who was momentarily speechless.

'I have never cashed a single check' Ruchitra Devi finally replied, her voice rising in anger. This puzzled the government official. 'Who is cashing all those checks'? He asked in bewilderment. 'I don't know' Ruchitra Devi replied as tears came down from her eyes. 'We have to find out' the official responded gently to the distraught widow. 'Have you ever been to the local post office'? The official asked Ruchitra Devi. 'No' Ruchitra Devi replied adamantly. 'There is only one way to determine the forged check cashier' the government official assured the young widow. 'How many adults do you have living in the house'? The official asked Ruchitra Devi. 'Four, counting me, my brother in law, his wife and my old mother in law' Ruchitra Devi replied to the official. The government official moved a little closer to Ruchitra Devi and lowered his tone. 'Can you get the entire family together'? The official asked the young widow who was still finding hard to comprehend the events. 'Well the family generally gets together during early lunch' Ruchitra Devi informed the official. 'You just missed it today by half an hour' she added further. The official made a note of this in his diary and tucked it in his pocket. 'I will be back tomorrow a little early along with someone from the post office' the official stated to Ruchitra Devi who listened anxiously. 'We have to find out who is cashing the checks' the official said firmly.

Ruchitra Devi shook her head in agreement. The government official requested Ruchitra Devi to keep the conversation between them private. 'You have to be discreet about the entire matter till I arrive tomorrow' the official concluded. The official sympathized with the young widow and departed.

After the official left, Ruchitra Devi had difficulty focusing on things. 'Who could be doing this'? The question lingered in her mind. Something that belonged to her had been snatched without her approval for years. Anger and anxiety filled inside her as she worked around the house. At times she wished the culprit could be identified immediately and faced her. Ruchitra Devi had lot of questions in her mind. Tomorrow was too long of a wait but she was helpless. The official had requested her to be discreet about the entire matter. More she thought about it, she realized the official was probably right. The culprit still had to be identified and this could be only verified by someone from the village post office. After all the person had been cashing check every month. 'Who is this person'? The thought refused to get out of her mind. As she was collecting firewood high above the village, a thought raced through her mind, 'Who collects the family mail from the post office'? It has to be either the brother in law or his wife. The mother in law was in declining heath to walk that far apart from being illiterate. She had an immediate urge to ask the family members but after some consideration dropped the idea. 'Tomorrow is not far' Ruchitra Devi assured herself. During the evening as the family was having dinner in the courtyard, Ruchitra Devi looked at them contemptuously from the kitchen. She quietly fulfilled their needs as they talked about petty things. Later she ate her dinner and pondered about the day's event. She hurriedly washed the utensils and cleaned the kitchen. Tonight she was in a hurry to go to sleep. Tomorrow awaited and Ruchitra Devi was anxious!

The sister in law usually had lunch after her husband every day, bathing and cleaning her daughters in the meantime. Today surprisingly Ruchitra Devi had taken care of that responsibility to her sister in law's delight. She had also served lunch to her mother in law who had lately been bed ridden. The sister in law was glad to join her husband for early lunch. 'It has been long since we are both eating together this early' she said to her husband who nodded his head silently. Ruchitra Devi was serving them slowly and kept looking in the direction of the village path. 'Are you expecting someone'? The sister in law finally asked Ruchitra Devi. 'Just a messenger from my older brother in Gauri Ghat' Ruchitra Devi assured the inquisitive sister in law. 'Like he is going to bring something for her' the sister in law whispered to her husband who quietly continued eating. They both were sitting in the courtyard facing the kitchen. A little later sound of footsteps was heard entering the courtyard. Ruchitra Devi almost froze in the kitchen as she peeped outside. The government official was accompanied by a clerk from the post office. The brother in law and his wife turned around and looked at the two visitors. 'It is him' the postal clerk pointed to the shocked brother in law. Food dropped from his mouth and his wife failed to comprehend the development. 'What is happening'? The sister in law demanded from the two visitors. 'This man has been committing forgery for the past few years' the government official angrily pointed to the brother in law. 'What.....What.......What are you saying' the sister in law fumbled. Ruchitra Devi now joined everyone in the courtyard.

The government official narrated the developments to everyone in the courtyard as the brother in law remained speechless. The culprit had been forging Ruchitra Devi's signature and cashing checks for years. It was a criminal offense and punishable under the law. The sister in law started crying hysterically as the official elaborated on the misdeed. A crowd started gathering around the courtyard. Sounds emanated from inside the house but Ruchitra Devi paid no attention to her mother in law. Anger was rising inside her but she kept it bottled. She listened to the government official who thanked her for keeping his previous visit discreet. This resulted in a disgusted look from the sister in law but Ruchitra Devi didn't care. She looked at her brother in law who was standing up with his head held down. Soon the small village witnessed a rare sight. Two police constables entered the crowded courtyard to the shock of onlookers. They talked to the government official and the postal clerk for few minutes. The police constables escorted the brother in law out of the courtyard amid shocked villagers. The government official walked towards Ruchitra Devi and said, 'From now on you will be required to collect the checks yourself from the post office'. Ruchitra Devi nodded in agreement and wiped tears from her face. 'You are a courageous woman and I thank you for your help' the official said to Ruchitra Devi and departed. 'It is you who has helped' Ruchitra said softly regaining her composure.

The sister in law was still crying and had followed the constables escorting her husband to the periphery of the village. She had to be held back by two women from going any further. Her husband was being dragged away and she stood helpless. 'What will happen to me and my children'? She cried as the two women from the village walked her back to the courtyard. When the sister in law entered the courtyard she saw Ruchitra Devi surrounded by a crowd of people. Some wanted to know more about the recent developments while others expressed shock at the disgraced brother in law. Ruchitra Devi was trying her best to satisfy everyone's curiosity. The sister in law's despair turned into rage as she came face to face with Ruchitra Devi. 'You knew all about this and kept it away from us' the sister in law screamed at Ruchitra Devi who was stunned by the sudden outburst. 'You wanted my husband locked away so you could control the family' the sister in law continued her tirade. Ruchitra Devi could hardly believe her ears as the villagers gathered in the small courtyard jostled each other for position. Everyone wanted to watch the spectacle unfolding closely. 'Who is going to take care of my children now'? The sister in law pleaded to the crowd some of whom sympathized with her. 'This witch has ruined the family since her arrival here' the sister in law screamed in anger. 'One by one she has taken them all' the sister in law cried.

Ruchitra Devi had been aghast listening to all the tirades hurled at her. The sister in law's continuous accusations had left her speechless for few minutes but she was ready to respond. Anger had bottled up inside her and it was about to spill out. 'Don't you ever call me a witch you wife of a thief' Ruchitra Devi erupted pointing to the sister in law who had never seen this form in the past. 'How dare you accuse me'? Ruchitra Devi yelled at her sister in law who moved a few steps away. The crowd now approved of Ruchitra Devi as they leaned forward to get a better look of the confrontation. 'Your husband stole money for years that belonged to me and you blame me for his condition' Ruchitra Devi angrily continued. 'You probably knew all about this but still kept quiet' Ruchitra Devi accused the sister in law. 'No….No… I ……didn't know' the sister in law mumbled facing an enraged Ruchitra Devi who showed no signs of calming down. 'Shut up, you liar' Ruchitra Devi screamed. 'They should have taken you away too' Ruchitra Devi motioned to her sister in law. 'All day long I take care of the house, cooking, cleaning and collecting firewood while you play with your kids and gossip with mother in law' Ruchitra Devi loudly stated in the crowded courtyard. The sister in law's anger had now turned into fear as she stood facing Ruchitra Devi in the courtyard. 'I will no longer cook or clean for you anymore' Ruchitra Devi said emphatically to her sister in law. Ruchitra Devi then turned to the crowd and observed them. 'You all find this entertaining' she remarked sarcastically to the large crowd in the courtyard who were taken aback by the comment. 'Most of you like watching tragedies unfold' Ruchitra Devi said crowd. 'You don't care about anyone's feelings' she scolded the crowd which was now thinning out. 'Now go back to your homes, there is nothing left here to see or watch' she angrily admonished the remaining crowd. 'Hypocrites' Ruchitra Devi yelled as the crowd emptied out of the courtyard.

When the news of her older son finally reached the mother in law, she jumped out of her bed in disgust. In doing so, she damaged her already weak body. She had been bed ridden for weeks due to poor health and the recent developments just worsened her condition. The sister in law was by her side and had detailed the day's events to her including the altercation with Ruchitra Dev in the courtyard. 'Who is going to perform my final rites now'? The mother in law moaned in the bed. 'I had two sons and they both have been taken away from me' she continued grieving. 'I must have done something terribly wrong in my previous life and god is making me suffer for this' the mother in law cried in her bed. The sister in law pleaded with her to be quiet for the sake of her health but the old woman continued grieving about her misfortunes. 'What is going to happen to our family'? The mother in law cried as the daughter in law watched closely. 'Who is going to provide for us now'? She moaned to her daughter in law. The daughter in law sympathized and wiped her tears. 'You have to rest or your condition will worsen' the sister in law stated, holding her mother in law's hand. 'My condition cannot get worse' the mother in law yelled again to the dismay of her daughter in law. 'That woman has cast a spell on the family' the mother in law pointed her finger outside to Ruchitra Devi who had gone to the cattle shed. 'First they took my dear Mohit Lal followed by his father and now they took away my only remaining son, the evil spirits have entered this household' the mother in law said shaking in her bed. 'I will be next' the mother in law stated looking at her scared daughter in law. 'No, No...' the daughter in law pleaded. 'The spirits won't spare anyone' the mother in law trembled in her bed. She soon fell asleep as the distraught sister in law sat by her side. Few hours later the mother in law was dead!

When Ruchitra Devi heard the news she hardly shed a tear. The sister in law and her kids had assembled in the dark room and were crying in front of the lifeless body. 'What are we going to do with the body'? The sister in law sobbed looking at Ruchitra Devi who had no answer. 'We have to get some men from the village' the sister in law pleaded to Ruchitra Devi. 'It has to be taken to the confluence of the holy rivers for the final ritual' the sister in law said wiping her face. 'I will go ask for help in the village' Ruchitra Devi stated and departed. 'She doesn't even have tears' the sister in law muttered to herself after Ruchitra Devi's departure. Ruchitra Devi went down to the village and explained the tragic family situation. The villagers expressed shock and grief but no one offered to help. Some men just didn't have time while others were scared to enter the family courtyard again. Ruchitra Devi's efforts in the village yielded no results and she ventured into the neighboring fields hoping for help. The mother in law's dead body had to be removed from the house. Ruchitra Devi knew the longer body remained indoors more difficult it would be for the family. Men from the village had refused assistance and her only hope was the poor farm laborers. It was with great difficulty she was able to convince two laborers at a field far from the village for the task at hand.

When the sister in law saw the two farm laborers at the house she was surprised. 'No one from the village wants to help in the ritual'! The sister in law exclaimed. 'No' Ruchitra Devi dejectedly replied. 'Did you ask everyone'? The sister in law asked slowly as the two laborers waited in the courtyard. 'Yes' Ruchitra Devi replied with a hint of anger. The local customs dictated males to perform funeral rituals of the deceased family members. In a family devoid of males this task fell on the men of the same village. Anything else was considered unfortunate. Ruchitra Devi and her sister in law had no option as the two weary farm laborers looked at them. 'We better get moving soon or these two will lose interest in helping' Ruchitra Devi informed the apprehensive sister in law. Ruchitra Devi had offered small piece of jewelry to the two hesitant laborers in exchange for assistance. She went upstairs in her room and opened the old closet. The sister in law motioned the two laborers to come inside the house. The two picked up a makeshift wooden shaft and followed the sister in law to the dark room. 'The old woman would have never approved this' the sister in law muttered under her breath. Women from the village had gathered in the courtyard as the mother in law's lifeless body was brought outside by the two farm laborers. Ruchitra Devi slipped a small bag to the two laborers and they anxiously looked inside. It was late in the evening and the confluence of the rivers was a long walk from the village. The two laborers hoisted the dead body which rested on the wooden shaft and began their march. It was hoped the body reached the holy confluence of two rivers as no one followed the two migrant farm laborers. The sister in law began weeping at the sight of the departed two carriers. Now she was all alone in the house! Ruchitra Devi watched the proceedings with little emotion. The two laborers could be seen carrying the wooden shaft high above the village. They soon disappeared from the view past the dense pine forest. 'Those two are not even from the village'! The women gathered in the courtyard whispered to each other.

Ten days after her mother in law's untimely death, the sister in law left the small village. Recent tragic developments had made her life difficult in the household. It had come to her notice that her husband was going to be locked away for years. There was no one left to provide for her and the small children. The villagers viewed her suspiciously after the arrest of her husband. Ruchitra Devi hardly communicated with her in the household. The sister in law had to cook for herself and her children in addition to taking care of them. Everyday life was taking a mental and physical toll on the sister in law in the household. She decided to move to her maternal village some ten kilometers from the present one. A paid messenger had been dispatched to her maternal village explaining her condition. Her parents were not thrilled at having her move back but understood the compulsions. A married woman with children moving back to her maternal home was looked down upon by the locals. Finally the younger brother was asked to get her and the children. The sister in law had kept her plans secret from Ruchitra Devi. She wanted to keep Ruchitra Devi out of her family business and secondly she was a little scared of her younger sister in law. 'God knows how she might react and create another scene' the sister in law thought to herself. The sister in law had been quietly packing her belongings for the departure. When her younger brother arrived at the house, it was still late morning. The sister in law was ready and had quietly assembled all her belongings in the courtyard. Her children were not prepared to leave and were crying. Their young uncle was trying his best to calm them down. Ruchitra Devi was in the kitchen and came outside upon hearing the commotion. 'We are leaving' the sister in law said sternly to Ruchitra Devi standing alongside her younger brother. 'Okay' Ruchitra Devi replied looking at them. The children looked at Ruchitra Devi and smiled extending their hands. Ruchitra Devi moved towards them but the sister in law pulled her children away who started crying. 'Let's go' she said to her brother and they all departed. Ruchitra Devi was now all alone in the household and she didn't mind.

Recent developments had changed Ruchitra Devi's reputation in the small village. Her courage and outspokenness had created fear among people and it spread around to surrounding villages. Some locals still viewed her as evil on account of her family tragedies while others considered her a form of goddess who had overcome severe obstacles in her life. Ruchitra Devi herself noticed changes when she was around other women. It mostly happened when she was collecting firewood high above the small village. Now women didn't whisper when she was around but her presence generated muted silence. Some women even helped her collecting firewood while others moved out of the way when she walked around. The new found respect was either due to contempt or fear but Ruchitra Devi started liking the attention. Collecting firewood had turned into social gathering and Ruchitra Devi looked forward to it every day along with other women. Soon the women held court high above the village and Ruchitra Devi had become the chief arbitrator. Matters relating to the village and other women were discussed and eventually it turned to plain gossip.

It was middle of the winter and trees high above the village held a mystic view. Some shedded leaves while others adorned new ones. The women still needed firewood for everyday cooking and hence collected it daily. A large group had gathered around a fallen tree branch and was chopping it in small pieces. When

Ruchitra Devi arrived at the spot they all moved a few steps away. Ruchitra Devi started collecting the dead wood and assembling it in her large wooden basket. 'We have a new one picking firewood today'! One of the women remarked to Ruchitra Devi pointing to a young woman further away from the group. 'I heard she is married to an old widower due to family compulsions' another woman in the group said moving a little close to Ruchitra Devi. The group along with Ruchitra Devi looked at the young woman who was busy collecting firewood. When she turned around the group of women gave her a sympathetic look. 'Poor soul, she is barely out her teens' one of the women from the group remarked. 'Where is she from'? Ruchitra Devi asked the group of women around her. 'The neighboring village, Mausi' the group said in unison. Ruchitra Devi had now become Mausi or an older aunt to everyone. 'Let us find out more about the young woman' Mausi said to the group and they moved towards the young woman further down.

The long road connecting number of villages to the big town of Kesar Khal was finally completed. The road circled around the periphery of most villages amid the surrounding hills connecting them to different small towns. A journey that took an entire day was now possible in a matter of hours for the villagers to the district headquarters. Buses and other vehicles were now operating on the newly built road on a regular basis. This brought changes to surrounding villages including the one Ruchitra Devi resided. Young men now started venturing out for jobs or just adventure. Goods and services that were rare in the past now started appearing in the villages. Electricity was expected to arrive soon! Times were changing, too fast for some.

Over the years, the messages from Gauri Ghat coming to Ruchitra Devi or Mausi as she was now known in her village started decreasing owing to various factors. Most people in the village had little time to spare as the young started moving out for a better life. Farming was considered old fashioned and laborious as young men looked for brighter prospects. Hence it was difficult to send someone to a far away village but Mausi's older brother still tried his best. A messenger from Gauri Ghat finally did arrive to meet Mausi. He narrated the events of Gauri Ghat to Mausi who was now advanced in age. Her older brother was in declining health due to lifetime of toiling in the fields. Like his father, farming had taken a heavy toll on him. Ruchitra Devi's younger brother had joined the army and was far away from the village. The new road had brought prosperity to Gauri Ghat resulting in better life for most of the villagers. The most prosperous was Dev Prasad courtesy of his thriving provision store. 'How is Dev Prasad'? Mausi asked the messenger from Gauri Ghat. 'He is doing fine under the circumstances' the messenger said with regret. 'What do you mean'? Mausi asked anxiously. 'His wife died during childbirth and his father passed away recently' the messenger informed Mausi. She looked away from the messenger and wiped her tears.

'Dev Prasad is a generous man and extends credit to the needy at his provision store' the messenger stated to Mausi. Few other tidbits about Gauri Ghat were also mentioned by the messenger.' I better get going, I've some work in Kesar Khal' the messenger said to Mausi. 'It will take you all day to get there' Mausi said to the messenger from Gauri Ghat. 'Not anymore, they have buses going to the big town every few hours' the messenger said with a smile. 'Oh yes, it almost slipped from my mind' Mausi said shaking her head, realizing besides the local post office she never ventured anywhere else. She thanked the messenger and gave him some coins on his departure. The messenger refused the generosity of the widow but Mausi persisted. 'Don't worry, I get check every month from the government' she assured the messenger.

Mausi had hired a young woman from the neighboring village for domestic help. Her financial condition made possible for this small luxury. The young woman cooked, cleaned and even attended the cattle shed for the monetary compensation. She performed her tasks gladly and liked talking to Mausi. 'I plan to further my studies from this money' the young woman said to Mausi as she cleaned the courtyard. 'All the colleges are in the big city and they cost a lot' Mausi informed her enthusiastic domestic help. 'I will work more and then move to the big city' the young woman said confidently. Mausi smiled and reminisced listening to the young woman. 'Make sure to further your studies' Mausi stated to the young woman. 'I definitely will' the young woman assured. 'Now go to the cattle she and check on the cows' Mausi said mischievously. The young woman smiled and disappeared from the courtyard. Apart from collecting firewood, Mausi hardly worked. She spent the day sitting around in her courtyard and part of the night in her verandah. 'How did I work so much in the past' she thought to herself. Working from morning till night she hardly had any time left. Now all she had was time and little else. She would talk with village women gathered in her courtyard about various things and the conversation eventually turned petty. 'Who is having problem in the village, whose husband is problematic? Whose mother in law is mean? Who is getting married? Who is in financial turmoil?' The women talked among themselves and kept busy. Mausi too had unknowingly become part of this as time passed. Sometimes when she was all alone in the courtyard, Mausi missed her hectic work days of the past. She also realized advancing age was catching up to her. During the night she sat in her verandah and looked at the small village. Light started appearing in distant villages and was coming soon to her own. The road was still far from the village but occasionally roar of the motor engine filled the quiet night. As she sat in the verandah Mausi wondered about her silent house. 'There is no one left here but me....'

When Dev Prasad arrived to meet Mausi one late afternoon, both had difficulty recognizing each other. 'Ruchitra'! Dev Prasad said looking at Mausi sitting in her courtyard. 'Yes', Mausi replied anxiously getting up from the edge of the courtyard. 'Dev Prasad', Mausi asked apprehensively. Dev Prasad nodded his head in agreement. Passage of time was distinctly obvious in their faces and they observed each other closely. Dev Prasad was now an old man with thick gray hair. His forehead was wrinkled but his face still carried the youthful charm. He was attired in white shirt and dark black pants. He resembled a man leading a comfortable life. His easy smile remained from his boyhood days. Mausi's long flowing hair had turned silver and almost reached her waist. Life had been hard to her and the lines on her face were clear proof. Her eyes still sparkled like Dev Prasad remembered from childhood. Whether they always did was debatable! As usual she was attired in plain white sari and her body displayed no ornaments. Years of bending and stooping had taken a toll on her but she tried her best to stand erect upon facing Dev Prasad. 'I've come here to inform you about the death of your older brother' Dev Prasad said after a long pause. 'When did this happen'? Mausi asked sadly. 'Few days ago, we have been busy with the funeral ritual' Dev Prasad informed. 'I know he had been in bad health for quite some time' Mausi regretted to Dev Prasad. 'I've lost touch with the family for a long time' Ruchitra Devi sighed. 'How is my younger brother'? She asked anxiously. Dev Prasad remained silent for a minute. 'Why didn't he come to inform me'? Mausi apprehensively asked Dev Prasad.

Dev Prasad cleared his throat and narrated the events of Gauri Ghat to Mausi. The younger brother had been released early by the army due to some medical condition and had returned to Gauri Ghat six months ago. He had married a woman while on duty and they had three young daughters. They had all accompanied him to Gauri Ghat. Dev Prasad asked for a glass of water and Mausi quickly fetched him one from the kitchen. 'You're younger brother is unfortunately addicted to vices and does not fulfill his family obligations' Dev Prasad continued. Mausi listened in shock as Dev Prasad took another sip of water. 'His poor wife has the responsibility of taking care of the entire household and the woman is stretched' Dev Prasad stated. 'The daughters will be of marrying age soon and need a stable household' he said to Mausi who listened closely. 'Your help will be greatly appreciated by them' Dev Prasad pleaded with Mausi. 'I've mostly come here to take you back to Gauri Ghat' Dev Prasad cleared his intentions. 'Your remaining family needs you Ruchitra' Dev Prasad said with slight smile. After listening to Dev Prasad, Mausi was in a predicament. What should she do? Should she move back to Gauri Ghat to help her brother and his family or should she continue living in her present village? The more she thought, the clearer were the answers. The three young daughters could be affected by an unstable family. Who was here for her to look after or vice versa? She was an old woman now living alone in small a village. 'You don't have to make the decision today' Dev Prasad interjected. 'I've made the decision but it will take some time for me to move back, I need to take care of few things' Mausi smiled. Dev Prasad was pleased with outcome.

'How are things with you'? Mausi asked Dev Prasad who was now sitting on the edge of the courtyard beside her. 'I'm doing fine' he smiled. 'How is your provision store and who is taking care of it in your absence'? Mausi inquired. 'The store is doing good business and my young son Manu Prasad is handling it in my absence' Dev Prasad replied. Mausi was both pleased and surprised upon hearing the news. 'I've another son lot younger than Manu; the poor boy suffers from respiratory problems' Dev Prasad stated to the surprised Mausi. 'I remarried since the demise of my first wife' Dev Prasad said softly. The two moved away from the late morning sun which was shining brightly. 'It is always easy for a man than a woman in our local tradition…..' Dev Prasad said as they moved to the shaded area of the courtyard. Ruchitra Devi choked as she listened to the man who had comforted her since she was a little girl. 'Should I send someone to come along with you'? Dev Prasad asked Mausi. 'No, now there are buses travelling between villages every few hours' Mausi replied with a smile. 'I can manage to travel on my own' she further added. 'I've to get back to my store, my son Manu Prasad is still a young boy' Dev Prasad said getting up from the courtyard. 'I hope to see you soon in Gauri Ghat' he said to Mausi said and departed. The words cheered Mausi and she bid Dev Prasad goodbye.

A week later Mausi was ready to move back to Gauri Ghat. She had informed the local post office about her plans and was assured by them of proper assistance. She had carefully packed her belongings from the house. The old cabinet in her room was cleaned of all the jewelry and her wedding gifts. She looked at the old bottle of herbs tucked in the corner of the cabinet and reminisced about Mohit Lal. Every night she used to mix the herbs with milk for her late husband. She placed the bottle along with her belongings. Mausi looked in the mirror attached to the old cabinet and wondered what Mohit Lal would make of her old self today. She walked through each room of the small house and observed closely. The kitchen and the courtyard held a special place in her heart. She had spent a lot of time in both! Later she asked her young domestic help to take care of the house. 'I will come back and check on you occasionally' she reminded the young woman who was sad to see the old woman leave. The road connecting the periphery of her village to Gauri Ghat was two kilometers away from her house. She picked up her bag like the firewood basket and started walking towards the long road. As she was waiting for the bus along with few others, Mausi admired the long unending road. Her Mohit Lal had a contribution in this amazing stretch and Mausi felt proud. A bus could be seen weaving through the mountain road and this brought smile on the faces of those waiting for the vehicle. Mausi gathered her belongings and got ready for the ride to her native village.

Chapter 6

When Mausi finally arrived back at Gauri Ghat, a lot had changed in her native village. Mausi had little time to notice things as she was quickly immersed in helping her younger brother and his family. Her brother was hardly home and his poor wife had been taking care of the household in his absence. The wife cooked, took care of the family farm, managed the cow shed and groomed her three young daughters. She had aged beyond her years and her body showed ample proof. The arrival of the older sister in law pleased her most in the family. Mausi reduced her burden in the household. She now cooked and looked after the young daughters while the brother's wife tended to other matters. The brother too was pleased to see his sister back at the village but he was rarely home, except for eating and sleeping. Since being released prematurely by the Army, alcohol had a strong hold on him. His meager pension barely supported the family. Mausi tried her best to straighten her younger brother but vice had powerful grips on him. The new road had brought prosperity to Gauri Ghat and the surrounding villages. It had also brought some cheap alcohol from towns and cities to the small villages. Some of the old along with young were drawn to this vice. For a few, there was no escape from the clutches of this cheap thrill. Mausi soon realized her brother was one of them. In spite of her advancing age, she did her best to keep the family moving. The three daughters were soon going be to of marrying age and Mausi wanted to provide a stable household for them. Any prospective groom in the future would first look at the girl's domestic condition. Mausi wanted the best for her nieces. It was one of the main reasons she had moved back to Gauri Ghat.

As she settled back to her new life in Gauri Ghat, Mausi started to inquire about her surroundings. The village had changed since her time as a little girl. The most obvious were the inhabitants. Mausi could only recognize few of them. Some had moved away while others had left for the heavenly abode. Most of the farming was now done by seasonal laborers. Goods and services were now readily available in the village, courtesy of Lorries moving up and down the road from towns and cities. Television and various household appliances adorned most family homes in the village. Telephone communication was just a few years away! As promised the road had definitely brought comfort to Gauri Ghat. This had led to idle time among the villagers which resulted in gossip. Who was doing what? Who had the most money in the village? Who was having difficulty getting his daughter or son married? These conversations occupied the elderly in the village. Mausi too was drawn to these chats in her idle time. There was one topic that consumed both the elderly and the young alike in the village. It was Dev Prasad and his family.

Mausi listened eagerly as the villagers narrated the events in her courtyard. Dev Prasad had become the most prosperous man in the village due to his bustling provision store. Actually it was his father who had done all the hard work and now the son was reaping the benefits. Dev Prasad was a generous man and this quality endeared him to the villagers in Gauri Ghat. He extended credit to poor souls who couldn't afford to pay for the purchased goods at his store. In fact people from the surrounding villages had also been the beneficiary of this kind act. Mausi listened as young and old would occasionally come to the courtyard and describe her neighbor. Dev Prasad had a dutiful wife and two sons. The younger one had a medical condition that required a monthly visit to the hospital in Kesar Khal. It was the older son that everyone talked about in the village. He was a strapping young man with an easy smile on his face. He was quick to help anyone in need and loved his younger brother. He was also born with a silver spoon in his mouth. Manu Prasad was indeed the prince of Gauri Ghat. Every week his father was presented with marriage proposals from the surrounding villages. Families even from faraway towns wanted Manu Prasad for their daughters. Manu Prasad wasn't interested in any of this. His mind was already made up about his destiny. He knew the girl he wanted to marry although few in Gauri Ghat were aware of his choice. A handful knew about the girl while others just gossiped. Mausi was curious about it after hearing the tale from the villagers. She along with the rest of the villagers was drawn to the saga of Manu Prasad and his mysterious girl.

The first time Leela and Manu Prasad met was at the provision store in Gauri Ghat. It was late in the afternoon and Manu Prasad was helping his father at their provision store. Dev Prasad was helping the customers while Manu was arranging the newly arrived items in the back. The store wasn't too busy and Dev Prasad managed his account books along with tending to occasional customer. Manu Prasad was whistling a tune as he neatly placed items in the shelf. 'I've got to stop lending credit to people, the books are not balanced properly' Dev Prasad said aloud. 'You always say that father and then melt easily' Manu Prasad commented and started whistling again. 'Some of these folks don't have much money and we have been blessed with plenty' Dev Prasad remarked looking away from his account book. Manu Prasad just shook his head and continued working. Deep down he knew, he was just like his father.

'I need a large notebook' a female voice requested Dev Prasad. He put away his account book and said 'Yes we have that here'. Three young women attired in their school uniforms were looking at Dev Prasad and slightly smiling. The one who had requested the notebook was standing in the front of them. She probably was seventeen or eighteen years of age while her two friends standing behind were slightly younger. 'Manu, can you get me a large notebook'? Dev Prasad asked his son. 'Are you there'? Dev Prasad asked as the whistling from the back had suddenly stopped. 'Yes, yes…., I'm here father' Manu Prasad stumbled. He had been looking at the girl up front since her arrival at the provision store. A flower bead adorned her head and a long pony tail came down almost to her lower back. She had light eyes and an innocent pretty face. 'Are you going to get the notebook or just stare at these young women'? Dev Prasad chided his son. 'Yes, in a minute' Manu Prasad finally started looking for the large notebook. He looked around but Manu Prasad was having difficulty finding the notebook. Dev Prasad finally got up from his seat and went in the back. A minute later he had the large notebook in his hands. 'My son is usually good with finding things but currently he seems lost' Dev Prasad said to the girl up front. The girl with the long pony tail collected the notebook and handed her dues to Dev Prasad. 'Haven't seen you before'? Dev Prasad asked all three of them. 'We are from the neighboring village and recently started attending school in Gauri Ghat' the girl with the notebook replied as her two other friends nodded in agreement. 'What is your name beautiful girl'? Dev Prasad asked with a smile. 'Leela', replied the girl with recently purchased large notebook. 'Hope to see all of you again' Dev Prasad concluded. As she walked away, Leela looked in the direction of Manu Prasad whose gaze had been fixed on her. Her two friends giggled and all three of them soon disappeared from the provision store.

For the next ten days, Manu Prasad discreetly followed Leela. Around 8AM every morning he would walk close to the higher secondary school located about one kilometer from his house and watch the students fill inside the facility. Corn fields adjoined to the school provided a nice cover for him as he watched Leela and her two friends disappear in the building. Every day Manu Prasad would start looking in the neighboring hills as the three of them made their daily descent to the school in the valley. He could always recognize Leela even from a distance with her long hair and flowery bead. Once the school started, Manu would get back to his daily routine. He would take care of his younger brother as his mother tended to household duties. Later Manu Prasad helped his father at the provision store which took most of his time. His father appreciated the help as Manu Prasad was now well trained to take care of the family business.

'One day you will have to take care of all this on your own', Dev Prasad said to his son with an affectionate smile. 'That day is still far away', Manu Prasad replied emphatically. 'I'm getting old' Dev Prasad sighed leaning back on his cushion at the front of the store. 'You are still in good health father' Manu Prasad said from the back of the provision store. 'You're younger brother occupies my thoughts' the father sighed. 'He is getting better and with proper medical care his breathing will be completely normal' Manu Prasad encouraged. 'I hope so, I hope so' Dev Prasad replied. It was getting early in the evening and Manu Prasad looked at the clock hanging in front of the store. 'I need to go out for some time' Manu Prasad requested his father. 'For the past week, you've been leaving around this time everyday! Dev Prasad exclaimed in surprise. 'I like to hang out with some friends' Manu Prasad said suppressing a smile. Dev Prasad gave his son a puzzled look. 'They have just come back to the village for their summer vacation from college in the big city' Manu Prasad said guarding his emotions. 'Okay go meet your friends but be careful, those city boys are not as naïve as the villagers' Dev Prasad smiled looking at his son. 'Don't worry father' Manu Prasad replied with a big smile as he departed the provision store. A bigger smile descended on the face of Dev Prasad. 'He thinks I don't know' the father mumbled to himself.

Manu Prasad knew well that after school was finished in the late afternoon, an hour later Leela and her friends grazed their cattle in the pasture high above the village. His family had hired a man from a neighboring village to graze their cattle. Manu Prasad had quietly arranged with this man to take over his responsibility. A pack of cheap cigarettes and plenty of free time was convincing enough for the poor man. For few hours in the evening, Manu Prasad was the cattle herder and he looked forward to it with enthusiasm. Like a seasoned herder, he would carefully take his cattle to the pasture. After more than a week, he was now enjoying the endeavor.

A young bull had separated from the herd and was running wild around the pasture. The bovine was full of energy as he zinged around the open fields. This had created quite a commotion among rest of the village herders. Young girls screamed at the sight of the advancing bull while the boys whistled in delight. The bull showed no sign of stopping and soon fear gripped most of the young village herders. Manu Prasad had been slowly chasing the bull for some time but was having no success in taming the animal. He knew something had to be done quickly as the young bull belonged to his cattle herd. Manu Prasad took off his shirt and gathered pace. He was now closing in on the bull but the animal was still proving elusive. A crowd had now gathered around the vicinity and was encouraging Manu Prasad in his pursuit. Manu got close to the bull and held his tail. The bull quickly shrugged his tail and left Manu Prasad flat on the ground. Moans and laughter echoed around the pasture as the bull took off again. Manu Prasad was now agitated as he gathered himself. He dusted his hair and ran ferociously towards the young bull. The bull was now running in circles and dodging the advancing Manu Prasad. This continued for few minutes as Manu Prasad carefully observed the young beast. A little later Manu Prasad ran towards the front of the bull and suddenly stopped. This surprised the bull and he froze in his tracks for a few seconds. As the bull was about to move again, Manu Prasad lunged at his horns and wrestled the animal to the ground. He held the bull tightly as the young beast lay on the ground. After a few minutes he released the young bull from his grip. The bull stayed on the ground for a while and then got back on its feet. He soon joined the rest of the herd. Young boys and girls clapped in admiration as Manu Prasad slowly got up from the ground. The crowd soon disappeared back to themselves and their herd. Manu Prasad started walking back to his cattle herd. His shirt was missing and he was drenched in sweat.

'Your shirt' a female voice said to Manu Prasad as he quenched his thirst from a nearby stream. Manu Prasad turned around and saw Leela standing in front of him with his dusty shirt. 'Thank you, I looked around but couldn't find it' Manu Prasad said accepting his shirt from Leela. 'The wind had carried it down the hill' Leela said with a smile. Manu Prasad shrugged his shirt and slowly put it on again. His arms ached as he stretched them. 'Are you okay'? Leela asked with a concerned look. 'I'm fine, just a little sore' Manu Prasad replied. His aches started disappearing as Leela stood close to him. 'Well, I'm going back to my cattle herd now' Leela said to Manu Prasad who suddenly felt refreshed. 'I'm going the same way' Manu stated and started walking alongside the young girl. 'Everyone was in awe of you today' Leela said after a minute of silence. 'It was crazy' Manu Prasad laughed. 'Yes it was, the bull was putting up a spectacle' Leela joined in laughter. For a few minutes both talked about the wild ordeal. 'Well my herd is right over there' Leela said pointing to her cattle. 'I guess I will see you again tomorrow' Manu Prasad said as Leela walked away from him. 'Okay, just make sure there are no cattle chasing' Leela smiled looking back at Manu Prasad. The look and the smile remained with Manu Prasad as he herded his cattle back home. He hoped the chasing had stopped for him.

Every evening Manu Prasad rounded up his cattle herd and eagerly approached the vast pasture high above Gauri Ghat. On his way to the pasture he whistled loud tunes as he kept his herd in tow. The pasture was a gathering place for young boys and girls from the surrounding villages. It also served as a playground for indigenous games. Once the cattle were left to graze, the young villagers roamed carefree around the pasture. The girls mostly stayed in a group while the boys played separately. Occasionally the two would play mingle and then disperse again. After setting his cattle free, Manu Prasad would look around the pasture. He would spot Leela with her friends and smile. Leela would smile back but continue talking to her friends. They both exchanged glances, conspicuous of their surroundings. When everyone gathered together for a game for marbles, Manu and Leela exchanged greetings. The noise created by others created a perfect screen for their verbal exchanges. 'How are you? How was school, Are you having fun'? Manu Prasad tried to keep his voice down. 'I'm fine, school is always interesting, and how is your business at the provision store'? Leela communicated with a smile. The conversation would end as the boys and the girls went their own way at the end of the game. Manu Prasad wished somehow he could talk longer with Leela. It was difficult for them to avoid the large group. Manu Prasad wanted to keep his close friendship with Leela a secret. He knew if the young villagers found out about their budding relationship, friendly ridicule would follow. He was more concerned about Leela than himself. Sometimes Manu would walk to the running stream away from the pasture even when he wasn't thirsty. Leela appeared at the stream whenever she could evade her friends. They both talked freely before loud calls to Leela by her friends from the pasture below would end their meetings. Once in a while the pine forest east of the pasture provided solace for the two of them. The late evenings always ended too quickly for both of them as their herd had to be steered back home after grazing. After countless evenings of hiding and seeking, Manu Prasad and Leela got to know more about each other. Manu Prasad wanted to spend time talking with Leela away from the pasture land in the evenings. He conveyed his thoughts to her regarding this conundrum. Leela too agreed with Manu but knew it was difficult for the two to meet for a longer period. She had school in the morning, back home in the late afternoon, cattle grazing in the early evening and home again for dinner and school work. Manu Prasad too was occupied for most of the day. He started thinking about ways to change the current predicament. Manu Prasad soon came up with an idea. One evening, he revealed this to Leela by the stream high above the village.

Mausi was now comfortable around her surroundings in Gauri Ghat. Her household was in order and the eldest of her three nieces was getting marriage proposals. The other two were soon to follow and this pleased Mausi along with her sister in law. The younger brother still remained mostly absent from the house but showed his appreciation to the family by weekly visit to the market. Mausi had ample free time on her hands and this led to more gossip among her newly acquired village friends. The talks ranged on various village topics but would eventually settle on Dev Prasad and his prosperous family. His son Manu Prasad was the most eligible bachelor in Gauri Ghat or for that matter in the surrounding villages. Marriage proposals were pouring in for the family from everywhere. There was also a strong rumor that Manu Prasad was in love with a girl from a neighboring village. Few had proof but everyone had their opinion. Who was the girl? This captivated everyone. Mausi too was drawn to this puzzle. She wanted to find out about the girl that had infatuated the son of Dev Prasad. She thought of different ways to accomplish this task. One day she noticed a young boy of twelve or thirteen passing through her courtyard. He seemed to be singing a broken tune and oddly twisting his head. Mausi stopped the young boy and asked if he wanted a transistor radio. The boy delightedly shook his head in agreement. A little later Mausi emerged with an old pocket radio from the house. The young boy danced in joy as the radio started playing. Soon Mausi's wish was his command.

The town by the confluence of two rivers hosted a large fair once every year. It attracted a lot of people from the entire district. Young men and women from surrounding towns and villages were especially drawn to the yearly carnival. They dressed up in their finest attire and headed to the town for a day of fun and frolic. The schools and colleges remained closed for this occasion along with some government offices. Manu Prasad and Leela had picked the carnival to spend the entire day together. The rest of the plan was well known to both of them. The day had finally arrived and the anticipation was building up among everyone. Gauri Ghat along with several surrounding villages seemed bustling with activity. There were extra buses running for this one day festivity. The road above Gauri Ghat resembled a bus depot. Scores of people had lined up on the road leading to the carnival town. Every time a bus filled up with passengers and departed, it released fumes into the crisp morning air. The crowd was in a hurry to catch the next available bus except one neatly dressed young man. He seemed to be looking around him.

Manu Prasad had arrived at the makeshift bus depot quite early in the morning. He had woken up three times during the night fearing he might have overslept. He had bathed and clothed his younger brother to the delight of his mother. After that he had finished his morning routine. A cleanly ironed shirt and pants waited for him in his closet. A crisp navy blue blazer hung by the wall in his room. Manu Prasad carefully attired himself and checked in the mirror several times. His father had given him a mischievous smile upon leaving the house. Manu Prasad had avoided the direct gaze of his father and headed to the road above the village. He could have left for the carnival long ago but he wasn't in a hurry. It was still early and Leela was nowhere in sight. The plan was to be in the same bus, just not in the same seats. Fort five minutes after he was at the makeshift bus depot, Leela arrived accompanied by her female friends.

She was dressed in a bright pink Sari with a matching blouse. A flower bead consisting of blue lilies adorned her head. Her long black hair was neatly combed and freely flowed towards the lower back. Red bangles circled around her each hand. Her friends too were impressively attired but Manu Prasad just stared at Leela who was standing few feet away from him. She slightly nodded at Manu being aware of her surroundings. Manu Prasad smiled and looked away. 'Are you going to move forward'? Someone yelled at Manu Prasad. 'You go ahead; I will take the next bus' Manu replied politely. Leela suppressed her smile as Manu Prasad moved back towards the long line. A little later Manu Prasad and Leela were in the same bus headed to the carnival. He was seated in the back while Leela was sitting in the middle of the bus with her friends. The vehicle picked up speed and rolled downhill towards the town by the confluence of two rivers. In the front seat a young boy twisted his head listening to the transistor radio hanging around his neck.

As planned Manu Prasad exited the bus few stops before the scheduled one in the heart of the town. On his way out of the vehicle he lightly tapped Leela on the back as he walked towards the front door. Five minutes later, everyone emptied out of the vehicle in the middle of the carnival town. 'I will be back in ten minutes, just have to make a quick visit to my Aunt who lives few blocks from here' Leela said to her friends and departed. At the post office few blocks away, Manu Prasad was eagerly waiting. He saw Leela waking towards him and his face glowed. They both had avoided suspecting eyes. His plan had worked! Now they both had to get away from the huge crowd.

The town's population had swelled because of the carnival. It seemed the entire district had descended by the confluence of the two rivers. Every square inch of space had been filled in the town. Numerous shops and makeshift stalls covered the ground. Banners and flags flew in the wind displaying various signs. Food, various kinds of clothing, amusement, appliances and much more were abundantly available at the carnival. Young and old from the surrounding small villages were struck by such opulence. Even while talking, people hardly looked at each other as their eyes darted from one thing to the other. It suited Manu Prasad and Leela perfectly as they kept moving forward. 'I'm hungry, let's get something to eat' Leela said softly. 'Okay' Manu replied looking around to make sure they were far away from their group of villagers. A stall close to them was selling hot potato and onion dumplings. Manu motioned towards the delicacy and Leela shook her head in agreement. Soon they were devouring the dumplings along with a side of mint chutney. They washed it down with an ice cold beverage. 'Are you still hungry'? Manu Prasad teased. 'No' Leela replied emphatically. They kept moving forward and looking at the sights, occasionally glancing at each other.

A shop advertised in authentic photographs caught the attention of Manu Prasad. 'Let's get a picture together' Manu said to Leela who anxiously agreed. 'A little closer' the man behind the lens directed. Manu Prasad and Leela moved nervously close to each other and smiled. It was third time the photographer had asked them to be relaxed. 'For a cute couple, you two seem to be distant' the photographer said at the end of the shoot. Manu and Leela smiled looking away from the photographer. 'Impending marriage jitters'? The photographer asked with a broad smile. Manu Prasad looked at the ground while Leela moved her head away and covered her face. As they walked out of the shop, both avoided conversation for a while.

A jewelry stall caught the attention of Leela and she observed it closely. Various ornaments hung from the makeshift tent and women had clustered around the stall. A necklace had drawn Leela's attention but she was having difficulty getting a closer look. She asked Manu Prasad to stay in the back as she moved closer to the necklace. Leela elbowed her way forward and finally asked the shopkeeper to see the necklace. She held the ornament in her hands and admired the craftsmanship. She gently put it around her neck and looked in the small mirror provided by the shopkeeper. She turned the mirror sideways and looked at the necklace again. Leela started bargaining with the shopkeeper as Manu Prasad watched away from them. It seemed she really wanted the necklace but couldn't agree on the price. The shopkeeper did not budge on the negotiating and Leela eventually gave the necklace back. She reluctantly walked away from the stall. 'I'm thirsty' Manu Prasad said upon rejoining Leela. 'Me too' Leela replied. 'I will get us some cold drinks'

Manu stated. 'I will wait for you around here' Leela
said eyeing another jewelry stall in the vicinity.

'Let's get away from the carnival' Manu Prasad asked
Leela. 'It is fun out here' Leela replied. 'After a while
it gets too hectic' Manu pleaded. 'Where do you want
to go'? Leela asked. 'I've a place in mind, up in the hill
at the end of the town' Manu Prasad stated excitedly.
'It is going to be difficult for me to walk that far in my
Sari' Leela said pointing to her attire. 'Don't worry,
we will walk slowly' Manu assured. 'I will show you
some amazing views from the hilltop' Manu Prasad
promised. 'Okay, just walk slowly, I still want to see
the rest of the carnival' Leela agreed with a smile. The
desired destination was about two kilometers away
and they both slowly headed in the direction. The
carnival sights and sounds soon gave way to small
houses and buildings. Manu Prasad and Leela walked
past them to the end of the town. He held her hand
as they climbed the hill overlooking the town. 'If it
wasn't for the Sari, I would race past you uphill' Leela
teased Manu Prasad. He smiled and looked back at the
town below. Leela too turned around and gazed at the
carnival from high above.

The summer was in full swing but it was cool on the
hilltop. It was late in the afternoon as Leela followed
Dev Prasad to his location. 'It is just around the corner'
Manu Prasad encouraged Leela who stopped and
took a sip of water from her container. 'I hope so' she
said, offering her container to Manu Prasad. After
a few minutes they were on the other side of the hill

and the town below was totally obscured. Complete silence greeted them both as they rested on a large boulder on the side of the hill. May be it was fatigue or the surroundings but they both remained speechless for few minutes. 'I've a feeling you have been here in the past' Leela spoke first. 'Yes, I have' Manu smiled. 'Me along with some friends came here two years ago' He confessed. 'The place is just stunning'! Leela exclaimed getting up from the large rock. 'Let me show something' Manu said moving away from the boulder. He asked her to follow him around the mountain trail. Wild flowers with intoxicating smell littered their path as they walked. 'Have some of this' Manu said to Leela as he plucked blueberries from a large shrub. She wasn't finished with the blueberries when Leela came across red berries on the path. She plucked them in bunches and tucked it away in her bag. 'I want you to close your eyes' Maun Prasad requested Leela. She obliged and he led her through a narrow path. 'Open your eyes and look below' Manu Prasad asked. The two large Himalayan Rivers were merging far down below but they resembled village streams from the hilltop. 'The holy confluence looks so small from up here' Leela remarked as her eyes stayed fixed below. 'Where do these rivers finally end'? Leela asked looking at the wide stretch of the confluence. 'They empty out in the vast sea thousands of kilometers from here after passing through numerous towns and cities on the way' Manu Prasad replied. 'The rivers originate from here but end up so far away'! Leela exclaimed. 'Do you like to travel to distant places'? Manu Prasad asked in anticipation. 'Not really, I like our surrounding villages' Leela replied. 'I guess I will have to visit the big city all alone' Manu Prasad exasperated. They both smiled looking in the direction of the highway below which led to the big city about two hundred kilometers further away. A large eagle flew above them and fluttered its wings. They watched the big bird soar high into the sky. 'There is something more I wanted to show you' Manu Prasad insisted. 'More surprises'! Leela exclaimed. 'I hope so' Manu Prasad smiled.

He led her through the mountain trail again, occasionally holding her hand when the path narrowed. They soon came to a stop and Manu Prasad motioned forward with his hands. 'The big town of Kesar Khal' Manu pointed with his finger. Even from a faraway distance high above, numerous buildings and structures could be seen by the naked eyes. 'I've never been to Kesar Khal' Leela remarked stretching her eyes forward. 'What about you'? She asked looking at Manu Prasad. 'I've been there plenty of times' Manu replied with a slight shrug. 'What work do you have in Kesar Khal'? Leela asked in surprise. Manu Prasad smiled and narrated the reasons for his numerous visits to the big town. He usually accompanied his parents along with his younger brother to Kesar Khal. His brother had a medical condition and required monthly visits to the government hospital in the big town. Leela moved closer to Manu Prasad as he divulged details about his brother. Due to his irregular breathing, the younger brother needed constant attention most of the time. His mother hardly left him out of her sight.

'He is getting better now' Manu smiled. The hospital in Kesar Khal had helped him immensely.

'I think my friends know about us' Leela said softly, turning her head away from Manu Prasad. 'Really'! Manu exclaimed sitting beside her on a large rock. 'They give me funny look when they see you coming to the pasture every evening' Leela revealed. 'Today they smiled as they saw you entering bus' Leela further added. The disclosure took Manu Prasad by surprise and for a minute he pondered. 'I think the only person who knows about us in Gauri Ghat is my father' Manu Prasad broke his silence. 'Of course your father knows, the first time I came to your provision store you were staring at me for a long time' Leela responded candidly. 'Can you blame me'? Manu Prasad asked looking at Leela. She turned away again and smiled. 'I don't care if people find out about us' Manu Prasad said firmly. 'I'm tired of meeting you secretly' He added. Leela looked at Manu Prasad who avoided her gaze. 'I would like to see you in the morning, day and night' Manu Prasad as his voice trailed off. Leela remained silent and just looked at Manu who turned his gaze towards her. 'I would like to marry you Leela' Manu Prasad said looking in her eyes. Her eyes got moist and soon started dripping. Manu Prasad pulled a handkerchief from his pocket and gently wiped her eyes. 'I hope that means yes' Manu Prasad said to Leela. She nodded her head in agreement and turned away from him. 'I've something for you' Manu Prasad said, pulling a wrap from his back pocket. She gently turned towards him. 'When did you get this'? Leela screamed looking at the necklace in front of her. It was the same ornament she had wanted at the carnival. 'I want you to put it around your neck' Manu Prasad said, handing the jewelry to Leela. She was too excited to say anything and carefully adorned the fine ornament. 'I wish I had a mirror' Leela lamented adjusting the necklace around her neck. 'Look in my eyes' Manu Prasad suggested. Leela looked in his eyes and admired her glowing necklace. Manu Prasad stood still as Leela continued looking in his eyes. He was glad he had bought the necklace along with cold drinks at the carnival.

The sun was slowly setting in the west behind the mountains and the temperature was dipping on the hilltop. 'We better start getting back to the town before it is late' Leela said looking at the sky. 'Don't worry, we have enough time' Manu Prasad assured. 'You know buses don't run after a certain time during the night' Leela said with concern. 'I know; my family comes this way every month' Manu stated. 'We almost missed the last bus to Gauri Ghat once during our visit to the hospital' Manu recollected with a smile. 'You are still not worried'! Leela said giving a slight push to Manu Prasad. 'Hey careful, I almost slipped downhill' Manu Prasad teased balancing himself. They both started walking back towards the carnival town. Even from the top they could see the activities were dwindling down below. The make shift stalls had been gradually pulled apart and loaded into the small trucks and Lorries. The multitude of humanity that thronged the carnival in the morning and afternoon was fast dwindling in numbers. People from the faraway villages wanted to be home before nightfall. 'Your friends are probably worried about you' Manu Prasad said to Leela walking downhill. 'I will tell them I got lost and couldn't find them among the large crowd' Leela smiled. 'You could tell them the truth' Manu said suppressing his smile. 'Don't worry, everyone is going to find out soon about us' Leela said adjusting her necklace. 'Yes they will' Manu Prasad said with conviction.

'What is that sound'? Manu Prasad wondered as they both approached the bottom end of the hill. It was a slow moan echoing from few feet away on the side. Leela rushed towards the sound holding her Sari firmly. 'Be careful' Manu Prasad yelled following her in the back. 'It is a boy; he has fallen in a ditch'! Leela screamed coming to a stop. 'Let's get him out of here' she said to Manu as he came close. 'What are you doing here Bal'? Manu Prasad asked looking inside the large ditch. 'You know him'! Leela asked in amazement. 'Yes, he is a boy from my village' Manu Prasad replied as he got down inside the ditch. Bal was too distraught at the moment and was sobbing. His small transistor radio still hung by his neck but it was partly covered in dust. 'How did you end up in the ditch'? Manu Prasad softly asked after safely rescuing the young boy. Leela offered him water from her container which he quickly drank. 'Your neighbor.......your neighbor.....asked me to follow you' Bal stuttered after a few minutes looking in the direction of Manu Prasad. 'Why'? Manu asked surprisingly with a smile. 'She wanted.........to find out……..about the girl' Bal stuttered looking at Leela. 'Mausi' Manu Prasad sighed. 'It seems people in the village want to know about us' Leela smiled. 'They do…… they do' Bal confirmed. 'Let's get out of this place' Manu Prasad said wiping his brow. 'Yes, let's go home' Leela added as the young boy smiled. Soon all three of them started walking towards the bus depot in the middle of the town.

Manu Prasad and Leela soon informed their families about each other. Dev Prasad was pleased his son had picked a future bride of his choice and approved of the decision. After all he had known about both of them from the beginning. His wife was hesitant in the beginning about the relationship. Manu Prasad had attracted lot of marriage proposals from the surrounding villages. Owing to the family's social and economic standing, some noble families from faraway towns in the district also wanted Manu Prasad for their daughter. His mother wanted the family to explore these opportunities. After lengthy conversations with both her husband and son, she agreed on Leela as her future daughter in law. Leela's family was overjoyed that Manu Prasad had asked their daughter to be his future wife. Dev Prasad was held in high esteem around the neighboring villages due to his generosity and wealth. Leela's family came from a moderate background and was thrilled about the possible union. Her parents gave their approval to the relationship. Soon the two families met each other to complete the formalities. Manu Prasad and Leela were set to marry in three months.

The villagers in Gauri Ghat reacted differently to the wedding announcement. 'Manu Prasad could have married into an equally rich family; some high ranking government officials in the big town wanted him for their daughters, that girl just cast a spell on him' commented some villagers. Mausi listened to all the gossip but was pleased to hear the wedding announcement. In her courtyard as she spread the grain to dry, her eyes darted across. Dev Prasad's wife tended to her younger son in the courtyard while he stretched in the morning sun. The young boy was going through various exercises as advised by his doctor. The mother looked in pride as the boy continued with his routine. Mausi observed the proceedings from her courtyard. She had met Dev Prasad's wife on numerous occasions since her return to Gauri Ghat. She was a petite woman and few years younger than Mausi. They both usually exchanged smiles upon seeing each other but little else. She was too busy with her younger son most of the time while Mausi remained occupied with her own work. 'Dev Prasad's wife' Mausi thought to herself looking across the courtyard as the mother watched her young son. 'She indeed is lucky, her older son is getting to marry the girl of his choice' Mausi mumbled slowly.

'We have to visit the hospital tomorrow' Dev Prasad informed his older son at dinner during the night. 'Manu, I need you to stay here and look after the provision store' Dev Prasad continued. 'Okay' Manu agreed nodding his head. 'It is just not economically viable anymore to keep the store closed while all of us make the monthly trip to Kesar Khal' Dev Prasad concluded. The rest of the family agreed in unison. The next morning Manu Prasad headed to the provision store as rest of his family prepared for the long trip. He was going to be all alone at the store for the entire day tending to customers and also arranging the arrived goods in proper order. In the late afternoon he would definitely catch a deserved break! Leela would come to the store after school and probably spend an hour helping him. The thought cheered him as he arrived at the provision store.

Dev Prasad, his wife and their younger son were now all ready for the trip to Kesar Khal. The journey was going to take up the entire day, eventually ending in the late evening. They had well planned for the trip, making sure food and water was appropriately stocked. Above the village all three of them waited for the bus by the long winding mountain road. Fifteen minutes later, all of them were on their way to the big town. The young boy smiled as the bus gathered speed and moved ahead. His parents gently rubbed his forehead. Cool crisp morning air was gushing inside the bus and some passengers rolled down their seat windows. The morning sun was shining brightly and the rays were piercing through the glass pane of the vehicle. The driver adjusted his screen and kept driving. Further away the mountains glowed in the sun and their snowy peaks glistened in the backdrop. The pine and rhododendron trees emanated their scent as the vehicle snaked through the mountain road. Monkeys could be seen on the side of the road picking up wild fruit from the trees. Dev Prasad and his wife were lost in their thoughts. What was the doctor going to say? What is he going to prescribe this time? Will he be satisfied with boy's progress this time around? They both looked at their young son who was fast asleep in his seat. 'I hope we don't have to make more of these trips' the wife whispered to her husband. Dev Prasad quietly nodded his head in agreement. The bus was going to make several stops before reaching the district headquarters in Kesar Khal.

They arrived in Kesar Khal little after eleven in the morning. Dev Prasad, his wife and their young son headed to the big government hospital. The doctor received them and examined the young boy. The parents anxiously waited outside as the doctor performed a series of tests on the young boy in a closed room. This continued for two hours. Finally the doctor emerged from the room along with the young boy. Dev Prasad and his wife walked towards the doctor in anticipation. 'Your son is improving and getting better' the doctor revealed to the anxious parents. They both hugged their child and thanked the doctor. They were required to pick up some medication from the hospital pharmacy and their visit to Kesar Khal was over. The doctor gave them more good news. The next visit to the hospital was required in two months. The wife was thrilled. Monthly visits seemed too quick. All three of them thanked the doctor and headed outside.

I'm going to relax a little' Dev Prasad informed his wife and son as he headed to a tea stall. The husband

and wife sipped hot tea in the late afternoon sun and their son quenched his thirst with a soft drink. 'Why don't we go to a nice restaurant for lunch'? The husband asked his wife. 'But we have brought lunch with us'! The wife exclaimed pointing to her bag. 'Don't worry you can save that for dinner' Dev Prasad stated. 'Okay, I won't have to prepare dinner' the wife smiled. Soon all three of them headed to a restaurant in the middle of Kesar Khal. They ordered choice delicacies and ate to their hearts content. 'You want some desert'? Dev Prasad asked his young son. 'No, he already ate enough and he is going to get sweets later' the mother interjected. 'We better get to the bus depot' Dev Prasad said getting up from his seat. 'There is one more stop before our return to Gauri Ghat' he said turning his eyes towards the wife. The wife just shook her head and smiled. On the way to the bus depot they picked up a large packet of sweets along with some flowers. A little later all three of them were on their way as the large vehicle moved away from Kesar Khal.

The town by the holy confluence of two rivers was approaching and Dev Prasad wished all three of them just kept moving along with the bus. That was not going to be possible! On every trip back from Kesar Khal his wife had a ritual of performing Puja at the temple by the holy confluence. 'Our boy has been getting better because of the grace of Almighty' this was her convincing argument to Dev Prasad. It didn't matter that the ritual took almost an hour of their time. The wife was adamant about the Puja. Dev Prasad had to relent which meant catching the last bus to Gauri Ghat after the ritual at the temple.

All three of them got off the bus by the confluence of two rivers. They slowly walked down the long steps that led to the sacred temple located right near the confluence. 'I just hope we don't miss the last bus to Gauri Ghat' Dev Prasad sighed as he walked down the steps. 'The last bus leaves in an hour and half' the wife assured her husband. 'I know but I don't like waiting for the last one' Dev Prasad said, carefully holding the large packet of sweets and array of flowers in his hands. 'We have been blessed by the Lord, this is our way of thanking' the wife replied as they neared the end of the steps. Dev Prasad shook his head in agreement. The holy confluence was a sight to behold in the evening. The water from the two rivers was splashing against the rocks that lay in the middle and making quite a spectacle against the setting sun in the west. Dev Prasad's young son was observing the phenomenon closely. 'We have to get moving' his mother said to the young boy. He reluctantly followed her to the temple. Dev Prasad had already managed to get the priest for their private Puja. Soon they were inside the temple chanting hymns and making offerings. Dev Prasad's wife had her eyes closed and was totally engrossed in prayers. Her head moved from side to side as she chanted hymns along with the priest. Dev Prasad too was praying but his eyes occasionally drifted towards the wrist watch. The young boy tried his best to stay awake. The ceremony lasted almost an hour. The young boy was the happiest of all as he devoured sweets at the end of the Puja. 'Let's hurry back to the top' Dev Prasad said to his wife and young son.

'Be careful climbing the steps or you will end in the river' Dev Prasad chided his young son who slightly slipped on the way to the top. 'Stop it' his wife lightly hit her husband who smiled looking at his son. 'Guess we have another twenty minutes before the last bus from Kesar Khal arrives for Gauri Ghat' Dev Prasad said looking at his wrist watch. They had now reached the top of the long steps and the small town was bustling with late evening activities. 'You want to look around for few minutes'? The wife asked her husband. 'No, I want all of us to wait here for the bus' Dev Prasad announced emphatically, standing in the middle of town. The bus arrived few minutes after its scheduled time and the three along with five other passengers got inside the vehicle. 'I feel better now' Dev Prasad said to his wife sitting alongside him in the middle seat. The young boy was sandwiched between them and was falling asleep. The bus was soon getting away from the small town and making its upward ascent towards the long mountain road. A light drizzle greeted the passengers and the driver switched on the windshield wipers. The visibility was poor and the vehicle was moving uphill at a slower speed. Dev Prasad closed his seat windows and his wife tucked a sweater on her son. 'It got dark quickly' the wife said looking outside the closed window. 'Yes it did' Dev Prasad added with concern.

A loud noise rattled the bus and it came to slow screeching halt. The driver and the conductor of the vehicle quickly departed outside with their flashlights. The bus had about twelve passengers and they were all anxiously looking at each other and talking about the unexpected event. The commotion had woken up Dev Prasad's son from his sleep and his parents tried to calm him. The driver and the conductor returned inside the bus to face the distraught passengers. 'The front tire of the bus is damaged' the driver informed the anxious passengers. 'It probably got hit by a sliding rock because of the rain' the driver further added. 'We will try our best but it is going to be difficult to fix the tire in the dark' the conductor said to the passengers. 'The wheel has suffered significant damage' the conductor sighed. The two operators started looking for their tool box as the passengers contemplated their predicament.

'They are not going to be able to fix a badly damaged tire in this rain and darkness' Dev Prasad said shaking his head. 'What shall we do' the wife said on the verge of tears. 'I'm thinking' Dev Prasad replied softly. 'Let me go talk to the driver and conductor outside' Dev Prasad said to his wife who had a shawl wrapped around her son. 'Be careful outside' the wife said as her husband exited the stalled vehicle. The rain outside had tapered off but the darkness was in full glow. Dev Prasad walked towards the front of the vehicle and talked to the two operators who were busy with their tools. He returned to his wife a little later. 'Looks like the bus might stay here till morning' Dev Prasad revealed to his wife. 'What do you mean'? She asked in exasperation. 'I mean they are not going to be able to fix the tire till morning' Dev Prasad replied with a hint of anger in his voice. 'We can't stay here till morning'! The wife exclaimed. 'I know' Dev Prasad agreed. The two contemplated for few minutes as the young boy watched them. 'We can just spend the night inside the bus' the boy finally broke his silence. 'It is going to get very cold during the night' His mother said putting her arm around him. 'We don't have any blankets to keep us warm during the night' Dev Prasad added with regret. 'Even the blankets won't help in this cold rainy night' the wife stated. 'Our son might get pneumonia spending the night in an open bus' Dev Prasad whispered in his wife's ears. The rest of the passengers had started stretching out in their seats. They were preparing to spend the night inside the stalled vehicle.

Dev Prasad looked at his wrist watch as his wife rubbed her tired eyes. 'There is a lorry that ferries goods to Gauri Ghat and few other villages during the night' he said in excitement. 'We still have time to catch it' he said looking at his wife. 'I don't know' the wife said shaking her head. 'It is our last chance in the night to get back home' Dev Prasad pleaded. 'The lorry is a small vehicle and drivers are mostly young and reckless' the wife said looking at her husband. 'Our son can sit on my lap and we can squeeze together' Dev Prasad assured. 'Don't worry I know lot of the drivers as they deliver goods to our provision store' he further added. 'Okay' the wife finally agreed. All three of them gathered their belongings and exited the vehicle. They could hear some of the passengers snoring on their way out. 'Let's stay huddled together to keep warm' Dev Prasad instructed his wife and son who obliged. The three of them started walking away from the vehicle which was parked on the side of the mountain road. The driver and the conductor had given up on fixing the tire and were reluctantly entering the vehicle. 'We should stand close to the bus; it will be easy for someone to notice us' Dev Prasad stated. All three of them rubbed their hands and waited for the last lorry of the night going uphill. It was cold but the rain had subsided.

Fifteen minutes later, sound of a motor engine cheered Dev Prasad as he leaned forward in anticipation. The small vehicle came uphill towards the bus and slowly stopped at the sight of a man who was vigorously moving his hands for help. The driver rolled down his window and looked outside. 'Oh, it is you' the driver said with a smile looking at Dev Prasad and his family waiting in the dark. Dev Prasad was glad to see a familiar face and explained his predicament to the driver. 'I have no problem giving you a ride to Gauri Ghat' the driver informed the relieved family. 'You might have to squeeze a little' he advised as three slowly entered the front of the lorry. 'You can put your belongings in the back' he said to Dev Prasad who quickly agreed. The lorry was on its way up the mountain road again to the relief of everyone. 'The rain has really slowed everything down' the driver said with a smile. 'Oh yes' Dev Prasad sighed holding his young son between his legs. The wife quietly nodded. 'I should be able to get you home before bedtime' the driver smiled as he picked up speed on the dark mountain road. These were the last words uttered inside the lorry!

The lorry was moving upwards on the road which was flanked by a mountain on side and a deep ravine on the other. Dev Prasad stretched his legs as far he could on the passenger side and was looking at his wife. The wife was unsuccessfully trying to fight off sleep. His young son rested in front of him. The bus with a broken tire was now just a memory. The small vehicle in which they were cramped together had rescued them during the cold night. The lorry had almost completed its upward ascent on the mountain road and was now approaching a sharp curve but the driver failed to adjust accordingly. A large rock had slid onto the road from the side of the mountain and was partially visible in the dark. When the driver finally noticed it upon nearing the curve, he suddenly applied his brakes to avoid the hazard. The lorry skidded off the road and plunged into the deep ravine below. It all happened in less than fifteen seconds!

When the last bus to Gauri Ghat and the surrounding villages failed to arrive forty five minutes after its schedule time, Manu Prasad was worried. He had closed the provision store early and arrived at the bus stop almost an hour ago. 'It is probably due to inclement weather' he mumbled to himself as he waited by the road above the village. He paced back and forth on the road and rubbed his hands to keep warm in the cold night. Another half an hour passed and still no sign of the large vehicle. 'The last lorry ferrying goods to the neighboring villages should be arriving soon' Manu Prasad thought to himself. 'I'm sure the driver probably has seen the bus on his way up' he muttered to himself. Another forty five minutes passed and neither the lorry nor the bus arrived. Manu Prasad was worried but he was helpless. What was he supposed to do? How was he to find out about the rest of his family? He stared at the dark empty road and contemplated. 'Maybe the road was shut down due to rockslide', 'Maybe my family missed the last bus', 'The doctor probably wanted to further examine my little brother, hence they all decided to stay overnight in Kesar Khal' the thoughts kept going in and out of his mind. It was getting late and cold. Manu Prasad realized standing all alone on the lonely road wasn't going to solve anything. He reluctantly started walking back to his house below.

'Where is rest of the family'? A voice asked Manu Prasad as he entered his courtyard. He looked around and saw Mausi staring at him from her top floor verandah. She was standing up from her customary chair and looking across her young neighbor. 'The last bus didn't arrive' Manu replied looking across. 'They probably decided to spend the night in town due to bad weather' Mausi offered her reason. 'Don't worry they will take the morning bus to Gauri Ghat tomorrow' Mausi encouraged the young man who seemed lost in thoughts. The conversation cheered Manu Prasad a little and he slowly entered his house. It was strange being all alone in the house as he switched on the lights.

Manu Prasad hadn't had dinner but he wasn't hungry. He went upstairs to his room and changed into his night attire. He tried to sleep but failed. He looked at the ceiling and wished Leela was with him at this moment. He closed his eyes and the images of his family kept appearing. 'Like Mausi said, they will be here in the morning' he assured himself opening his eyes. Soon he was overtaken by exhaustion and fell asleep.

Mausi continued to observe her surroundings from the top floor verandah. She was now seated in her chair and leaning back. Every night after dinner she would spend hours in the verandah rocking in her favorite chair. Her eyes and ears watched and listened to the sights and sounds of her village. Who is going where? Who is coming at late night? Mausi had a good idea. She knew the last bus to Gauri Ghat didn't arrive and neither did the goods lorry. Even from down below she could hear the ramblings on the road above Gauri Ghat. Mausi could even point a house emanating a child's cry in the stillness of night. She knew when her alcoholic brother stumbled home in the dark and quietly went to sleep. Occasionally sound of an animal from the forest high above still scared her like a little girl growing up in the village. The neighboring villages twinkled in lights and Mausi reminisced about her time without electricity. Those days seemed so distant! The little girl was now an old lady. Eventually Mausi would retire back in her room from the verandah. Tonight before going to bed she prayed Dev Prasad and his family were safe somewhere.

Manu Prasad was up well before dawn. He prepared himself a hot cup of tea and changed his clothes. He washed his face with some cold water and was on his way to the road on top of the village. The first early morning bus to arrive in Gauri Ghat was still fifteen minutes away. Two elderly men were waiting for the bus along with Manu Prasad on the side of the road. It was a crisp and cool early summer morning and the sky was spotless blue. The overnight rain had cleared everything. The ground was still a little damp but Manu Prasad was focused on the road in from him. The first bus was about to arrive any minute and he anxiously looked in the direction of the vehicle. The cluttering of the large engine signaled the arrival of the bus and Manu Prasad ran towards it to the surprise of the two elderly gentlemen waiting alongside. He got inside the vehicle and eagerly started looking for his parents and the younger brother. The bus only had five passengers seated in the middle. Manu Prasad walked towards the end of the bus and looked closely. He was disappointed in his search. The rest of his family was not on the bus. 'Maybe it is still early; they will probably take the next bus' Manu Prasad consoled himself. He slowly exited the vehicle. On his way out he asked the driver about the bus schedule. The next bus was still two hours away.

As he stood on the road, Manu Prasad contemplated about his time. 'Should I just go home for few hours? I should get some rest, I woke up early' his mind kept thinking. He thought about walking down and meeting Leela on her way to school. He should let her know about his family. It would probably calm his mind informing Leela. 'No, I can't tell her, she will get worried and skip school to be with me' he argued. 'It is better if I deal with this alone, I'm sure they will be here on the next bus' Manu rationalized. He kept walking up and down the road, hoping time would pass quickly. The provision store was supposed to be open soon but Manu Prasad was least concerned about his family business. 'They have to be on the next bus' was the only thought on his mind. Down below the temple bells were ringing and prayers offered. Further away young boys and girls were laughing and talking on their way to school. Men ploughed their fields while women tended to their respective cattle shed. It was just another day in Gauri Ghat. Manu Prasad pacing back and forth on the road wished it was so!

The sun was now shining brightly and surrounding hills glowed in the light. About ten people were waiting for the next bus alongside Manu Prasad on the road. The bus finally arrived and everyone waiting jostled for position. The large vehicle was almost filled to capacity and the driver loudly instructed everyone on the ground to stay clear off the door for the exiting passengers. Manu Prasad apprehensively moved forward to get a close look at the exiting passengers. Eight passengers exited the bus but Manu Prasad's family wasn't one of them. He was now nervous and slightly angry. He brushed aside everyone and rushed inside the vehicle. 'Wait your turn' the driver yelled at Manu Prasad. 'I'm looking for my family' Manu Prasad apologized to the driver. He elaborated about his family to the driver who was now sympathetic to the distressed young man. 'My family was supposed to be the on the bus last night' Manu Prasad detailed to the driver as the conductor joined the conversation. 'Your family was on this bus last night' the driver revealed to Manu Prasad who was now shaking. 'The bus sustained a broken tire coming up last evening and was stalled roadside overnight' the conductor intervened. From Manu Prasad's description, the driver informed him about his parents and his young brother. 'I saw them get off our bus last night and get inside a goods lorry about twenty minutes later' the driver concluded to Manu Prasad who listened in stunned silence.

After getting off the vehicle, Manu Prasad aimlessly walked down the road. His thoughts were incoherent but he kept walking forward. 'What happened to the lorry'? This just consumed him as he moved further away. Manu Prasad was now determined. He started looking for any sign of the lorry on both sides of the mountain road. Manu Prasad was breathing heavily but he kept searching. He had moved far away from Gauri Ghat and was now approaching downward descent on the long mountain road. His tongue was sticking out of his mouth in need of water but Manu Prasad continued walking. From a distance he could see three people gathered on the side of the road which sharply curved. They seem to be examining the edge of the road. Manu Prasad started walking faster. 'What are you all searching'? Manu Prasad asked almost running out of breath as he got close to the small group.

'We presume our goods lorry went down this deep ravine last night' one of the men said pointing to the tire marks on the edge of the road. 'Our driver didn't report back in the night, hence we three have been combing the road since morning' the man who was probably the owner of the small vehicle concluded. 'What time in the night.................what time in the night'? The words were barely audible as Manu Prasad slurred. 'You okay'? The man standing close to Manu Prasad asked with concern. Manu Prasad was now shaking and uttering broken phrases. 'Let's give him some water' one of the three said thrusting a cool container in front of Manu Prasad who quickly started drinking. He splashed some on his face and returned the container back to its owner. 'You seem better now' the man said to Manu Prasad who started looking around the edge of the road. Manu Prasad tried to compose himself but his hands were shaking uncontrollably. He followed the skid marks of the lorry to the edge where the road ended and the deep ravine stared him in the face. The skid marks were firm on the side of the road but deep and haphazard as they neared the ravine. Manu Prasad walked a little further and saw sacks of wheat and flour lying slightly below the ravine. He walked further down as the three men looked at him puzzled.

Manu Prasad looked in front of him and his heart sank. The utensils were splattered on the ground and food was spilled everywhere. He clearly identified his family utensils his mother used for lunch! 'My mother and father and my brother, my mother and father and my brother' Manu Prasad started crying hysterically upon discovering the unfortunate obvious. The three men rushed towards him but poor Manu was inconsolable. He picked up the utensils scattered on the ground and held them tightly. The three men watched from the top edge that separated the road from the ravine as Manu kept crying further down from them. Manu tucked the utensils in his shirt and started going down. 'What are you doing' one of the men yelled from the top. 'I need to find them, I need to find them' Manu Prasad cried in anger. 'The ravine is extremely deep, you can't go any further' the three men pleaded from above him. 'I don't care', Manu Prasad continued crying and descending. At this point one of the three men slowly walked down the ravine. He grabbed Manu Prasad from the back and dragged him away. 'You keep going down and you will end up dead' the man screamed at Manu Prasad who was still crying. 'The ravine is really steep and no one has seen its end' the man said firmly holding Manu Prasad. 'What I'm I supposed to do'? Manu Prasad cried. 'My family is no more' he kept sobbing. 'We have also lost a driver, he was part of our family' the man said holding back tears. 'There is nothing we can do right now' the man consoled Manu Prasad. He put his arms around Manu and the two started walking back up the ravine. When the two reached the edge of the road, a goods lorry had stopped on its way to Gauri Ghat. The driver was busy talking with the other two men about the incident. 'The driver here can give you a ride' one of the men said to Manu Prasad. 'I don't need a ride' Manu Prasad calmly replied with tears fading from his eyes. 'Poor boy, he lost his whole family last night' one of the men said softly to the driver of the lorry who soon departed on his journey to Gauri Ghat and the surrounding villages.

When Manu Prasad finally staggered home late in the evening, the entire village along with Leela and her family had gathered in his courtyard. The lorry driver had conveyed the bad news to everyone hours ago. It was a somber gathering and some were still wiping tears. Leela saw Manu Prasad entering his courtyard and rushed towards him. She held him tightly and started weeping. Manu Prasad held Leela close to her but it seemed he had run out of tears. His eyes were swollen from crying and walking for hours. They held each other for few minutes and then the rest of the villagers offered their condolences to Manu Prasad. The grieving lasted for almost an hour and then everyone left the courtyard except Leela, her family and Manu Prasad. Very little was exchanged between them as night approached. Leela offered to stay with Manu Prasad during the night but he kindly refused. 'We are not married yet', was his simple explanation. He thanked Leela and her family for their support and urged them to leave before late. Leela was still hesitant to leave him alone in this time of grave distress but ultimately agreed to depart after prolonged persuasion. 'I will be here early in the morning' Leela firmly stated as she bid a tearful goodbye to Manu Prasad. Soon she along with her parents was gone. Now Manu Prasad was all alone in his courtyard.

He hadn't eaten all day and wasn't in the mood to feed his empty stomach in the night. As he sat on the edge of his courtyard, Manu Prasad wished to sleep and wake up from this nightmare facing him. Maybe this was just a bad dream and everything would be fine in the morning. His mother would prepare hot tea for him as usual, his father would start getting ready for the provision store and he himself would play with his younger brother. Manu Prasad tried to fight off sleep as the moonlight lit up his courtyard. The night was getting cold and he slowly rose from his seated position in the courtyard. His house looked dark in the night as no one had switched on the lights. Now he was the only one responsible for his house! Manu Prasad shuddered to think as he quietly entered his dark home.

Across the courtyard, Mausi had been observing everything about her distraught neighbor from the top floor verandah. Along with rest of the villagers she had been grieving in Manu Prasad's courtyard once the tragic news reached her late in the day. She wanted to talk personally with the grief stricken young man once he arrived in his courtyard late in the evening but the situation was overwhelming. Everyone was offering their condolences at the same time and the poor young man seemed disoriented with the response. She realized it was better to leave him alone at the moment and talk to him later. She had come home after the grieving and prepared dinner for everyone except herself. Mausi just wasn't hungry. As she rocked from her chair in the top floor verandah, her thoughts remained with her young neighbor. Poor young boy was now all alone in this world after losing his family. Her childhood friend Dev Prasad was no more! She couldn't come to terms with the brutal fact. The night was still early but Mausi didn't feel like spending long hours in her verandah tonight. The engine of a goods lorry could be heard cranking on the road above the village. Mausi slowly rose from her chair and walked inside her room. She started walking back and forth in her small dark room. A little later she looked in the direction of the road from her room and started screaming. 'Why did they build this road, why did they build this road'? Mausi cried in the darkness of her room. When she was a little girl the road took away the wide green pastures from Ruchi, later the road took away her Mohit Lal when Ruchitra Devi was barely a young woman. Now her only true friend Dev Prasad was also a victim of the long road.

Chapter 7

After the sudden and tragic demise of his family, Manu Prasad stayed at home for a week. Every morning before going to school, Leela spent an hour with him. She brought him breakfast, prepared lunch and talked with Manu Prasad while he stayed in his room. Leela tried her best to cheer him up and Manu appreciated the genuine care along with the effort. 'You have to start going to the provision store' Leela encouraged. 'I just don't feel like opening the store so soon' Manu would reply. 'Our pending marriage is not far away, we need to get things in order' Leela stated. 'I know, I know' Manu Prasad would respond. Leela knew that he was in shock and needed some time to recover from his current state. After spending an hour in the morning she would walk to her school, promising to come back again in the late afternoon. Once Leela departed Manu Prasad would leave his room and walk down to his courtyard. He would sit on the far edge of his courtyard and gaze in the direction of his fields. Sometimes he would turn around and look at his empty house. The man hired by his family to look after the cattle herd would arrive with milk from the shed. Manu Prasad would quietly nod at the man who would place the milk container along with some other purchased items in the kitchen. The man would later clean the house and the courtyard. He would silently look in the direction of Manu Prasad before departing for the day. Manu Prasad would continue spending his time sitting in the open courtyard. Across from her own courtyard, Mausi would keep an eye on her young neighbor as she worked. Late afternoon would arrive along with Leela in Manu Prasad's courtyard. They would talk about school and other things for a while which eased his mind. Leela would then prepare an early dinner for him and Manu Prasad would return in his upstairs room. 'I've to go home now' Leela would inform him frustratingly. 'I understand, you practically spend the entire day helping me' Manu Prasad would comfort Leela. 'I would like to spend more time' Leela always replied. 'You will soon, you will soon' Manu Prasad would encourage her before leaving. She would smile and depart, leaving Manu Prasad all alone in his house. This continued for a week.

It was late in the morning and Manu Prasad was idling in his courtyard. 'You just can't keep going like this' Mausi said softly walking towards Manu Prasad who had his back towards her. He slowly turned around and faced his old neighbor. As a mark of respect Manu Prasad rose from his seated position. 'Please sit down Mausi' he asked his neighbor clearing the edge of the courtyard. 'Why don't you sit down too'? Mausi asked firmly. Soon the two were seated alongside on the edge of the courtyard. 'I understand your pain son' Mausi began as Manu Prasad listened with his head down. 'I too have lost things near and dear to me all my life' Mausi continued. She elaborated about her time as a little girl growing up in Gauri Ghat and her marriage to a distant village. Manu Prasad listened intently as Mausi described her own loss in life. 'After a while no one feels sorry for you, in fact they despise you' Mausi revealed to her young grief stricken neighbor. Tears came back to Manu Prasad as he watched and listened to his old neighbor. 'It is difficult Mausi' Manu finally let out.

'Yes it is but you have to keep moving forward' Mausi stated. 'You just can't hide from everyone and stay in your house all day' Mausi said to Manu Prasad. 'Your provision store is closed for more than a week' Mausi continued as Manu listened. 'I just don't feel like going to the provision store' Manu Prasad said softly. The two sat in silence for few minutes. 'You have to re -open the store Manu' Mausi continued. 'It is the only way for you to make a living; you don't have other skills' Mausi emphasized. Manu Prasad shook his head in agreement as his wise old neighbor narrated the truth. 'You did not pursue college in order to help your family business, the provision store is your economic lifeline' Mausi said to him. 'I understand' Manu nodded looking at his old neighbor. 'It has been more than a week since the horrible tragedy, you have to slowly get back on your feet son' Mausi said softly. 'People in the village are saying things behind your back' Mausi stated. 'What kind of things'? Manu Prasad asked in surprise. 'They say you've lost your mind and can't seem to function normally' Mausi further elaborated as Manu listened. 'The fools don't understand a close loss' Mausi said shaking her head. 'The people also talk about Leela' Mausi stated. 'Really'! Manu Prasad exclaimed with surprise. 'They say she is not yet married to you but still spends all her time in the house' Mausi continued. 'Man and a woman spending time together before marriage is not part of our culture, the villagers look down upon this arrangement' Mausi informed Manu Prasad. 'I've told Leela not to spend so much time here but she won't listen' Manu Prasad informed Mausi. 'It will be fine once we both get married in a few months' Manu Prasad said with a relief. Mausi put her arms around Manu and said, 'Son you better get married sooner'. Manu Prasad reluctantly replied, 'But I still have to finish lot of work'. Mausi looked at Manu Prasad and took a deep breath. 'You've lost both your mother and father' Mausi again continued. 'Who is going to perform the ceremonial marriage functions'? Mausi asked and Manu Prasad listened closely. 'Don't forget we live in small villages where certain customs are still followed' Mausi emphasized. 'Right now people still have sympathy for you but longer you wait............' Mausi wondered. Manu Prasad tried to comprehend as he sat beside his old neighbor in the courtyard. Mausi slowly rose from the edge of the courtyard. 'I've to get going now son' she informed Manu Prasad. 'Thank you' Manu said putting his arms around Mausi. 'You will be okay son' she said accepting his embrace. 'Now don't forget to open the store tomorrow' Mausi stated to Manu Prasad as she departed. Manu smiled and nodded his head. It was the first time he had smiled in nine days.

The next day when Leela arrived, Manu Prasad was already preparing his morning tea. 'I've prepared an extra cup for you' Manu said to her as she entered the kitchen. 'I'm pleased' Leela said to him as they sipped hot tea together. 'You are dressed early today' Leela noted looking at Manu Prasad. 'I'm going to open the store' Manu stated. 'Really, can I join you'? Leela asked in anticipation. 'Not now but you can come after school' Manu Prasad replied calmly. 'There is lot of work in the house after school' Leela said raising her hands. Manu Prasad was quiet for a minute and then stated, 'Leela, I don't want you to spend so much time here in the house everyday'. Leela gave him a puzzled look and asked, 'Who is going to cook and clean then'? Manu Prasad moved closer to her and said, 'We are not married yet, it doesn't look appropriate for us to be together most of the time'. Leela gave him a stern look for thirty seconds. 'Are people in the village talking about this'? She asked looking in his eyes. Manu Prasad turned around and said, 'If they are talking, they are not wrong'. Leela put her tea cup away along with the pot. 'I don't care about what people say; I will help as I please' Leela stated thumping her foot on the ground. Manu Prasad tried to conceal his smile but failed. 'Okay, do as you please' he said softly looking in her eyes. Leela smiled and Manu Prasad was pleased. 'Now I've to go to the provision store' Manu Prasad said to Leela. 'Yes, you do'! She exclaimed in delight.

Three days after re-opening his provision store, things were slowly getting back to normal for Manu Prasad. He was working all alone in the store which kept him busy most of the time. Leela would join him late in the afternoon and ease his workload for an hour. The rest of the time Manu Prasad was taking care of the customers as well as stocking items in the back shelf. It was overwhelming at times but it kept his mind away from incessant thoughts. The customers also appreciated re-opening of the provision store which was the largest of its kind in the vicinity. Communicating with his customers pleased Manu Prasad. His father and his grandfather had worked hard for the success of the provision store. As a child he remembered going to the small store with his father and watching his grandfather work diligently. Over the years the provision store had expanded and prospered. It had become a household name in Gauri Ghat and the surrounding villages. Manu Prasad realized it was now incumbent upon him to continue this legacy.

It was late in the morning and Manu Prasad was tending to customers. It was quite hectic at the store as he would first take orders from a customer, get the item from the shelf and then collect the necessary dues. This continued for a while and eventually the customers trickled down. Manu Prasad wiped his brow and took a sip of water from his container. From the corner of his eye he noticed a familiar sight for the past few days. Bal, the young village boy was listening to his small transistor radio by the side of the provision store. He would shake his head listening to the tunes emanating from the radio and occasionally smile looking in the direction of Manu Prasad. 'You've have nothing to do Bal'? Manu Prasad asked loudly looking at the young boy. 'No' Bal replied calmly. Manu Prasad smiled hearing the reply. Like everyone else in the village, he knew the young boy had a speech impediment and was mostly ignored. 'Every morning you come here and listen to the radio for hours' Manu Prasad stated to the young boy. 'No one wants me......... around' Bal said softly. 'You are the only one who......... doesn't object' Bal further added. Manu Prasad contemplated for a few minutes as he looked at the young boy. 'Why don't you come inside and help me in the store'? Manu Prasad asked the boy with a smile. 'Okay' Bal replied gleefully and rushed forward. 'Just make sure the volume is turned down on the radio while you are working in the store' Manu Prasad asked the young boy. Bal quickly obliged with a smile. Manu Prasad now had an employee!

The goods lorry was filled to capacity when it arrived at the provision store late in the evening. The driver got off the vehicle and greeted Manu Prasad. 'Do you have all the items I ordered' Manu Prasad asked the driver. 'Not really' the driver replied sheepishly. 'What do you mean'? Manu Prasad asked in surprise. 'I just have few things for you' the driver replied looking away. 'Where is the rest of all this going' Manu Prasad asked the driver pointing to the packed lorry. The driver remained silent for ten seconds. 'The merchants in town are threatening to stop your supplies unless their dues are cleared' the driver said looking at Manu Prasad. 'We pay our dues in time' Manu Prasad emphasized to the driver. 'I'm sure you do, I'm just an employee who does what he is told' the driver said to Manu Prasad. 'You know my father took care of all the accounts in the past but now........' Manu Prasad stopped himself.

'I know, I know....' The driver started sobbing. 'Hey it is okay' Manu Prasad said putting his arms around the driver. 'My older brother was driving the lorry that fateful night' the driver confided wiping his tears. The two looked at each other and embraced. 'It feels good to finally meet you' the driver stated after sharing his pain. Manu Prasad silently nodded in agreement. 'Tell the merchants I will settle their dues soon' Manu Prasad said to the driver as he was departing. The driver acknowledged with a smile and drove away. 'I've to find the account ledger' Manu Prasad mumbled to himself upon getting inside the provision store. 'Can you get me a small sack of wheat'? A customer asked Manu Prasad. 'Sure' Manu replied and asked Bal to get the item from the back shelf. 'Hey, you haven't paid for it yet' Manu yelled at the customer as he was walking away with the sack of wheat. 'I will pay you in a week like I usually do' the customer smiled and walked away. Working alongside his father in the past, Manu knew that week almost meant a month for most customers. 'I've to stop lending credit' Manu Prasad said to himself stretching back in his seated cushion. 'Can I go home now......... it is getting late' Bal asked from the back of the store. 'Yes you can leave' Manu Prasad agreed from the front. The young boy was soon on his way home dancing to the tunes coming from the transistor radio. A little later Manu Prasad too was home bound and whistling a slow tune.

One early morning, Leela failed to appear at Manu Prasad's home. She had been coming regularly for the past twenty days since the sudden demise of his family and helping before heading her way to school. 'Probably running a little late and hence decided to go straight to the school' Manu Prasad thought to himself as he prepared his morning tea. 'She will come straight to the provision store after school' Manu Prasad mumbled softly sipping his hot brew. Manu Prasad finished his morning routine and walked towards the provision store. Bal was already waiting for him when he arrived at his business. Soon both of them were busy. Bal was stocking the newly arrived goods in the back shelf while Manu Prasad helped the customers. 'Turn it down further' Manu Prasad smiled looking in the direction of the young boy listening to his radio. 'If I slow it down any further.............there will be no sound' Bal stuttered from the back. 'Maybe you will work faster' Manu Prasad replied and the two laughed. The flow of the customers to the provision store trickled down as morning gave way to afternoon. Manu Prasad stretched back in his seated cushion and looked outside the provision store. Late afternoon soon arrived but Leela didn't! Now Manu Prasad was puzzled.

'Is she sick'? Manu Prasad wondered sitting inside the provision store. Her absence since morning remained in his mind as he tended to customers. As evening approached, Manu Prasad contemplated about his Leela. He wanted to visit her home which was about twenty five minute uphill walking from his store. It meant leaving Bal in charge of the business and the prospect discouraged Manu Prasad. He could leave after closing the store but it would be too dark upon his return. He pondered his other options and decided to wait till the following morning. The next morning Manu Prasad had two cups of tea ready in anticipation of Leela. He decided to have his hot brew along with her and hence covered the two cups with a large saucer. When Leela did not arrive at her scheduled morning time, Manu Prasad walked out in his courtyard. He reached the far end of the courtyard and looked above in the direction of her village. Except for few women collecting firewood, there wasn't anyone coming down the hills. The school was still an hour away from opening and it was early for young boys and girls from the surrounding villages to walk down the trail. 'Who are you looking for'? Mausi asked from across her courtyard. Manu Prasad turned around and said 'Leela'. He walked towards Mausi with a concerned look on his face. 'She hasn't been here in two days' Manu Prasad said to his old neighbor. 'I know' Mausi calmly replied spreading a sack of grain on the floor of her courtyard. 'Where should I look for her'? Manu Prasad asked Mausi after a minute of pondering. 'I've to open the provision store soon' He further added. 'First you go to the school and find out about Leela' Mausi stated looking straight at Manu Prasad. Manu Prasad slowly nodded his head in agreement.

When Manu Prasad reached the higher secondary school further down from his house, he was informed Leela had stopped attending school for the past two days. Now Manu Prasad was worried! He looked around for her friends in the school but failed to see them. He walked around the school for ten minutes hoping to get some information regarding Leela without any help. Manu Prasad realized that the provision store needed to be opened soon and he was running late. He was expecting the goods lorry to arrive in the morning and Bal was in no position to handle the merchandise alone. Manu Prasad left the school and started walking towards his provision store. When he arrived at the store, the goods lorry along with Bal and some customers were already waiting for him. He said sorry to everyone and hurriedly unlocked the shutter of the provision store. The goods lorry delivered less than he was expecting but Manu Prasad was in no mood to argue with the driver. He knew the merchants in the town wanted their dues settled before normal services were restored. He had been planning a trip to meet the merchants but time had not been on his side. He knew sooner or later the dues had to be settled. Right now he was more concerned about Leela than his outstanding balance. Once the driver departed, Manu Prasad tended to the customers while Bal stocked the arrived goods in the back. 'I need you to do something for me in the afternoon' Manu Prasad said to Bal twenty minutes later. 'Okay' Bal stuttered from back of the store. Manu Prasad was planning to send Bal to Leela's village. He hoped the trip would clear things. 'I wish I knew where the outstanding accounts are kept'? Manu Prasad said opening his drawer. For the past week he had been trying to find the ledger in which his late father had detailed debts of the customers. He was low in cash and needed certain customers to pay their past debts. It was the only way his dues with the merchants were going to be settled. Manu Prasad kept looking for the ledger in the store unsuccessfully. Just before noon an emissary from Leela's family arrived at Manu Prasad's provision store. 'I've been sent here on behalf of the family' the man said to Manu Prasad. 'Is Leela okay? Where is she'? Manu Prasad asked the emissary getting up from his seated cushion. 'She is fine' the emissary calmly replied looking at anxious Manu Prasad. 'The family requests you not to see her anymore' the emissary added looking away from Manu Prasad. 'What'? Manu Prasad asked shockingly. There was an awkward silence between the two for few seconds. 'I'm just here giving a message' the emissary said lifting his hands in innocence. He soon departed unconvincingly, leaving Manu Prasad speechless.

Manu Prasad made up his mind to visit Leela's home up in the hills. He was going to close the store early in the evening an idea which thrilled Bal. The customers were not pleased at this but Manu Prasad didn't care. The emissary from Leela's family had shaken him with shocking news. Manu Prasad wanted answers. He wanted to talk to Leela, he wanted to talk to her parents. The recent developments just didn't make sense. He kept himself busy in the store, hoping for evening to arrive soon. Manu Prasad hardly talked to Bal which surprised the young boy. 'I will not..............bring the radio to the store........if it bothers you' Bal eventually stuttered to his boss. 'Oh, the radio is fine' Manu Prasad replied assuring the young boy who smiled. 'Do you.......still want me to go uphill'? The young boy asked. 'No, I will go there myself' Manu Prasad assured Bal. The early evening arrived and Manu Prasad bade goodbye to the young boy along with the provision store.

A twenty five minute walk up the hills to Leela's village only took Manu Prasad fifteen minutes. He ran half the time going uphill without realizing. When he arrived in front of Leela's courtyard, Manu Prasad was drenched in sweat. Her younger brother was playing in the open courtyard and he asked him to get Leela. 'She is not home' the boy replied looking at Manu Prasad. A few minutes later Leela's father walked out in the courtyard from inside the house. As a mark of respect for his future father in law, Manu Prasad rushed forward and touched the older man's feet. Leela's father slightly moved away from Manu Prasad hence leaving the respect incomplete. The gesture surprised Manu and he looked up at Leela's father. 'How are you'? He asked his elder. 'I'm fine' Leela's father replied rather firmly. 'Where is Leela'? Manu Prasad asked wiping his brow. 'I haven't seen her for two days and worried' he further added quickly. 'Let's sit down on the edge of the courtyard' Leela's father motioned to Manu Prasad who was now apprehensive. The two sat on the edge of the courtyard as Leela's mother arrived with a glass of water for Manu Prasad. 'Leela has moved with her relatives far from here' the father broke the silence as Manu Prasad finished his glass of water. 'What, why'? Manu Prasad blurted. 'It is for the sake of the family' the father said as his wife stood quietly beside him. 'I don't understand' Manu Prasad said with a hint of anger. Leela's father looked at his wife and then turned his attention towards Manu Prasad. 'Leela has been spending time in your home which has raised lot of eyebrows in the community' the father said dejectedly. Manu Prasad tried to respond but the father raised his arm in protest. 'In our tradition men and women are not supposed to be together before marriage' the father stated firmly. 'I understand, I understand' Manu Prasad consoled the father. 'I will ask her not to visit my home anymore' Manu Prasad said looking at Leela's parents. 'In fact we should just move the marriage closer than the usual date' Manu Prasad suggested with a smile. 'Our family is against this marriage' the father stated getting up from the edge of the courtyard. Manu Prasad tried talking but words deserted his mouth. He mumbled something and rose from his seated position. 'You had promised my parents'! Manu Prasad exclaimed in disbelief looking at the father. 'Unfortunately your parents are no more here' Leela's mother said standing close to her husband. Manu Prasad looked at the two and remained speechless. 'What does Leela make of this'? He finally asked in anger. 'Leela is young and naïve, she doesn't understand norms of the village' the father stated looking away from Manu Prasad. 'It was for her own good my brother took her to his home' the mother said covering her mouth with one hand. 'Did she cry when she was forcibly moved'? Manu Prasad asked softly looking straight at Leela's parents. The two looked away from Manu Prasad who shortly departed from the courtyard. The walk downhill took Manu Prasad almost an hour!

When this news eventually reached Mausi, she was sad but not surprised. After the demise of Dev Prasad and his family, she had shown great interest in her orphaned young neighbor. Mausi's own behavior was also affected by the sudden tragedy. She was now prone to bouts of impatience and anger. Her younger brother was barely home hence the sister in law bore the brunt of her mood swings. Mausi's oldest niece was getting married in two weeks and it was hectic around the household. She was in charge of planning everything and the rest just followed her commands. Few times she dragged her younger brother away from his merry making friends to prove her point. The sister in law had almost become mute in her presence. The poor woman did what she was told without any objections. In spite of her busy schedule, Mausi did not forget about Manu Prasad and his Leela. She was determined to find out more about Leela and her sudden disappearance. During her free time she chatted up with the villagers regarding this matter.

After talking to various people Mausi was able to come up with certain facts regarding Leela. She eventually conveyed them to Manu Prasad who appreciated the concern. Leela was currently staying with her Aunt in the town by the confluence of two rivers. One evening her Uncle had arrived at her village and taken her to his home on the pretext of his ailing wife. Leela was apparently confused and hesitant to leave her home but wanted to see her beloved Aunt. Her mother convinced her to leave in order to assist relatives during the time of need. No one in her village had seen her since her departure and it was assumed Leela was well guarded in her new home. Her parents had apparently made a trip down to the town by the holy confluence. They did not want their young daughter spending morning and evening at Manu Prasad's home. The villagers were talking behind their back and maligning the family name. Rumors slowly started spreading. 'What are Leela and Manu Prasad doing together before marriage? How can her family allow this? When they do get married who will perform the ceremonial duties of the groom's parents? She is marrying a person who has no one left!' Leela's parents eventually got an account of all this from their neighbor. They eventually consulted a priest regarding this matter. 'It is a bad omen to marry a person whose parents have recently deceased' the priest had opinioned. Leela's parents had an embarrassing problem on their hands. What were they supposed to do? They consulted their relatives and came with the possible solution. They couldn't afford to malign their family name any further. It was going to be difficult but their daughter had to be moved away from the village and Manu Prasad for her own good. Hence she was relocated with her Uncle and supposedly sick Aunt in the town by the confluence of two rivers. Her parents faced another problem after her departure. The surrounding villages now knew about her broken relationship with Manu Prasad. It was going to be difficult for Leela to find a suitable groom in the future. Leela's parents wanted a young man far from the surrounding villages for their adorable daughter. Along with their relatives, they started looking for a suitable match. According to the accounts of the villagers, they seemed to have found one! The details were still sketchy but Leela's family was pushing hard for her marriage. The young man was supposedly ten years older than Leela and was employed by the government in the big city some two hundred kilometers from the village. The prospect of a government job and a faraway city enticed Leela's family. The groom's family lived in the town by the confluence of the rivers and Leela's Uncle and Aunt did their best to persuade them for a quick matrimonial union. Leela's mother and father too had moved to the town for bonding with the groom's parents. Their joy knew no bounds when the young man himself drove down in his car from the big city and approved of the marriage proposal. Mausi accounted all this to Manu Prasad who listened in silence. 'Did Leela approve of the marriage'? Manu Prasad asked his old neighbor. 'I don't know' Mausi replied shaking her head. 'I do know from the accounts of the villagers that the marriage is scheduled in a month' Mausi stated firmly.

Leela's wedding day finally arrived! She had been brought back home to her village just a few days prior to the marriage by her Uncle. Everyone in Gauri Ghat was aware of the wedding day including Manu Prasad. Initially Manu Prasad wanted to close his provision store for the day and travel far away from Gauri Ghat. It was the only way he could avoid seeing the festivities in the neighboring village. He thought about Bal accompanying him on the day long trip to the mountains. The night before the wedding, he abandoned the idea. He realized the further he got away from the village the more his mind would think about the day's events. If he kept his store open during Leela's wedding day, he would at least be occupied helping the customers most of the time. Also financially it wasn't viable any more for his business to remain closed for the entire day. Thus Manu Prasad worked at his provision store as preparations for Leela's wedding started at her house from the morning. The provision store was busy as morning progressed due to arrival of wedding guests from outside. The store was located close to the road and hence drew customers who had arrived on rented buses and other vehicles. Some whispered to each other while others gave Manu Prasad long looks as they refreshed themselves with snacks and cold drinks. They eventually trekked uphill to Leela's village.

'Leela is getting............... married today' Bal innocently stuttered from the back as afternoon approached. 'Yes' Manu Prasad replied with a smile looking back at the young boy. 'Where is your radio today'? Manu Prasad asked apologetically for failing to notice earlier. 'I didn't............want to bring it' Bal replied looking away from his boss. 'I need a bag of sugar' a customer interrupted Manu Prasad from his thoughts. Before he could turn back and ask, Bal had produced the bag in front of the customer. 'I guess not having the radio is a good idea' Manu Prasad smiled looking at the young boy who failed to suppress his smile. As the day progressed more rented buses filled with wedding guests arrived on the side of the long village road. The evening hour was approaching and the drum beats from the village high above filled the cool air. A little later a car adorned with flowers pulled up by the side of the road. Songs and dance followed as the groom exited the nicely decorated vehicle. It drew Bal's attention who walked outside the provision store. 'He is......here' the young boy yelled to Manu Prasad who froze for a minute. 'Should I go out and have a look? What does he look like? Is he really ten years older than Leela'? The thoughts crossed Manu Prasad. He later decided against going outside and remained inside his provision store. The groom and his party soon embarked on an uphill trip aided by relatives of Leela. 'Let's close the store little early' Manu Prasad said to the young boy. 'Okay' the boy replied showing no emotion. The late evening gave way to night and Manu Prasad was sitting on the edge of his courtyard. The pomp and festivities from Leela's village could be seen and heard down in Gauri Ghat. The drum beats got louder as the departure of the bride arrived. A little later night lamps and makeshift halogen bulbs aided the bride and the groom downhill to the parked vehicle on the side of the road. Manu Prasad sitting on the edge of his courtyard tried looking away but the sounds from the road above reverberated in his ears. Leela's hysterical cries bidding her family goodbye could be heard in the quiet night. Soon the sound disappeared as she got inside the parked car along with her husband. Leela who loved her surrounding villages was now on her way to a faraway city. The engine roared in the night and the vehicle departed on the long journey. Manu Prasad slowly got up from the edge of his courtyard. He pulled his wallet from the back pocket of his pants. He carefully took out a photograph and observed the picture. Leela and Manu Prasad were standing close together in the photograph taken at the carnival just a few months ago. Manu Prasad slowly ripped the photograph and tossed it in the night wind. From across her top floor verandah Mausi watched and wiped her eyes.

The goods lorry suddenly stopped delivering items at Manu Prasad's provision store. This led to disruptions in the normal functioning of the business. The provision store was running low on supplies and had to be replenished soon. Manu Prasad had two options. Either get hold of the elusive lorry driver or talk to the merchants personally who were responsible for the predicament. The lorry driver had informed him in the past about the displeasure of the merchants regarding their past dues. Manu Prasad had avoided the problem for long due to time constraints and his personal circumstances. He finally got hold of the lorry driver after chasing him down the long road. He was told by the helpless driver that the merchants simply refused to supply further goods to the provision store. Manu Prasad was required to meet the merchants personally to clear his outstanding debts. He pleaded with driver that it was difficult for him to leave the store for the day and meet the merchants in the town further down. The driver threw up his hands regretfully. After much persuasion he was asked to bring one of the merchants along with him on his next trip uphill. 'I assure you I will clear my debts' was Manu Prasad's final message to the lorry driver.

When the lorry driver arrived next morning with one of the merchants by his side, Manu Prasad thanked them both. The driver soon departed, leaving the merchant and Manu Prasad together inside the provision store. 'We have been your loyal client for years' Manu Prasad said to the merchant standing by his side. 'I know' the merchant replied sipping water from the glass provided by the young boy standing further away. 'I will clear all my debts, it has been tough lately' Manu Prasad confided to the merchant. 'I understand but you haven't paid your dues in the past five months' the merchant responded. 'Really'! Manu Prasad exclaimed in surprise. 'The dues go back to your father's time' the merchant said apologetically looking away from Manu Prasad. The two remained quiet for a while as young Bal watched from a distance. 'I didn't know the debts went back that far' Manu Prasad said softly. The merchant shook his head in affirmation. 'Your father extended generous credit to his customers which sometimes stretched for months' the merchant said after a pause. 'You need to collect the dues from your customers' the merchant further added. 'I know, I've been trying hard to find the ledger unsuccessfully that details the debts of the individual customers' Manu Prasad stated to the merchant. 'We also have a business to run and just cannot afford to lend indefinite credit' the merchant explained to Manu Prasad. 'Your family has been our old and loyal customer and hence we have been generous but now it is very difficult to continue if the accumulated debts are not settled soon' the merchant stated firmly. 'I understand' Manu Prasad assured the merchant. The merchant produced a notebook from his front pocket and pointed to the total debts of the provision store which startled Manu Prasad. 'Excuse me for a minute' Manu Prasad said to the merchant and walked to the back of the provision store which led to a seldom used small door. The merchant and young Bal watched Manu Prasad disappear inside the small door. He later appeared with a small bag in his hands. 'Currently I can only offer you this much' Manu Prasad stated handing the bag to his creditor. The merchant slowly started counting the money inside the small bag. 'There is still a lot of debt' the merchant said after counting the money. 'I will clear it soon' Manu Prasad replied apprehensively. 'It has to be soon otherwise unfortunately the deliveries will be suspended again' the merchant said throwing his arms up in the air. 'Okay' Manu Prasad replied with relief and thanked the merchant for restoring his services. The young boy's radio started playing again as soon as the merchant departed.

The first order of business for Manu Prasad was to stop lending any further credit to his customers. This led to displeasure among the customers but Manu Prasad was adamant. 'He has changed, Manu has become greedy and the provision store is just not the same anymore' the villagers whispered behind his back. Some of the customers just stopped coming due to their financial constraints. Secondly and more importantly Manu

Prasad started collecting the past dues of his customers. He knew some of the debts stretched past for months and had to be cleared. Manu Prasad faced one problem regarding this matter. The ledger in which his father had detailed the debts of individual customers was still missing from the provision store. He had tried his best to find the hand written ledger but was unsuccessful in his efforts. He even searched his house but failed to find the ledger. Without the ledger it was impossible for him to pin point the customer debts. He knew the customers that owed him money but the amount was unknown. Something had to be done! He was now aware of the total debt of the provision store and merchant's warning. Manu Prasad finally decided to confront the customers individually regarding the debts.

To his great surprise some of the customers suddenly had no idea about their past dues. When confronted further they offered various explanations. 'I only borrowed few items from the store, I had settled my past dues with your father, I will soon clear all my remaining debts with you' some of the customers remarked to Manu Prasad. He got agitated and demanded the proper dues to be settled soon. 'Where does it state that we owe you this amount of money' the customers with bigger debts finally shocked Manu Prasad. Without the store ledger there was no proof! There was little Manu Prasad could eventually do but just persuade his debtors. Few obliged but most turned the other way. Manu Prasad now had a bigger problem on his hands. The merchant debts had to be cleared soon and his cash supply was eroding. His emergency cash stashed in the back of the provision store by his late father could sustain the business only for few months. 'What should I do'? The thoughts occupied him for days. The provision store was the only thing he had remaining. His grandfather and father had worked hard to maintain the business for years. He wanted to keep the family legacy alive. After much pondering Manu Prasad came up with a solution. His family owned vast stretches of land in the village. Manu Prasad was forced to sell the ancestral property to the merchants and clear all his debts. It was the only way the provision store would remain afloat. Now apart from the provision store, Manu Prasad had his house along with the cattle shed and a small tract of land to his name.

'You need to find a wife soon' Mausi confronted Manu Prasad one morning in the courtyard. He just smiled on his way to the provision store. 'You have aged beyond your years' Mausi said to Manu Prasad who stopped and listened. A year had passed since the sudden demise of his family and Manu Prasad definitely looked frail. 'You cook your food, take care of the household and run the provision store on your own' Mausi stated to Manu Prasad who listened in silence. 'You need someone Manu' Mausi said softly. Manu Prasad looked away from his old neighbor. 'You have to move forward' Mausi added gently. 'I know, I know' Manu Prasad replied with a slight smile. 'You are still a young man son' Mausi assured him. Manu Prasad thanked his caring neighbor and departed for the provision store. He realized the workload was taking a physical toll on him. Sooner or later he needed a wife! Could he be with someone? Could he get close to someone again? Images of Leela still haunted him occasionally. Like Mausi stated he had to move forward. Marriage was the only way he could keep his family name going!

Manu Prasad's search for a wife first began in his surrounding villages. The local customs usually dictated parents of a girl or a boy looking for a suitable match. Unfortunately Manu Prasad's both parents had deceased and the responsibility of finding a wife fell on his shoulders. In some instances the relatives also helped in this matter but Manu Prasad's close ones had lately withdrawn from his life. It seemed after he was forced to sell vast tracts of ancestral land to the merchants, relatives from both side of his family stopped talking to him. Thus Manu Prasad had to find his own wife! It wasn't easy as he worked from morning to evening at the provision store and was in no position to personally meet a prospective bride and her parents. He initiated his search from the provision store which meant talking to various customers. Mausi also helped in this endeavor as she announced him as a possible suitor to her friends from the village and around. Eventual lack of interest surprised both Mausi and Manu Prasad. It seemed most people still considered the tragic demise of his family a bad omen. 'He is all alone', Moaned some of the inquiring suitors. After years of flourishing in the past, Manu Prasad's provision store was currently just staying afloat and loss of his ancestral land had diminished his social standing in the community. It was hard to believe the same young man was deluged with marriage proposals just over a year ago. Manu Prasad did receive two offers from the neighboring villages! He had to unwillingly close his provision store and make the long trip. His first prospective bride was deaf and mute, a fact that was hidden from him by the girl's family. The second girl was ten years older than him and had a child from broken marriage living far away with her relatives. Needless to say Manu Prasad wasn't interested. His further search for a suitable match proved futile. The most eligible bachelor in the surrounding villages, now just couldn't find a wife!

'There is a girl about ten kilometers west from Gauri Ghat' Mausi approached Manu Prasad one morning as he was drying his clothes in the courtyard. 'I don't know' Manu responded with a shrug. 'Her uncle was passing through the village yesterday afternoon and approached me' Mausi revealed with a smile. 'Just listen to me' Mausi said to Manu Prasad before he could speak. She walked closer to him and requested to be seated. Soon they both were sitting on the edge of his courtyard. 'I understand your hesitation but I had a long talk with the girl's uncle yesterday' Mausi assured her apprehensive neighbor seated beside. 'The girl is few years older than you but otherwise fine' Mausi continued. 'Her family is stable and have shown interest' Mausi stated as Manu Prasad listened quietly. 'Now you just have to pay a proper visit' Mausi said to Manu Prasad. 'It is a little far from here' Manu Prasad finally spoke. 'Yes but this is the best prospective match so far…..' Mausi said looking at Manu Prasad. 'I probably will have to close the store for the entire day' Manu Prasad sighed looking at his old neighbor. 'I know but you might end with a future wife' Mausi said. 'Son your current options are limited so don't waste time' Mausi said putting her arm around Manu Prasad. Manu Prasad nodded his head in agreement. Mausi was overbearing at times but no one cared so much for Manu Prasad.

Janki Devi was the eldest of her three sisters. Her village was located about ten kilometers away from Gauri Ghat. She lived with her mother and father who were homemaker and farmer respectively. Her middle sister was already married and the youngest one had two prospective offers to be a bride. Janki Devi the oldest sister still remained unmarried! Like her two sisters she was pretty but unlike them she was overweight. This last fact turned away lot of prospective suitors. The predicament had troubled the family and turned Janki Devi slightly bitter. The family wanted the eldest daughter to get married soon. This even meant postponing marriage offers for their youngest daughter who had plenty of suitors. The search for a possible suitor proved to be difficult. Prospective suitors would come to see Janki Devi and disapprove of the match upon seeing her in person. In some cases Janki Devi herself dismissed the overzealous suitors to the dismay of her parents. 'I'm not ready to get married to just anyone' she would scold her parents. Eventually the task of finding Janki Devi a proper match fell on her uncle. It took him a while but after much travelling the uncle found a suitable match in the village of Gauri Ghat. The two sides soon agreed to meet formally.

When Manu Prasad arrived to see Janki Devi he was exhausted. The bus dropped him off on the periphery of her village. He still had to complete a twenty minute uphill walk to Janki Devi's home. After some inquiries Manu Prasad was now in the middle of Janki Devi's courtyard. He took out a napkin from his pocket and wiped his perspiring face. From the top floor of her small room Janki Devi peeked through the window and looked below in the courtyard. She had known about the arrival of her possible suitor for days in advance from her uncle. Unknown to her family Janki Devi had screened most of her previous suitors in advance through her small window. She had carefully observed them as they entered her family courtyard. Her eyes were currently focused on the man wiping his forehead in the courtyard. She slightly moved across the window to get a better look down below. Something about the man dressed in grey slacks and blazer struck Janki Devi. The young man looked old beyond his years but his eyes suggested otherwise. He had an innocent smile on his face as he waited in the courtyard. Sweat still party covered the side of his forehead and dripped slowly on the collar of his neatly ironed blazer. 'Someone please give him water' Janki Devi said out loud and then covered her mouth disappearing from the window. Janki Devi's father soon came out in the courtyard from inside the house and welcomed Manu Prasad. His wife was waiting inside the small living room and kindly requested the guest to be seated.

After drinking a full glass of water, Manu Prasad requested another. 'It is a long walk up here' Janki Devi's father said to the seated guest. 'Yes' Manu Prasad nodded finishing the second cup of water. Would you like more water'? Janki's mother asked Manu Prasad. 'I'm fine now' he thanked the hosts. 'My brother has mentioned good things about you' the father said to Manu Prasad. Janki Devi's uncle had met Manu Prasad on two occasions in Gauri Ghat and talked in detail about the possible union. The uncle had asked Manu Prasad some questions but was surprised when Manu himself raised few. 'I will just come and see the family myself' was the only response uncle got from Manu Prasad. The uncle knew about the demise of his parents and informed Janki Devi's family about the tragedy. Janki Devi's parents were shocked to hear about the tragedy but did not consider it a bad omen. More than a year had passed since the unfortunate incident. The parent's main concern was to get Janki Devi married quickly to a decent young man. The one sitting next to them in their living room impressed both. 'It is now for you two to decide' Janki Devi's father said with a smile. 'She should be coming out soon with tea and snacks' Janki Devi's mother said looking behind the kitchen door.

Janki Devi was dressed in a bright red Sari as she walked towards the living room from the kitchen. Her forehead was partially covered with the fine garment and she was holding a small tray in her hands. She walked past her parents towards Manu Prasad who straightened himself in his seat. Janki Devi lowered herself and offered a cup of tea to Manu Prasad. As he took the cup of tea from the tray, Janki Devi slightly pulled the Sari from her forehead. She looked at Manu Prasad and smiled to his surprise. Manu Prasad smiled back and spilled the tea in the process. Some of the hot brew stained his pants. Janki Devi pulled a part of her long Sari and slowly wiped his pants apologetically. Manu Prasad didn't mind and thanked the kind gesture. Janki Devi's parents watched in amazement. She had never been this kind to any of her past suitors! After the incident Manu Prasad noticed little else about Janki Devi. The rest of the formalities were fulfilled. Manu Prasad and Janki Devi were getting married soon.

Manu Prasad had one request regarding the marriage. He wanted it to be a simple and private affair. Janki Devi's family gladly accommodated his wish. Mausi's younger brother performed the ceremonial duties of a father for Manu Prasad and accompanied him to Janki Devi's village for the wedding. Mausi herself stayed back in Gauri Ghat but was pleased Manu was represented by an elder at his wedding. A handful of villagers from Gauri Ghat also made the wedding trip along with Manu Prasad's best friend Bal. Manu Prasad had rented a goods lorry for the wedding journey to Janki Devi's village. The small vehicle was neatly decorated with flowers and Mausi's younger brother volunteered to be the designated driver. The mood was festive inside the vehicle as it moved away from Gauri Ghat. A two man band was practicing drums in the back of the vehicle and Bal dressed in matching green jacket and slacks was enjoying the music. Mausi's younger brother too was dressed sharp since the marriage of his two young daughters six months ago. Manu Prasad was attired in an all white suit, one his mother had chosen few years ago. 'This is going to be your wedding dress' she had stressed to Manu Prasad after the purchase. A freshly plucked flower adorned the front pocket of his suit. Manu Prasad seemed calm as the vehicle moved ahead westward on the mountain road. When the groom and his small wedding party arrived at Janki Devi's village in the early evening, the mood was festive.

The little village perched on a hill was bustling with activities. 'Where is the rest of the wedding party'? The villagers whispered to each other upon seeing Manu Prasad and his entourage. The groom smiled after overhearing the comment as he made the uphill trek to the bride's home. Janki Devi's house was moderately decorated for the event which pleased Manu Prasad as he entered the family courtyard. He was warmly welcomed by her parents in the middle of the courtyard. The rest of his wedding party was courteously seated in front of the makeshift wedding stage set up on the north end of the courtyard. Manu Prasad was led on to the wedding stage by Janki Devi's father and requested to occupy one of the two neatly adorned empty chairs. He seated himself on the chair and looked around. It seemed the entire small village had descended around Janki Devi's family courtyard. Everyone was anticipating arrival of the bride! Soon Janki Devi arrived in the courtyard led by her two sisters. She was clad in a bright yellow Sari and a matching blouse. Her hands were covered in bright red henna and matching bangles. A gold ornament hung from her neck and her forehead was partly covered with edge of the Sari. Janki Devi slowly made her way to the wedding stage. The empty chair next to Manu Prasad was now occupied. Janki Devi slightly moved the Sari from her forehead and got comfortable on the chair. She was looking straight ahead into the courtyard. From the corner of his eye Manu Prasad tried to catch a glimpse of his bride. All he caught was the smile as Janki Devi avoided a direct gaze.

Soon the bride and the groom were lead to a holy ritual by the priest. The ceremony consisting of various chants and hymns lasted for almost an hour. The wedding feast followed and no one was more pleased than young Bal. He ate to his heart's content asking for several serving of sweets in the process. 'Who is that boy' Janki Devi softly asked her husband. 'He is my best friend' Manu Prasad whispered in her ears with a smile. The bride's departure was approaching and the guests were lining up to wish the newlyweds goodbye. Janki Devi's friends and relatives from the village and around gave her their final blessings. Her family gathered around her for their last goodbye. Her middle sister hugged Janki Devi tightly and wept. 'Now you better get married soon' Janki Devi said to the youngest sister wiping her tears. She embraced her father and touched his feet as the old man fought off tears. When Janki Devi finally bid goodbye her mother, they both cried for few minutes. 'I was difficult at times' Janki confided to her mother. 'We are going to miss you' the mother cried wiping her tears. Manu Prasad and Janki Devi were soon led away by the beating drums. The two man band did their best as Bal danced on the way downhill to the parked vehicle.

Janki Devi was seated in front of the vehicle along with Manu Prasad as it moved towards Gauri Ghat. The nightfall was approaching and the stars were appearing in the sky. When they reached Gauri Ghat everyone was exhausted from the festivities and the long journey. Manu Prasad slowly led Janki Devi into his courtyard. 'Our home' he said to his wife upon entering the courtyard. 'I like it' Janki Devi responded with a smile. Manu Prasad looked up in the night sky and hoped someone was watching. 'Let's go inside our house' Manu Prasad said to his bride. 'Okay' Janki Devi agreed. The two soon disappeared inside the house. Across from her top floor verandah, Mausi had obscured herself from the couple but was watching them. She never got a good look at the bride and this bothered the old neighbor.

Janki Devi was out in the courtyard sipping her tea during the morning hour. Her husband was still in the kitchen emptying the tea pot. 'Your courtyard is amazing' Janki Devi said out loud. 'I will be out there soon' Manu Prasad smiled from inside the kitchen. Unknown to Janki Devi, Mausi had been observing her from across the courtyard. She finally got a good look at Manu Prasad's new bride. 'She is a big woman' Mausi muttered to herself observing Janki Devi. The new bride was enjoying her surroundings and suddenly turned around directly facing Mausi in the process. She covered her head and slightly bowed as a mark of respect for her elder. 'This is our beloved Mausi and neighbor' Manu Prasad said to Janki Devi as he entered the courtyard from his kitchen. 'You should walk over and pay proper respect to her' Manu Prasad whispered in the ears of his new bride. Janki Devi walked in the direction of Mausi standing close to her courtyard and touched the old neighbor's feet. 'How are you'? Mausi said to the new bride facing her. 'Fine' Janki Devi mumbled nodding her head. 'It is a little late for a morning stroll Mausi' Manu Prasad said with a smile. 'All the noise coming from your courtyard got me intrigued' Mausi replied with a straight face. Manu Prasad smiled and looked at his bride who rolled her eyes looking away from Mausi. 'We will see you later Mausi' Manu Prasad said to his old neighbor. 'Yes you will, I'm not going anywhere' Mausi replied. She gave another look to Janki Devi as the couple walked away from her.

'I have closed the provision store today' Manu Prasad said to his new bride. 'Really'! Janki Devi exclaimed. 'Yes two days in row the business has been shut' Manu revealed to his bride. 'We got married yesterday so I understand' Janki Devi smiled. 'There are plenty of things I need to show you' Manu Prasad stated to his wife. 'Let me prepare some breakfast and then we will get going' Manu Prasad stated to his bride. 'I will not let you work anymore in the house' Janki Devi firmly said to her husband. 'Preparing morning tea is not work' Manu Prasad smiled. 'From now on I will do everything around here' Janki Devi said uncovering the Sari from her head. 'I just need a day or two to locate things in the house' she further added. 'What would you like for breakfast'? She smiled looking at her husband. Manu Prasad just stood there looking at his wife. His late mother always said that to him in the morning. 'Are you hungry'? Janki Devi gave him a puzzled look. 'Oh yes, oh yes' Manu Prasad apologized for the pause. 'Today I'm going to make you pancakes' Janki Devi stated. Manu Prasad's mouth watered as he pointed various ingredients in the kitchen to his wife. Soon Janki Devi was busy preparing pancakes.

After a hearty breakfast Manu Prasad took his new bride to the cattle shed. 'The cows are not in a good shape' Janki Devi lamented upon inspecting the herd. 'It has been hard since the cattle herder left' Manu Prasad revealed. 'I've tried my best' he further added. Janki Devi looked at her husband in silence. Later Manu Prasad led his wife to a small patch of land he still owned. The field was covered in weed and wild brush pointing to neglect. 'As you can see I haven't had much time' Manu Prasad said looking away from his wife. 'Don't worry I will make the field green soon' Janki Devi comforted her husband. 'We had lot more land' Manu Prasad confided to his wife. He detailed the struggles of his provision store to Janki Devi who listened closely. She had already known about the tragic demise of his family but deliberately kept quiet on the subject. 'You have been managing everything on your own for more than a year? She asked her husband in amazement. 'Pretty much' Manu Prasad smiled looking at his wife. 'What about your relatives'? She asked anxiously. 'They helped a little in the past but now have suddenly withdrawn' Manu Prasad stated to his wife. Janki Devi looked away and slowly started sobbing. 'Hey, hey' Manu Prasad put his arms around Janki Devi. 'Has it been hard for you'? She asked wiping her tears. 'Yes but not anymore' Manu Prasad said to his wife which brought a smile on her face. 'Do you like this place'? He asked his wife. 'Yes' Janki Devi replied. 'I don't like your neighbor though' Janki Devi stated firmly. Manu Prasad started laughing. 'I think she is mean' Janki Devi said with a hint of anger. 'You barely know her' Manu Prasad mediated. 'I can tell by just looking at her' Janki Devi added. 'She can be overbearing but means well' Manu Prasad assured his wife. 'Let me show you the provision store' Manu Prasad said to his wife. 'I'm eager to see the business' Janki Devi replied. The couple started walking uphill towards the provision store located by side of the mountain road.

Manu Prasad tended to his provision store from morning till evening while his wife took care of the household. Janki Devi prepared hot breakfast for her husband every morning and then slowly made her way to the cattle shed. She milked the cows and cleaned the crowded shed. After providing fodder to the cattle she was back home again. She cleaned the dirty utensils and swept the house while her husband was away at the store. Janki Devi would then spread wheat in the courtyard along with lentils for drying in the late morning sun. She would comb her hair and keep an eye on the produce from preying birds. A little later she would start preparing lunch and look forward for Manu Prasad to join her in the afternoon. During late afternoon lunch the husband and wife would detail each other's activities. After a little rest, Janki Devi would head uphill from her house to collect fodder for the cattle. She was glad her new home unlike the previous one did not require firewood for cooking. Manu Prasad's family had installed cooking appliance years ago in the house. Janki Devi would store the fodder in the cattle shed and then walk towards her small field located downhill. She would spend an hour in the field tending to various needs. Janki Devi would return home in the late evening and prepare hot tea for herself. Soon she was busy preparing dinner. Manu Prasad would come home after closing the provision store and have dinner with his wife little later. At night the two would sit together in their courtyard and gaze at the surroundings. The day's events would be recounted to each other by the couple. They would eventually retire for the night in the bedroom, eagerly looking forward to the next day. The past slowly seemed distant.

It was early in the morning and Janki Devi was facing the sun with her eyes closed in the courtyard. Her husband was inside the house going through his morning routine. 'Feels good' Janki Devi mumbled to herself as the morning rays splashed on her face. From her own courtyard Mausi was observing the neighbor. She curiously walked closer towards her neighbor's courtyard to get a better look. Janki Devi's back faced Mausi as she enjoyed the morning sunshine. After facing the sun for few more minutes Janki Devi slowly turned around. She was surprised to see Mausi looking straight at her and slightly smiling. The old neighbor then moved her gaze and looked around the courtyard. 'Do you need something'? Janki Devi asked slightly agitated at the intrusion. 'Just wanted to make sure everything is okay' Mausi replied nonchalantly from the edge of her courtyard. This irritated Janki Devi but she maintained silence. 'Wondering how Manu is doing'? Mausi added. 'He is doing fine' Janki Devi said firmly. 'I just worry about him sometimes' Mausi said looking at her feisty neighbor. 'You don't have to worry about him anymore' Janki Devi angrily stated. 'He has me now' she loudly screamed across to her old neighbor. The two exchanged long uncomfortable stares for ten seconds. The commotion brought Manu Prasad into his courtyard from inside the house. 'What is happening'? He asked in bewilderment looking at the two women staring at each other. 'Ask her' Mausi said to Manu Prasad pointing at his wife. 'You need to mind your own business' Janki Devi blurted in anger looking at Mausi. 'Hey, come on ......' Manu Prasad tried comforting his wife. 'Looks like she really cares for you' Mausi smiled looking at Manu Prasad. 'Mausi please.......' Manu Prasad tried to persuade. Manu Prasad mediated for few more minutes. The two women slowly walked away and avoided each other in the future. 'Mausi just cares' Manu Prasad said to his wife over breakfast. 'Not as much as I do' Janki Devi smiled looking away from her husband.

Every alternate year Gauri Ghat hosted a religious festival. The daylong event involved worshipping of a local goddess considered pious by the devotees. The festivities started early in the morning with prayers at the village temple and culminated on a hilltop high above Gauri Ghat with a grand feast. The event attracted thousands of villagers from Gauri Ghat and surrounding villages some of whom travelled from out of town to connect with their roots and traditions. The current event held special significance as telephone towers were being erected along the mountain road above Gauri Ghat. Telephone communication now was just a few months away for Gauri Ghat and the surrounding villages!

Manu Prasad and Janki Devi woke up early on the auspicious day in Gauri Ghat. The provision store remained closed in order for both of them to attend the day long festivities. After finishing their morning routine and having a quick breakfast, the couple was on the way to the temple located further down from the house. When Manu Prasad and Janki Devi arrived at the temple, a large crowd had already gathered at the holy site for morning prayers. The temple bells were ringing loudly and Puja was being performed by the head priest. Scent of incense and smoke filled the air around the vicinity of the temple. Long line of devotees stretched from the temple to the field's further outside. Manu Prasad and Janki Devi attired in blue and yellow respectively stood somewhere in the middle of the long stretch. 'People really arrive early for the prayers' Janki Devi whispered to her husband. 'Yes, some are present before dawn' Manu Prasad said to his wife. Janki Devi looked around as the crowd swelled. She had never witnessed anything this size in her small maternal village. 'People just keep coming' she said in amazement. 'It is just the beginning; soon it is going to get bigger once the procession commences' Manu Prasad stated to his wife. 'You have been part of this in the past' Janki Devi smiled at her husband. 'Yes' Manu Prasad slowly nodded, remembering the time two years ago with his parents and younger brother at the festival. The number of devotees now stretched further back but Manu Prasad and Janki Devi were almost in front of the temple.

They both removed their footwear on the steps of the temple and walked inside towards the shrine. Manu Prasad rang the large bell hanging overhead on his way forward. The couple was now in front of the small shrine and bowed their heads to the deity attired in garlands. The priest applied a small sandalwood paste on the couple's forehead and they bowed as a mark of respect. Janki Devi took out some money from her purse and gently left it in front of the shrine. 'You should now ask the goddess to fulfill your wishes' the priest urged the couple. Manu Prasad closed his eyes and sought continued happiness for him and his wife. Janki Devi closed her eyes and wished a little longer. 'Please bless us with a child' she muttered at the end, loud enough for her husband to listen. 'Now we have to each circle the temple five times separately' Manu Prasad informed the local ritual to his wife. 'I will circle first' Janki Devi excitedly stated to her husband. 'Okay' Manu Prasad smiled.

The number of devotees inside the temple had multiplied and everyone was almost elbowing each other to move around. Manu Prasad was patiently waiting for his wife to complete her ritual. He knew it was going to be a while in the crowded temple. Manu Prasad was standing in the middle of the packed temple and wanted to be towards the edge where the devotees dwindled. He slowly elbowed his way towards the desired spot. He finally reached the edge of the temple and breathed a sigh of relief. He looked in the direction of Janki Devi who still needed to circle the temple one more time. Soon it was going to be his turn and he stretched his neck slowly. His eyes caught a sight and Manu Prasad just stood still. It was Leela standing few feet away from him. A small baby hung in her arms and she was looking straight at Manu Prasad who momentarily lost track of time. He wanted to say something but just stared at Leela and the baby. Leela's eyes welled up and she slightly moved towards Manu Prasad. 'Just too many people here' Janki Devi complained coming towards Manu Prasad. 'Oh yes, oh.........' Manu Prasad stuttered looking at his wife. 'You okay' Janki Devi asked her husband. 'Yes' Manu Prasad replied wiping his brow. 'Now it is your turn to pray' Janki Devi smiled. Manu Prasad nodded in agreement as he moved towards the middle of the temple. He slightly turned around and looked back. His eyes searched for Leela but she had disappeared. He noticed Janki Devi sitting on the edge of the temple and observing the large crowd in amazement. Manu Prasad slowly began his ritual around the temple, occasionally searching the crowd. The daylong event took a physical toll on Manu Prasad and Janki Devi but they gladly participated in the festivities.

Few years passed. Manu Prasad's provision store was gradually profitable again due to his efforts. His employee and friend Bal still entertained and assisted in the business. Against his own will, Manu Prasad occasionally lent credit to few desperate customers. He was just proud to keep the family legacy alive in the village and around. Janki Devi's hard work ensured the household ran smoothly. The cattle herd had multiplied due to her supervision and the shed was slightly remodeled. She had employed a herder to collect fodder and graze the cattle in the evening. The couple's small patch of field had turned into a green oasis due to Janki Devi's daily work. It yielded wide variety of seasonal crops. Janki Devi had even created a small vegetable garden on the side of her courtyard. Manu Prasad and Janki Devi were content with their lives but something was missing. In spite of various attempts, Janki Devi couldn't conceive. The failure to have a child affected Manu Prasad and his frustrated wife. Janki Devi felt empty in her life and the villager's gossip just added to her sorrow. Manu Prasad and Janki Devi went to great lengths in search of a remedy.

Initially the couple consulted an astrologer who left them dissatisfied. A village doctor was next on the list for Manu Prasad and Janki Devi. He prescribed some medicines and suggested various exercises prior to intimacy. According to him this would sure lead to desired results for the couple. The couple diligently followed his advice for months. This led to many awkward moments for Manu Prasad and Janki Devi but they were determined. All the medicines and work failed to produce the desired result. In the end Janki Devi was frustrated again and abandoned the practice along with her husband. 'I'm not going to seek anymore help' Janki Devi said to her husband. She immersed herself in work to keep her thoughts at bay. Manu Prasad was pained to see his wife in the current state. He realized something had to be done. A young man few years older than Manu Prasad had recently returned back to Gauri Ghat from the big town of Kesar Khal. Both were friends growing up and knew each other well. His friend was also married and had a young boy. He would occasionally visit Kesar Khal and spend time at Manu Prasad's provision store before his bus departure. One day Manu Prasad confided his problem to the friend from Kesar Khal. The friend listened patiently and promised to help.

He later visited Manu Prasad and Janki Devi at their home. He informed them about the big government hospital in Kesar Khal which assisted in fertility. Manu Prasad and Janki Devi informed the guest about their previous experiences. The friend stressed that the hospital was best of its kind in the region and provided all the modern facilities. He himself had witnessed the amenities at the government hospital during his wife's childbirth. Manu Prasad and Janki Devi were impressed hearing about the hospital and decided to seek assistance. They requested the friend to keep it a secret. It was their personal matter and they wanted to keep it away from rest of the villagers. Manu Prasad thanked his friend and started making plans for the trip to Kesar Khal. 'This looks promising' He whispered to his wife. 'I hope' Janki Devi replied apprehensively. The friend soon departed. Hidden from a plain view Mausi watched the proceedings from the corner of her courtyard. 'Who is the young man visiting them'? She mumbled to herself. She designed a plan to approach the young visitor.

Manu Prasad and Janki Devi made several trips to the government hospital in Kesar Khal. It wasn't easy. Manu Prasad had to close the provision during the visit and endure long trips on the mountain road something he normally avoided. Janki Devi too never looked forward to the day long journey. The hospital and the doctor had convinced the couple on a monthly trip for a positive result. Hence Manu Prasad and Janki Devi visited the government hospital once a month with high expectations. They had kept the trip a secret from everyone in the village but somehow Mausi had unearthed the mystery. One night when Janki Devi was away at the cattle shed, Mausi confronted Manu Prasad in his courtyard about the secret. Manu Prasad had been avoiding his old neighbor for quite some time and was surprised facing her in the courtyard. 'I ask because I care' Mausi comforted the nervous Manu Prasad. Initially he was reluctant but eventually Manu Prasad explained everything to his curious old neighbor. He knew she meant well and had helped him in the past. 'We are having difficulty conceiving hence seeking help from a doctor in the big town' Manu Prasad confided to his old neighbor. 'We have tried various things in the past without any results' he further added. 'Janki really wants to have a baby and so do I' Manu Prasad sighed. Mausi listened intently but expressed her doubts about the hospital. She had more faith in the traditional village approach. 'I have some old herbs that can help you in this matter' Mausi stated to Manu Prasad. 'Don't worry, your wife won't know about it' Mausi assured. 'I'm going to stick with the hospital for now' Manu Prasad firmly stated. 'Let me know if you need help in the future' Mausi informed Manu Prasad. 'Okay' Manu Prasad smiled. 'I better leave before your wife arrives' Mausi rolled her eyes and bid goodbye.

Manu Prasad and Janki Devi visited the government hospital in Kesar Khal for eight long months. The couple carefully followed the doctor's advice and his medications. Janki Devi failed to conceive! The couple was frustrated and grudgingly abandoned the government hospital in Kesar Khal. 'I'm not seeking anymore help' Janki Devi stated to her husband who listened in silence. 'The almighty doesn't want me to have a baby' she said wiping her tears. Manu Prasad helplessly looked at his heartbroken wife. For days he looked for a solution. He finally decided to approach Mausi for assistance. Manu Prasad remembered his old neighbor mentioning some herbs to him a while back. 'What is the harm in trying'? He thought to himself. 'We have tried everything else' he rationalized. One late morning he left Bal in charge of the provision store and headed home. He knew his wife was away in the field further down from the house. Manu Prasad entered Mausi's courtyard in search of the old neighbor. Lately Mausi had been keeping indoors and her mostly mute sister in law worked in the courtyard. 'I will get her' the sister in law motioned to Manu Prasad standing in the middle of the courtyard. Soon Mausi arrived from inside the house and almost stumbled walking towards the courtyard. Manu Prasad rushed forward and held his old neighbor. 'Are you okay'? He asked anxiously. 'I'm fine, just losing my right eyesight' Mausi stated. Manu Prasad held her hand and walked towards the edge of the courtyard. 'What brings you here'? Mausi asked sitting beside him. Manu Prasad looked away from the old neighbor in the direction of his field far below. 'I guess the hospital and the doctors were of no help' Mausi sarcastically smiled. Manu Prasad slowly nodded his head in affirmation. 'Do you want those herbs'? Mausi softly asked. 'Yes, it is our last hope' Manu Prasad looked in his neighbor's eyes. 'I will be back soon, just wait here' Mausi said to Manu Prasad. She slowly made her way inside the house to her room. Mausi opened an old cabinet and searched closely. She pulled out a small glass jar and reminisced. Inside were ancient herbs her mother in law had gifted decades ago. Mausi remembered serving them to her late husband Mohit Lal and got misty eyed.

'Here are the herbs' Mausi said to Manu Prasad handing over the old glass jar. 'Thank you' Manu Prasad said looking at the small glass piece. 'Make sure you take a small amount of herbs every night with warm milk' Mausi stated to Manu Prasad. 'Don't mention this to your wife' Mausi further added. 'Okay' Manu Prasad replied and thanked his old neighbor. 'I've to cook now' Mausi said to her neighbor. 'Don't you have problem in your eyes'? Manu Prasad asked apprehensively. 'Just one eye, I can see with the other' Mausi replied and disappeared from the courtyard. Manu Prasad squeezed the small glass jar in his pocket and hurried back to the provision store.

During the night he stayed downstairs in the kitchen a little longer and heated some milk. He poured the milk in a glass and carefully mixed a small amount of herbs inside. Manu Prasad slowly started drinking the warm mixture. He later joined his wife in the upstairs bedroom with a smile. Janki Devi was a little surprised at her husband's enthusiasm but pleased. This continued for months. 'I think I'm pregnant'! Janki Devi revealed to her husband one morning. 'What'? Manu Prasad asked in amazement. 'Yes' Janki Devi replied with tears rolling down her cheeks. 'Oh heavens' Manu Prasad stuttered containing himself. In the coming days, Janki Devi's pregnancy was confirmed at the village clinic by a local doctor. Manu Prasad and Janki Devi's joy was boundless. Manu Prasad hired a domestic help to assist in the household and spent enormous time away from the provision store to be with his wife. Eventually Janki Devi left for her maternal home for childbirth. Manu Prasad accompanied her on the long trip in a goods lorry along with his delighted friend Bal. Janki Devi was going to stay in her old village with her parents for few months. Manu Prasad was alone in Gauri Ghat but he didn't mind. He was soon going to be a father! Mausi's magical herbs had done wonders. Mausi mostly stayed inside her house due to deteriorating health but had been informed about her neighbor's joy. When Manu Prasad finally thanked her for his blessings, Mausi could barely walk. She embraced Manu Prasad as he visited the old neighbor in her room and expressed gratitude. Lately Mausi spent the days in her small room and the nights sitting in the upstairs verandah.

Winter had arrived in the hills leading to long and cold nights. High above Gauri Ghat the mountains were experiencing snowfall. It was a moonlit night twinkling with numerous stars. Manu Prasad attired in woolen pants and a long fur coat was sitting on the edge of his courtyard. He was looking westward towards Janki Devi's village and rubbing his hands to keep warm. His wife was due to give birth any day and Manu Prasad was imagining the possibilities. Finally he was going to be father! Manu Prasad turned around and looked towards Mausi sitting in her top floor verandah. He smiled looking in her direction knowing well that Mausi could barely see him. Mausi was wrapped in a thick blanket and sitting in her favorite rocking chair. Her vision had almost disappeared but she was looking around from her verandah. She could still feel and hear things as her head slowly turned from side to side in the dark night. Sound of a vehicle from the road above the village garnered her attention. Occasional scream from the forest high above made her shiver in the cold. A child's cry in the winter night drew her sympathy. The village was mostly asleep but Mausi was still fully awake. Her sister in law was fast asleep from the day's work. Her alcoholic younger brother came home whenever he wished. Mausi's three nieces were married long ago to her delight. She was in poor health for sometime but strangely content. Lately Mausi had been spending her entire night in the open verandah. Her sister in law usually woke her up in the morning and helped getting inside the room.

Manu Prasad was cleaning his courtyard in the early winter morning. He was diligently picking up things settled in the courtyard from the night. 'She is no more, she is no more' the screams from across his courtyard startled Manu Prasad. His rushed towards his neighbor. From the upstairs verandah Mausi's sister in law was crying hysterically. Manu Prasad motioned to her from the courtyard and ran towards the verandah. 'She has passed away, she has passed away' the sister in law cried upon seeing Manu Prasad in the verandah. 'I came to see her in the morning and she didn't respond' the sister in law continued crying as Manu Prasad looked in shock. Mausi had fallen from her chair and was lying face down on the verandah. Manu Prasad stooped down and examined Mausi. Her hands were ice cold and her eyes were shut. She had been dead for hours! Manu Prasad shook his head and trembled with tears. 'What should we do'? The sister in law pleaded. 'Where is your husband'? Manu Prasad asked. 'I haven't seen him for two days' the sister in law replied with tears running down her face. 'We have to move the body' Manu Prasad stated. With great difficulty the two slowly dragged the lifeless body inside the room. 'We cannot leave the body in the room for too long' Manu Prasad said to the shell shocked sister in law. 'You need someone from the village to help you' the sister in law said wiping her tears. 'I thought you were mute' Manu Prasad said to the sister in law. The sudden tragedy had overtaken his senses. 'I played mute because I was scared of her' the sister in law pointed to the lifeless body. 'Whom do I have to be scared of now'? The sister in law cried. Manu Prasad listened in silence. 'I will get some help and be back soon' he assured the distraught sister in law.

Manu Prasad went door to door looking for help in the village but failed. It seemed all the young ones were either at work or away at school, leaving the elderly behind. Manu Prasad's attempt to locate Mausi's younger brother also proved futile. In the end his friend Bal was the only one available. Manu Prasad realized Mausi's body had to be removed from her home. The longer it stayed, more difficult it would be for the helpless sister in law. He asked Bal to get hold of a goods lorry by the long road while he made his way back to Mausi's lifeless body. 'We have to perform the last rites soon otherwise the body will be here for long' Manu Prasad said to the sister in law. 'Okay' the sister in law agreed wiping her stained face. 'I'm sorry I can't be of any help' the sister in law stated. 'You have helped enough' Manu Prasad assured. 'I've to make some more arrangements, I will be back later' Manu Prasad said to the sister in law and departed.

Bal had eventually got hold of a small lorry along with the driver. After a financial agreement with Manu Prasad, the driver offered his lorry and help. Manu Prasad explained the task at hand to both Bal and the driver. They would have to load the body onto the lorry and take it down to the confluence of the holy rivers for final ritual. All three of them started gathering wood and other materials. When they arrived with a makeshift wooden casket, a sizeable crowd thronged Mausi's courtyard. The crowd was mostly elderly barring few infants and was mourning Mausi's death. Manu Prasad along with the lorry driver and Bal placed Mausi's body onto the open wooden casket as the sister in law watched from a distance. The cries around the courtyard got louder as the three hoisted the wooden casket on their shoulders and moved towards the road above. It was with great difficulty the three were able to load the body resting on the casket in back of the small lorry. Soon the lorry was on its way to the confluence of the rivers. 'Mausi is.........no more' Bal stuttered to Manu Prasad and he put his arm around the young boy.

The winter fog was rising from the mountains and spreading around. The driver was maneuvering the small vehicle through the mountain road, occasionally looking back at the wooden casket. Manu Prasad and Bal were silently seated in the front. The vehicle was approaching a sharp curve on the road and Manu Prasad looked away. A large sign recently installed by the local administration greeted the small vehicle few feet away from the sharp curve. 'Drive carefully, this curve has taken many lives including the men who built this long road' the sign stated in capital letters. The lorry driver slowed down as he maneuvered the sharp curve. A large plaque had been fitted on the side of the road that faced the mountain and it drew Manu Prasad's attention. The plaque listed the names of workers who had perished building the mountain road. Manu Prasad peeped out of his passenger window and looked at the long list of names carved on the plaque. 'Mohit Lal' was carved on top of the list. Manu Prasad never bothered to look on the other side of the road. The deep ravine was all too familiar to him. The lorry picked up speed and was now on its downward descent towards the holy confluence of the rivers.

It was late in the afternoon when Manu Prasad along with Bal and the lorry driver brought the wooden casket carrying Mausi's body on the banks of the holy confluence. A partial fog covered the banks and visibility was poor. Manu Prasad had picked up necessary supplies for the ritual along the way. He slowly walked to the farthest end of the confluence as Bal and the lorry driver followed along. He lit up a sacred pyre on the banks of the confluence and placed the open wooden casket on top with help from Bal and the driver. Manu Prasad watched from a distance and cried as Mausi was given her final rites. A little later everything turned into ashes. Manu Prasad picked up the ashes and immersed them in waters of the holy confluence. 'Where will…..they go' Bal stuttered pointing to the ashes. 'In a faraway sea' Manu Prasad answered wiping his eyes. Mausi who had never ventured out of her native Himalayan hills was in the end moving thousands of miles away.